DEE
MACOMBER
SUSAN WIGGS
JILL BARNETT

That Summer Place

MIRA

$7.99 U.S.
$7.99 CAN.

ISBN-13:978-0-7783-2713-4
ISBN-10: 0-7783-2713-2

EAN

PRAISE FOR THE AUTHORS

DEBBIE MACOMBER

"Popular romance writer Macomber
has a gift for evoking the emotions that are
at the heart of the genre's popularity."
—*Publishers Weekly*

"One of Macomber's great strengths is her insight
into human behavior—both admirable and ignoble."
—*Romantic Times BOOKreviews*

SUSAN WIGGS

Wiggs writes "a flawless story
touched by real emotions."
—*Publishers Weekly*

"Susan Wiggs is a superb storyteller."
—*Romantic Times BOOKreviews*

JILL BARNETT

"Barnett has a rare knack for humor.
Her characters are joyously fresh and her style
is a delight to read—a ray of summer sun."
—*Publishers Weekly*

"Five Gold Stars! This is one delightfully funny read
with witty, witty dialogue."
—*Heartland Critiques* on *Surrender a Dream*

DEBBIE MACOMBER
SUSAN WIGGS
JILL BARNETT

That Summer Place

MIRA

MIRA®

ISBN-13: 978-0-7783-2713-4
ISBN-10:   0-7783-2713-2

THAT SUMMER PLACE

Copyright © 1998 by MIRA Books.

The publisher acknowledges the copyright holders
of the individual works as follows:

OLD THINGS
Copyright © 1998 by Jill Barnett.

PRIVATE PARADISE
Copyright © 1998 by Debbie Macomber.

ISLAND TIME
Copyright © 1998 by Susan Wiggs.

www.MIRABooks.com

Printed in U.S.A.

CONTENTS

OLD THINGS

Jill Barnett

Dear Reader,

Have you ever visited a place you've never been to before and found that you felt as if you were home? That's what happened to me the first time I came to the Pacific Northwest. It doesn't seem that long ago that I stepped off a ferry and found a paradise.

A few months later I'd bought a house overlooking a lovely harbor where the eagles fly and the sailboats drift by, where there is a sense of utter peace and quiet. Although I was born and raised on the West Coast, for me, my small chunk of this wonderful island is the most beautiful place I've ever lived.

Writing about an area that has captured my heart so completely has been very special for me. Oh, I've written about islands before. I've set four books on small islands and have even joked that I must have been an island in a past life. But this is my first contemporary work of fiction, and it's set in a place where I live.

I feel so fortunate to have the opportunity to write for a collection with two fabulous and talented Northwest writers, who are now my good friends. Both Susan and Debbie welcomed me here with open arms and graciousness.

So I hope, as you read the stories, you will see a little of what we get to see every day—trees so lush and tall they can block out the sunshine, water so still you are afraid to breathe, and sunrises so perfect you think you must have dreamed them.

Enjoy!

Jill Barnett
c/o Rowe Enterprises
P.O. Box 8166
Fremont, CA 94536

To the readers who wanted an older couple,
particularly to Barbara,
who wrote and sent me one of the
funniest poems I've ever read.

One

Catherine Wardwell Winslow spent a week last winter at a time management seminar where the experts stood up on a big stage and told her that Wednesday was the slowest day of the work week.

They lied.

Catherine rested her chin in her hand and stared at her phone. It was a Wednesday, barely nine in the morning, and already four of the five phone lines were frantically blinking. She didn't know which one to answer first. So she didn't answer any of them.

Her life would be so much easier if she were one of those robots you see in the cartoons, the kind with slot machine eyes, a ball-bearing nose, and those spindly metal arms and slinky legs that jerk with every movement.

Like Rosie the Robot in The Jetsons.

But Catherine wasn't in a space-age home that looked

like the Space Needle. She was in her San Francisco office on the third floor of a restored Victorian. The building was just one of many candy-colored, gabled houses on a steep and narrow street that now held offices for dentists, attorneys and other professionals.

The last line buzzed obnoxiously and began to blink like the others. She groaned and closed her eyes to escape. Her imagination took over. In her mind's eye she was Catherine the Robot rolling around her office on feet made of rollers that looked like brass sofa balls. She jammed report folders under her robot arms with the clawlike hands of a carnival toy machine, then she spun around her messy office, grabbing files and reports, adding up cost sheets and filing.

But the more paperwork she handled, the larger the piles on her desk grew. So the faster she rolled, here and there.

Hectic. Hectic. Hectic.

The desk phone suddenly morphed into an old fashioned black switchboard. The switchboard was filled with little glowing golden dots that blinked and buzzed and only stopped if she stuck one of a hundred black spiderlike plug cords into them. No matter how fast she plugged in the cords, the telephone lines kept flashing away like those warning lights at railroad crossings.

Warning overload! Warning! Warning!

Then…

Pow!

She suddenly blew up in a cloud of springs, bolts and flying nuts.

"Are you all right?"

Catherine sat upright in her desk chair, startled. She blinked. Myrtle Martin, her secretary of fifteen years, was standing in the doorway, staring at her.

"I'm fine." Catherine quickly looked down, embarrassed. She busied herself by shuffling the papers all over her desk.

Myrtle gave Catherine's desk a pointed look, then shifted her gaze to the blinking lines. "You aren't answering the phone."

"I know." Catherine spent an inordinate amount of time fiddling with an already neat stack of the papers. She felt as if she had just blown up, like her nuts and bolts were scattered from here to kingdom come.

"What are you doing?"

"Looking for my nuts," Catherine muttered.

"You divorced your nuts eight years ago," Myrtle said without a beat, then closed the connecting door.

Catherine shook her head and bit back a smile. She picked up a handful of papers and tapped them on the desk until their corners were neatly aligned.

Myrtle was staring at her.

She glanced up trying to look calm and collected and in complete control, as if nothing was out of the ordinary.

Her secretary just stood there with her rigid back pressed against the door jamb, a knowing look on her face.

It was impossible to ignore her. Impossible because Myrtle Martin had a new hair color. Orange. Blindingly bright orange.

Catherine never knew a hair color could actually hurt your eyes. For just one instant she had the sudden urge to whip out her sunglasses.

Back in January Myrtle had dyed her hair jet black, painted a mole on her cheek and drawn on thickly-arched, Night-of-the-Iguana eyebrows, then wore animal prints and huge faux diamonds. At the time she was dating a Welshman named Richard.

Myrtle walked toward her with one of her "you-need-me-to-tell-you-exactly-what-you-need-to-do" looks. She had been gone for two weeks and the office looked as if she'd been gone for a year.

Catherine braced herself for a lecture, but instead Myrtle just hitched her hip on the desk corner, picked up the phone, and began pressing buttons. "Ms. Winslow is unavailable today."

Poof! Line one was gone.

"Ms. Winslow is in a meeting and cannot be disturbed." Line two gone.

"Ms. Winslow will get back to you as soon as possible." Line three gone.

Line four got the same treatment.

She punched line five. "Yes? Uh-huh. That's right. Who? Oh, hi! Yes, I'm just fine. Uh-huh. Uh-huh… I changed it last night." Myrtle smiled and patted her French twist. "Red Flambeaux. Yes, it's very vibrant. I like color, too. Catherine? Yes, she's right here." Myrtle studied Catherine for a long moment. "She's wearing a suit…of course. Black," she added as if she were describing cockroaches.

Catherine glanced down at her tailored black suit and frowned. She liked this outfit; it fit her mood.

"What's she doing?" Myrtle repeated, then gave Catherine a wicked smile. "Your daughter is looking for her nuts."

Catherine snatched the phone out of Myrtle's hand and glared at her.

Ignoring her, Myrtle just sank into a chair opposite the desk and began rifling through the papers on Catherine's desk.

"Hi, Mom. Myrtle was just being funny. No, I don't need any almonds. Yes, I'm sure."

Catherine paused, listening to her mom because she was her mom. There were some things you never outgrew.

Finally she took a long breath and said, "I know almond oil is good for the skin." She covered the mouthpiece and made shooting noises and gestures at Myrtle while her mother listed all the reasons nuts—almonds in particular—were good for her.

Five minutes later, when her eyes were glazed over and she now knew the complete history of the almond, she said, "Yes, I heard the whole thing. Every word, Mom." She took a deep breath and spoke rapidly to sneak a few words in, "I have to go now. Have a good trip, okay? No, I don't want any smoked almonds."

She winced and rubbed a hand over her pounding forehead. "I remember they were Dad's favorite. I love you, too. I promise I won't forget to tell the girls." She paused and added more softly, "Almonds make me cry, too, Mom."

She sighed. "You don't have anything to worry about. They give out pretzels on planes nowadays." She paused and pinched the bridge of her nose. "I don't know why." She stared down at her desk blotter. "I know Dad hated pretzels.

"No!" She jerked upright in her chair. "Don't cancel your flight!" She looked up at Myrtle, panicking. She ran a hand through her hair in frustration, then said more calmly, "Please, Mom. You need to go. This trip will be good for you."

There was a long, drawn out pause. Catherine sat still, holding her breath while she listened to the silence on the other end. Then her mother agreed.

Catherine exhaled and sagged back against her chair. "Yes, it would be difficult to cancel now. You'll have a good time. And the girls will miss you, too. Bye, Mom." She hung up the phone and gave Myrtle a look that should have cooked her.

Myrtle leaned forward and slapped some money on the desk. "Ten bucks says a case of almonds arrives before the week is out."

Catherine opened her desk drawer and threw out a wadded-up bill. "Twenty says it arrives tomorrow morning." She paused, then added pointedly, "About the same time you get your pink slip."

"You? Fire me?" Myrtle just ignored her. "Anyone else would bore you to death. Besides which, you need me."

"I also needed hard labor to give birth."

Myrtle burst out laughing.

Firing Myrtle was a ludicrous threat, since they both knew Catherine would be lost without her. Just one look at the cluttered office was proof enough.

Over the years she and Myrtle had become more than business associates; they had become friends. Catherine's daughters called Myrtle Martin "Aunt Mickie." It was Myrtle Martin who'd kept Catherine laughing through each difficult day after her husband, Tom, had walked away from her, and even more heart-wrenchingly, walked away from his young daughters because they caused too many complications in his life. Myrtle was the first person Catherine called when her ex-husband died two years after the divorce, and just six months ago, when her father was killed suddenly in an accident.

While Myrtle set about cleaning the office and filing papers, Catherine shoved away from her desk and stood. She crossed the room and opened the door to her small bath, where she dumped out an old cup of coffee, then rested both palms flat on the edges of the pedestal sink. She leaned into the mirror and wondered if that was really her face staring back.

She looked like her mother. And her grandmother. Blonde hair, brown eyes. Just like theirs except she had a dash of freckles across her nose that had never faded, even though her skin hadn't been exposed to the sun for years. They just stayed there, reminders of a summer when she had been badly burned.

She heard Myrtle mumbling out in the office and stepped into the doorway. "Are you talking to me?"

"Yes." Myrtle looked over her shoulder at Catherine. "I was saying that you're the one who needs a trip to the Greek Isles."

Catherine closed the adjoining door and crossed the office. "What I really need is to hire someone efficient while you're out on vacation." Catherine sat down.

Myrtle turned around. "At least I take vacations."

"I take vacations."

"When?"

Catherine raised her chin. "I took the girls to Disneyland."

"They were two and six."

Catherine's daughters were now eleven and fifteen. "I went to New Orleans, remember?"

"Yes, I remember."

"Good."

"Reagan was president."

"He was not."

"Well…" Myrtle gave her hand a dramatic wave and slapped a file drawer closed. "It must have been Bush. I know it was one of those good ol' Republican boys."

Catherine glanced down at the paperwork on her desk. She had so much to do. "I can't get away right now…." She let the last word fade out when she realized that Myrtle was silently mouthing the very same words.

Catherine stared at her, half in surprise and half in shame. Even to her own ears it sounded like something she'd said a dozen times. Nothing but the same old excuse.

She closed her eyes for a second, feeling as if she'd been hit with a huge anvil, one painted with the words Bad Mother. She ran a hand over her eyes. She could still see Aly and Dana's eager young faces as they'd stood outside Sleeping Beauty's castle.

Once upon a time they had been awestruck by Goofy, Mickey and the other Disney characters. Only last week Aly had hung a Hanson poster over her prized *Beauty and the Beast* print, and Dana had come home from a sleepover with a third hole pierced high in her ear.

Catherine sagged back in her chair and gave her secretary a direct look. "Has it really been that long?"

"It's been a few years since you went away with just Aly and Dana."

Her daughters' last vacations had been with their grandparents or a random week each year at summer camp. Catherine was hit hard by a working mother's guilt.

It had always sounded so perfect when her parents chose to take the girls some place special. And those trips always seemed to coincide with Catherine's important presentations. Now, in retrospect, she felt selfish.

When she was growing up, her parents had spent almost every summer in Washington, in a wonderful Victorian clapboard house on a small San Juan island. Those summers had been easy and free, a time past when the air was clean, the sky was blue, and you woke up to the aching call of the gulls or the soft sound of rain on the roof. A place where your schedule was dictated only by the rise of the sun or the moon.

On Spruce Island, when she was seven, she had learned the names of all the stars and constellations, because there was no television to teach her that stars were merely people made by Hollywood.

On dark summer nights at the water's edge, she had roasted her first marshmallow and heard her first ghost story around the golden flames of a beach fire. And on that same island, on a chilly Northwest morning she caught her first fish—a six inch bottom-sucker that her father didn't make her throw back in spite of the game laws.

It was there where she had learned to swim, to sail, and to kiss, for it was on Spruce Island during a bittersweet summer in the Sixties—the days when she used Yardley soap, dressed like Jean Shrimpton, and ironed her long hair straight—that she had found her first love.

With Michael.

She felt that old wistful feeling you have when you remember something that might have been. His image was bittersweet as it formed in her mind, and she wondered if he really had been that tall, intense young man she remembered.

Michael Packard had been twenty years old, incredibly mature and mysterious to a seventeen year old late bloomer who'd had a crush on him since she was eleven.

At twenty he'd had a man's strength and a man's gentleness, qualities she had seen in her father, but never in any of the young men she knew. The boys in her hometown craved fast cars and even faster girls. They drank Colt 45 malt liquor, carried hard-packs of Marlboros in their madras-shirt pockets, and cruised the streets in shiny cars with loud engines and big tires.

But Michael was so different from those boys. Even today, some thirty years later, she could still remember things about him: his voice saying her name, his long tanned legs stretched out on the small sloop they'd sailed in the cove, his wonderful hands and the way they could haul up a boat anchor, carve her initials in a piece of wood, or just as easily wipe a tear from her cheek.

That June she had fallen hard for him, fallen hard for the dark-haired young man with a deep, quiet voice that sounded as if it came from his soul. He had a poet's eyes, the kind of eyes she had seen in black-and-white photos of Laurence Ferlinghetti and Bob Dylan, eyes that could look right through you, especially if you were only seventeen. His hungry looks made her dreamy young heart melt like the cocoa butter they slathered over their suntanned skin. And he gave her long, hot kisses that could have burned the fog off Puget Sound.

"Good God... Whatever are you thinking about?"

Catherine straightened a little and stared at Myrtle. "Nothing. Why?"

"You look as if you just got lucky with George Clooney."

Catherine laughed and shook her head. "I was remembering a summer from a long, long time ago."

"It must have been one hot summer."

It was hot, she thought, so hot that all her youthful dreams had burned right up. She glanced up and gave Myrtle a wry look. "It couldn't have been too hot. I was only seventeen."

Myrtle held up her hand and began to count off. "Cleopatra, Lolita—"

"Well, now I'm forty-seven," Catherine said, cutting Myrtle off before she got going. She didn't want to talk about things from a long time ago. She wanted to keep them locked away in that secret part of her heart, the place where her daydreams began and a lifetime of what-ifs were hidden away.

"I'm fifty-five," Myrtle said. "And that doesn't stop me."

"Nothing stops you."

"I know." Myrtle grinned.

"Looking for someone or trying to start a relationship is too much hard work. I don't have time, especially now when I have the biggest presentation of my career less than a month away."

"Letni Corporation?"

Catherine nodded.

"I thought they weren't ready to talk seriously until September."

"So did I, but I got a call just before you came in. They want the presentation meeting scheduled for the first Tuesday in July."

Now Myrtle appeared to be stunned silent, looking as surprised as Catherine had been this morning when she'd heard from Letni.

Catherine tried not to smile when she said, "John Turner's been fired."

Myrtle did smile, one of those wicked cat-in-the-cream kind of smiles.

"With Turner gone we actually have a chance to beat out Westlake for the first time." Catherine could hear the excitement in her voice. "The company needs a big account. This is the chance we've waited for."

The largest computer chip manufacturer in the world, Letni was expanding into two states, moving from the high tax locations of California to better locations in Washington and Arizona. Thousands of employees would be moving over the company's ten-year plan.

Her heart raced a little at the thought that this deal could really happen. "The relocation accounts alone could keep us in the black for the next ten years."

The desk phone buzzed and began to flash yellow.

Myrtle glanced down at the phone at the same time as Catherine.

Within seconds four more lines lit up.

Catherine closed her eyes and leaned back against her chair with a sigh of disgust.

Myrtle crossed the room and opened the door. "I'll take care of those lines. For the rest of the day, I promise I'll only put through the most urgent calls."

Catherine gave her a weak smile as the door snapped closed, then sat there feeling lost and preoccupied and confused, as if she didn't know where to start. After a stretch of seconds where the only sound was the wall clock ticking away, she grabbed a pile of research files, put on her bifocals, and opened the first file folder.

The words grew foggy and a handsome face from her youth flashed across her mind. For one rare and tender moment, just before she began to read, she wondered what had ever happened to Michael Packard.

Two

He stood at the end of a long dock. The breeze off the water whipped through his hair the same way it had thirty years before. He was fifty now, and though his hair was still dark, there were streaks of gray near his temples, ears, and just above his brow. Each and every one of those gray hairs had been earned over two decades of international flight miles.

His eyes were ice blue, and those who were foolish enough to have crossed him over the years could tell you that there was a sharp and coldly decisive mind behind those eyes, the mind and strength of a man who could put you in your place with a single hard look.

Deep in the corners of those cool eyes were laugh lines that his few close friends saw often. But those same lines also showed anyone who shook his hand for the first time that he'd lived, long enough to know exactly how to get what he wanted.

His stride was easy and loose, the gait of someone comfortable with the power he possessed. The old dock creaked every so often, as if the wood protested him walking on it. He headed for the boathouse, which stood at the end of the dock and was more gray and weathered than he was.

The boathouse had been there a long time. It had been there the first day he'd stepped foot on Spruce Island, when he was thirteen and orphaned and angry at a world where parents could be sitting around the breakfast table one morning and die in a car crash that same night.

His first day on the island he had walked past the old boathouse with his pride on his sleeve and a chip on his shoulder. He was on his way to meet a grandfather he'd only heard of the few times his father had talked about his past.

At thirteen Michael had thought the island was just some backward hayseed place stuck out in the tulles. To him his grandfather was a stranger who lived in a strange place, someone he didn't know, yet who had the power to control his life. The island seemed like Alcatraz. And Michael had been scared.

But now, standing on the dock, he was older and wiser. World-weary. He didn't have any of those feelings he'd had when he was young. Now he could feel the freedom of the island. He saw the rarity of this place that had never been coldly dissected by freeways.

It was lush and green, surrounded by silver glassy water instead of silver-glassed high-rise buildings. Fir, cedar, maple and hemlock towered along the jagged ridges that rose from the center of the island, and even along the sheer cliffs and quiet inlets where birds wheeled in the clean air.

He didn't move for a minute, but stared out at the sharp blue sky above Cutters Cove where a large dark bird floated overhead. He did a sudden double-take. The bird had a majestic white head. With one hand, he shielded his eyes from the sun and stood there watching the eagle fly.

When the bird was out of sight, he shoved his hands back in his pockets and took a deep breath of cool, damp mid-morning air. The things that had been plaguing his mind suddenly fell into perspective in a way that was humbling and strangely welcome.

He had no idea how long he stood there, and it didn't matter because there was no plane to catch. No meeting to get to. No stockholders to appease. No do-or-die deal to close. Here he could just…be.

When he finally did move, it was slowly and with purpose. He opened the boathouse door, which creaked loudly and scared away the black crows perched on the old shingled roof. He ducked down and stepped inside.

The late afternoon sun slipped though the panes of rustic time- and weather-frosted windows and cast shafts of milky light on the floor in a checkered pattern that looked like an oversized circuit board. Spiderwebs drifted in the light. He could smell the metallic and wet scent of algae that always grew on the wood in the Northwest.

He stepped over a few teak oars and tossed aside an old orange life vest that water, air, and the seasons had turned hard as concrete. He took a few more steps and ran his hand over the old boards along the windows. He leaned closer, squinting at the wood siding because he'd left his glasses in the cabin sitting next to his cell phone, electronic daytimer and briefcase.

He ran his hand over the old cedar boards carefully and

more tentatively than any of his business associates would have thought possible. He was certain they thought he never did anything tentatively.

Yet his hands moved with care, the same way he'd wiped away her tears almost thirty years before. He stopped suddenly, his hand freezing in one splintered spot.

There, in the boards, were the ragged letters: M P + C W.

Summer, 1960

The first time he'd ever seen her he was fourteen and she was eleven. He was on an errand for his grandfather, walking down the gravel path that cut from his grandfather's cabin, through the forest, and on to the old summer place.

She was hanging upside-down from an old pine tree, her skinned knees hooked over a low thick branch. She was swinging back and forth, so her long blond braids dangled like Tarzan's jungle ropes. The whole time she hummed "Alley Oop" while she blew the biggest pink bubble he'd ever seen.

He didn't know you could hum and blow bubble gum at the same time. As he walked past her, there was a loud pop!

"Who are you?" She swung up so she was straddling the branch with one leg, while the other dangled down. Her palms propped up her body and she stared down at him.

Needles and pine dust fell all over him and scowling he wiped off his face and head. On the same level as his nose was a pair of red canvas shoes with no shoelaces and the word Keds on the scuffed rubber tips. He slowly looked upward along her gangly freckled legs and scabbed-over knees to her small indignant face, which looked like a troll doll.

"I asked you who you were," she repeated as if she were the queen of the island.

"I'm looking for a Mr. Wardwell."

"Oh." She blew another bubble, sucked in and popped it in an obnoxious way, then asked, "Why are ya lookin' for him?"

"None of your business, Squirt." Michael turned his back on her and started to walk down the gravel path that led toward the old house.

She jumped out of the tree and appeared beside him. "My name's not Squirt. It's Catherine."

He grunted some response and kept walking.

"Hey! What's your name?" she called out after him.

"It's Mr. Packard," he said to annoy her.

"You're not Mr. Packard," she said, skipping alongside of him. "Mr. Packard is taller and older and he has gray hair and a dog named King Crab."

Michael ignored her.

"And he's not a grump. Like you."

He stopped and looked down her.

Her expression dared him to ignore her again.

"He's my grandfather," he told her and started walking away again.

She kept up with him, not saying anything, but he could feel her studying him. He looked at her finally. All he saw was an expressive face and a pair of frowning brown eyes that were the same color as root beer.

They were on the narrowest section of the sea cliff trail

where it paralleled the water. He slowed his steps. "Watch it there, Squirt." He grabbed her arm. "There's a cliff on that side of the path. Fall down it and you'll land in the water. Really cold water."

She frowned down at his hand gripping her arm, then wriggled free with a stubborn independence and looked up at him. She stared for the longest time. "We come here every summer. I've never seen you here before."

He wasn't going to tell some kid why he had to live here.

But she wouldn't shut up. "Where'd you come from anyway?"

"The stork dropped me down the chimney."

"Funny." She called him a dork under her breath.

He almost laughed then.

When he said nothing she piped up, "I'm not a baby, you know."

He snorted and walked on.

"I know all about things like why the ocean is blue."

He didn't say anything.

"I know how planes fly and why engines need oil—" She paused as if she were waiting for him to make her prove it.

After a moment she announced, "And I know all about sex."

He stopped and looked down at her. Then he did laugh. Loud and long, because she was so silly.

She planted her hands on her boyish hips, raised her chin, and said, "I do."

He just shook his head and moved farther down the path. He could hear her running after him.

"Go ahead. Ask me something."

"No."

"But I know…" Her voice suddenly changed to a scream. Michael turned.

One instant she was wobbling on the edge of the path, and before he could reach out, she tumbled down the hillside toward the water, hollering all the way.

Michael swore under his breath and went after her, sliding down the steep hillside feet-first.

She was still screaming. Below him he saw her hit the water. Rock and dirt and mud tumbled down ahead of him. The whole time he was watching for her silly head to pop up out of the glassy surface.

It didn't.

He panicked and shoved off the hill in a half-dive. He hit the water just a foot away from where she'd sank. He dove down deeper.

The water was deep here and icy cold. She was frantic, kicking out and waving her arms like someone who couldn't swim.

He clamped his arm around her wiggling, scrawny body and pushed upward. She stopped kicking and he felt her small hands tightly grip his forearm as they rose through the water.

Their heads broke the surface and he heard her gasp for breath. He swam through the water, pulling her with him to a rocky beach. He crawled onshore with her hanging limply under one arm.

Once they were safely on the gravel beach she stiffened and rolled away from him. She just lay there. She had her face buried in her folded arms, and her back rose with each gasp for breath. He knew she was going to be all right when she began to cough.

He sat up, resting his arms on his knees, and watched her. After a minute he could see one brown eye peeking out from her arms. He shook his head and gave her a stern look. "You need to watch where you walk, Squirt."

She buried her head deeper in her arms and muttered something.

"What did you say?"

She scowled over at him. "I said I fell on purpose." Her chin jutted out like a mule he'd seen once. "I wanted to see how cold the water was."

They both knew she was lying.

She was too proud to admit she'd slipped and fallen in.

He stood, then looked down at her wet face staring up at him with a look that dared him to argue with her. He could have called her bluff. But he didn't. Pride was something he understood. He turned away and started to walk toward the cove just beyond the rocky beach.

Behind him he heard her mumble that she wasn't some squirty kid, that she was Catherine Wardwell and she did know all about sex.

He stopped and turned back around. "Hey, Squirt."

She was standing now, looking right at him.

"If I were you, I'd stop trying to learn 'all about sex' and just learn how to swim."

Three

The Wardwells were coming back to Spruce Island. For the past three years they had returned every June, and each year Catherine Wardwell spent most of the month bugging him. He'd discovered she had an annoying habit of popping up at the worst possible moment, like when he was in the woods drinking the beers he'd found in a boat his grandfather had loaned to some sportsmen. Or when he was making out with a girl named Kristy behind the old well house near the cove where her parents had moored their boat.

It was June again, and like Dylan had sung, the times they were-a-changing. The Coca-Cola Company made a major move in packaging, from bottle containers to aluminum cans. The Beach Boys hit number one on the pop charts, and *Dr. Strangelove or Why I Learned to Stop Worrying and Love the Bomb* opened in theaters with *My Fair Lady.*

But for Michael, June was hell month. Catherine Wardwell was back.

She was fourteen now, and she wore something called Erase for lipstick; it made her look too pale. She'd cut her hair short like some *Seventeen* magazine cover model. She looked pudgy and awkward and silly, as if she were trying too hard to be older.

He told her she wore too much makeup and looked half-dead. She told him his oxford shirt was buttoned too high and made him look like a geek.

It didn't take long for her to get in his hair again. During that first week he woke up one morning and caught her peeking in the cabin window. He slipped outside and turned the hose on her.

The second week she stole a pack of cigarettes from him and had broken them all in two. He hadn't cared much about smoking, just carried them to be cool, but to spite her he smoked all the stubs and blew the smoke in her face. She was so pig-headed she stood there and refused to run away.

But the worst incident was the afternoon he'd found a letter his dad had written to his grandfather on the day he was born, a letter that was filled with a father's pride and dreams, things that only reminded Michael of the family he had lost.

No one had ever seen him cry; his pride would not let him show that he hurt.

But she saw him cry that day, when he was seventeen and sitting on a rock in a deserted section of the island.

He thought he was alone when he sat there and sobbed in his knees.

That day she had walked right up to him and picked up the letter.

He cursed at her and tried to grab it away from her, but he could only see blurred images through his wet eyes.

She quickly stuffed it in her bra and ran away.

He didn't have the energy to chase after her, so he just stared off into the distance, trying hard to picture his dad's face and seeing nothing but the shadow of a tall man.

In a few minutes she came back, walking quietly.

From her tentative steps and her somber manner he could tell she'd read the letter.

She sat down next to him and handed him the crumpled paper.

He didn't take it. Didn't look at her. He only wanted to be left alone.

She began to smooth the paper against a rock, a lame effort to try to flatten it back to the way it had been.

It was a stupid thing to do. Like not having his dad anymore would hurt less if the letter weren't creased.

She stopped after a minute and said nothing. Time passed in awkward and tense seconds that seemed to last an hour, one of those moments where you want to run away and hide from everything.

But she just sat there right next to him, so close that he could feel the warmth from her where their shoulders almost touched. She folded her hands in her lap and hung her head. Then she did the one thing he'd never expected.

She cried with him.

Summer, 1966

For the first time since 1963, the Wardwells had come back to the island. It was the same day he got his draft notice.

Dear Mr. Packard,
Greetings from the President of the United States…

There was no doubt the letter would change his future. The draft situation had newspapers and television stations full of protests and debates where activists argued against war, declaring the draft was archaic and unfair. Claiming you couldn't buy beer, but you could die for your country. You couldn't vote for the president of the United States, but you had to kill if he ordered you to.

Some who got the same letter went off to war. Some ran to Canada. But Michael just read the notice and set it down. He didn't know how he felt about any of it. To him war seemed so far away, farther away than Vietnam. He went off into the woods to work so he wouldn't have to think.

He hadn't known the Wardwells were back this year. They hadn't been back for two years so there was no reason to expect them. The moment Michael saw her leave the old house and walk down the beach toward the dock, he forgot all about the draft notice.

He was hidden in a group of cedar and maple trees that circled the cove. He was cutting wood from a tree that had fallen during the winter when he heard the hinges squeak and a screen door slam. He cast a quick glance toward the old Victorian rental house where a girl in a bright pink bikini came down the front porch steps and crossed the lawn.

He leaned a shoulder against a tree and just watched her. She had a body that was better than last month's centerfold.

Then he recognized her face.

Gone was the pudgy and awkward blonde teen who wore too much makeup and followed him everywhere. She was taller now, a good three inches, and her shape blew him away. He remembered a poster he'd seen in Seattle, one of a soaking wet Ursula Andress dressed in a wet skin-colored bikini, her hair slicked back and her face and body guaranteed to make a man wake up in one helluva sweat.

He shook his head in disbelief. Gawky little Catherine Wardwell—the pest who knew all about sex, spied on him through windows, and had seen him cry—could have put the sexy Ursula to shame.

He felt a stab of something earthy and carnal go clear through the center of him. The ax slipped from his hand and hit the ground with a dull thud. He swore under his breath and shifted slightly.

He couldn't take his eyes off her. And he didn't want to.

Her hair was lighter, longer and straighter; it brushed her shoulders as she walked down to the end of the dock where a red and blue nautical beach towel lay spread out and a transistor radio with a tall silver antenna played the Lovin' Spoonful.

He leaned against the tree and crossed his arms, then blew out a breath slowly, kind of a half whistle of amazement that a girl could be put together that way.

She bent over and tossed something on the towel.

He groaned and closed his eyes. He heard the music throbbing through the air with the same beat that his heart pounded. He opened his eyes because he couldn't hide any longer. He had to see her.

She was standing with her toes curled over the edge of the dock, her stance stiff and straight, her arms raised high, ready to dive.

He shoved off from the tree and moved down toward her. This year things had changed; he was following her.

She dove in.

When she hit the water, his breath caught and held as if he had to hold his own breath along with her. He walked faster, down the dock toward the water. But when he reached the towel, he stopped. He stood there staring at the rings of water she left behind, while the music from the radio blared out over the cove.

Her head broke through the surface, sleek and golden and wet. He bent and flicked down the volume on the radio, then he straightened and waited until she turned in the water.

She froze the instant she saw him. "Michael?"

Her voice was older and throaty. It made him think of things like smooth soft skin. Hot deep kisses. And Trojans.

He took two steps to the edge of the dock and squatted down, resting a hand on his thigh. He just looked at her and enjoyed the view. The air grew hotter and tighter and felt heavy.

She swam toward him.

He reached out a hand to her. "Hi, Squirt."

She put her hand in his and he straightened, pulling her up with him while he watched the water run down her body.

She stood close to him, so close that all he had to do was lean forward and their bodies would touch. Chest to chest. Hip to hip. Mouth to mouth. He had a strange and laughable vision of them touching and steam suddenly fogging up the air around them.

She was five foot ten or so. No longer a little squirt. But it didn't matter because she still had to look up at him. He was six foot two.

She slid her hand from his grip, turned away and grabbed the towel. She used it to cover herself while she awkwardly pretended to dry off.

He hadn't moved, only watched her. He said nothing until she finally glanced up at him. He gave her a long look she'd have to be blind not to understand.

She got it. Her face flushed and she looked down quickly, rubbing the hell out of her legs so she missed the grin he had to bite to hide. She straightened then, still holding the towel. She raised her chin a little, defiant and challenging, the Catherine he remembered.

A moment passed. A minute maybe two. Neither said anything. They just stood on the dock and looked at each other under the warm and unpredictable sunshine. He felt like a thirsty man staring at an icy cold beer.

She dropped the act and returned his look, then whispered his name in that raspy grown-up voice he felt go all the way through him. "Michael."

Just Michael.

And he was lost.

Time seemed to pass quickly after that. On days when it rained that misty rain that sometimes clouded the islands, they walked on the beach together, not minding the moodiness of the weather. The sunsets grew later and later as summer crept into the Northwest, and they fell in love.

They swam in the cove where the water was shallow and warm enough to enjoy. He taught her to sail. The first time a heavy summer rain hit, they moored and took shelter inside the sailboat's small cabin, laughing at the foolish weather and eating a lunch of egg-salad sandwiches and barbecued potato chips she'd brought along.

The flavor of salt and barbecue spices lingered on her lips. Years later he could still not eat barbecued potato chips without thinking of that day, where a six-foot by six-foot sailboat cabin was too small and things quickly grew intense, so much so that they ended up moored to an old buoy and necking for most of the afternoon.

After that day, whenever they took the boat out he silently prayed for rain. Finally, rain or not, they spent afternoons in the cabin of his boat, where things got hot and heavy, where they would steam up the small mirror above the hard bunk and leave the sloop with their lips swollen and their bodies tense with need.

Michael learned the true meaning of wanting a woman that month. He learned the dark side of sex: the forbidden guilt and hunger that was teenage love. He would lie awake at night so hard from the mere thought of her that he couldn't sleep. And when she would look at him in that way she had, as if he knew the answers to all the questions in the world, he felt real and alive, as if he could take on the world just for her. He learned that when you were young, nothing else mattered but the girl you loved.

One day he oiled the hinges on the old screen door because it gave him an excuse to be near her. She slipped out of the old house for the first time that night and met him walking in the woods where he pinned her against a tree and kissed the hell out of her, unhooked her bra and felt her up.

All he had to do was touch Catherine and both of them burned up. But they didn't just touch and kiss and steam up the glass. Sometimes they would sit, hidden by those big old gray rocks near the cove, and watch the night drift by them.

And they would talk. About her hometown. About the war. About the poetry she loved. About the music he loved. About how Bob Dylan and Paul Simon were both poets and musicians. They talked about life and death and dreams.

She taught him the names of the stars because she said when he touched her and kissed her she always felt as if he took her clear up to those stars.

He didn't care that she was seventeen and he was almost twenty. He didn't care that the world thought he was a man who was ready to go to war, while she had one more year of high school and was jailbait.

He didn't care because when he kissed Catherine Wardwell, nothing else in the whole goddamned screwed-up world mattered. Until the night they couldn't stop and went all the way, the same night he'd carved their initials in the wood.

The same night her father caught them in the boathouse.

Four

Catherine slipped off her glasses and sagged back in her chair, staring out at the pink Victorian across the street from her office. It was four o'clock and almost every ten minutes there had been an urgent call.

She pinched the bridge of her nose and saw stars. When her vision cleared, she was looking at her desktop, where a cluster of silver-framed images of her daughters Alyson and Dana were grinning back at her.

In a frame with delicate ballet shoes decorating the corners was a photograph of Dana, her oldest daughter, dressed in a pink tutu, her blonde hair scraped back off her small heart-shaped face. She had been six then and had no front teeth. Her gummy smile looked almost too big for her face. There was another shot next to it of her sitting on Santa's knee, her eyes turned up to him in complete awe. And the last photo was taken only a few months ago when Dana went to the Sadie Hawkins dance.

She turned to Alyson's pictures. There was her second-grade photo taken the day after she'd tried to cut her own bangs; she looked like she'd had a fight with a lawnmower. Every time Catherine saw that photo she smiled.

There was no picture of Aly on Santa's knee. Aly had always preferred animals to humans. She had liked Disney's *Robin Hood* better than *Sleeping Beauty*. She wouldn't go near Santa because when she was three the older kids at her preschool had told her there was no such thing as Santa Claus. After that day, Santa meant nothing to her.

Now the Easter Bunny, well, that was different. Those kids hadn't said anything about the Easter Bunny. So instead of a Santa photo, there was one of Aly sitting on top of the Easter Bunny's furry knee, her hands cupping his pink fuzzy cheeks while she demanded to know how he got around to all the houses in the world and managed to hide all those eggs in only one night. One of Aly's typical questions—the kind that were hard to answer.

Catherine glanced back at the stack of report folders in a jagged pile on her desk, then up at the smiling images of her daughters. She picked up the phone, punched in a series of numbers and got Seattle information.

Fifteen minutes later she had rented the same quaint Victorian house in the same cove on the same secluded San Juan island where she'd spent so many summers.

This June, she vowed, would be different for her girls.

It was different. Her girls didn't want to go.

Dana had to turn down a free ticket to a rock concert at Great America and Aly was going to miss a birthday party at the boardwalk in Santa Cruz. Aly had eventually accepted Catherine's decision to go to the island, especially after Catherine had bribed her by letting her bring along her cat Harold. But fifteen year old Dana was still scowling at the world. Nothing worked with her. If there had been a high school course in sulking, Dana would have aced the class.

Over an hour ago they had left the ferry at Orcas, purchased their supplies and loaded everything into a boat run by Blakely Charters. Until January, when daily ferry service would start to Spruce Island, the charter company made two runs a week. Sundays and Thursdays. Other than by seaplane, hiring a boat was the only way to get to the more remote and secluded islands of the San Juans.

It was late and the sun was sliding down the horizon; it turned the cotton clouds in the western sky gold, purple and red. Catherine leaned over the bow of the boat and pointed west. "Girls! Quick! Look at that sky!"

She had forgotten how gorgeous the sunsets were here. The color. The sheer beauty of nature. No one could possibly visit this part of the world and not believe in the perfect hand of God.

She turned toward her silent daughters to share their first sight of a Northwest summer sunset, and her heart sank.

Dana sat with her back to her, staring out at the water like a prisoner heading for death row. In her lap was an open copy of Stephen King's Green Mile series. Without looking at Catherine, she blinked once, then buried her nose back in the book.

Dana's sulking hurt Catherine. She didn't want to let on

that Dana had gotten to her, so she looked away. Aly had on a set of headphones. She was head-bopping to some song that shrieked through the headphone earpieces.

Catherine reached over, picked up the empty CD case, and read the name.

Alanis Morrisette.

She felt as if she were a hundred years old. She hated that music. Then she remembered how much her dad had disliked her Bob Dylan albums. She asked herself the question she always asked when she was dealing with the girls.

Will it matter in five years?

Dana's sulking wouldn't matter and hopefully some other hot young singer would be Aly's favorite—if she still had her hearing.

The generation gap between her and her daughters felt as if it were as wide as the Grand Canyon. But she did know one thing—her relationship with her daughters would matter in five years.

She wanted her girls back, not these two young people she didn't know anymore. She desperately wanted what few memories they could make this month, something special for them to look back on the same way she looked back on the island and those summers from her childhood.

She thought of this trip as a fresh start; she needed to be a mother again.

Catherine reached across and snatched the book out of Dana's hands. "You can read this later." She tucked it inside her duffel bag, then she punched the off button on Aly's CD player and gestured for her to take off the headphones.

Both girls gaped at her.

She pointed ahead of them. "That's Spruce Island," she told them in a classic mother's tone that demanded their attention—now.

Against the horizon the island was a camel-shaped lump of rocks and trees and natural coastline that grew larger the closer they got.

"I loved that island when I was your age. My favorite memories are there and it's important to me that we spend time together so you can see what a wonderful place it is."

They continued to look at her, then turned in unison to look at the island ahead of them.

"There are no houses," Dana said in a voice that implied it was the very ends of the earth.

"There are summer houses, a few cabins and a village on the other side of the island. You can't see them on this side. It's more isolated. The island has always been a place where people go to get away." She paused, then added, "Like us."

They turned back around. From the looks on their faces you'd think she had just spoken Greek.

"The first houses were summer homes built late in the nineteenth century. Those hills are parkland and there are hiking trails."

Dana frowned at her. "You hate hiking. You said you'd rather chew on foil than traipse up some mountain."

"Yeah," Aly said, siding with her sister. "You said smart people leave mountain climbing to the goats."

Catherine realized she would never have to worry about losing her memory. She had her daughters to remind her of every single thing she had ever said.

"Fine. Forget about hiking. As I was saying, the house

is on a cove on the western side of the island. There's a private dock and a mooring. The rental agent said the owners still keep a sailboat. We're free to use it. There are supposed to be bikes, too. When we used to come here there was a handyman's cabin on a nearby inlet and a small harbor where boats from the mainland could moor. Other than that the island is pretty isolated."

Twenty minutes later they stood at the end of a gray weathered dock, their bags and supplies stacked like building blocks and Harold whining in his cat carrier. There was nothing before them but silvery water. Catherine watched the boat turn around in a wide swath and head back for the mainland.

For just one moment she looked around her and was a little scared. It was secluded, and they were three women alone.

She raised a hand to her forehead and scanned the island. The large house was partially hidden by cedar and maple trees, but Catherine could see the sharp roofline. The old shingles were green with algae and moss, the way everything grew green in the dampness of the islands.

She took a deep breath, bent down, picked up a duffel and two plastic bags of groceries, then she marched bravely down the dock toward the rocky beach. Over her shoulder she called out, "Grab something and let's go, girls. It's getting dark."

Five

It wasn't dark enough.

Not to hide what time and weather had done to the old house. It was painted the same color yellow with the same white trim. Catherine walked toward the house and the closer she got the more she realized that the house looked the same because it was probably the same coat of paint as in 1966. It certainly looked about thirty years old.

Behind her she heard Dana's shoes crunching on the gravel. A second later she heard a gasp.

"Mo-ther!"

"What?" Catherine snapped and turned around. She wasn't ready for a confrontation.

"What are those?" With her horrified expression, Dana stood pointing at the ground. Next to her Aly clutched the cat carrier to her chest the way one holds a child after a close call.

Catherine looked at the ground. "They're slugs."

"Ugh!" Both girls shivered and stepped back.

"Oh God! I stepped on one!" Dana dropped her backpack and jumped around, shrieking.

It was the most life she'd shown since Catherine told the girls about the trip and she'd given her best Mother-you-are-going-to-ruin-my-life act.

"Get it off! Get it off!"

"Stop hopping all over the place. You'll step on another one."

Dana froze.

"Just wipe your shoe off on the grass."

Dana moaned, then hobbled over to a patch of wet grass and made a big to-do about wiping off her shoe.

Aly had shifted her cat carrier and was scanning the ground. "Do they travel with a mate?"

"I have no idea. They're just like the snails we have at home only without the shells." Catherine quickly checked the ground for slugs, then set down her bags. She had forgotten about those huge slugs that slithered all over the place whenever it rained.

"This place is awful," Dana muttered from behind her.

"It's not awful. It's rustic and quaint," Catherine told her, trying to keep her voice light but not feeling light at all.

Dana snorted.

"Follow me." She could hear the girls whispering behind her and Harold began to whine. She didn't really blame them. She had a bad feeling about this. She opened the screen door and held it with her shoulder while she pulled the rental envelope with the key out of her pocket and unlocked the front door.

Please, she thought, please let the inside be better than the outside.

* * *

Better was a relative term.

The inside wasn't the Four Seasons. Catherine looked around the room. It was clean and neat and furnished in an odd mishmash of styles. There was an eastlake style sofa upholstered in a brown and red western print with bronco-riding cowboys, red and black lariats, and a smattering of green horseshoes. There were throw pillows scattered across it—one was yellow gingham, one was needlepoint bulldogs, and the other was black and white and shaped like a soccer ball. A Blackwatch plaid stadium blanket with the Mariners emblem embroidered in the corner was thrown over the edge of a brown recliner. Next to it was a white French provincial chair that looked exactly like one her grandmother had in front of her bedroom dressing table.

The coffee table was a huge wooden piece with burned edges, something you see in a roadside stand next to the velvet paintings of Elvis. In the center of the table was a monkeypod bowl with a silver nut cracker and a chrome and black leather ashtray. The end tables weren't end tables at all, but small dressers. One was painted aqua and the other canary yellow. The aqua dresser had a white milkglass lamp with a beige ruffled shade. The only other light in the room was a red and orange lava lamp.

"Who decorated this place?" Dana said with a disgusted voice.

"Dale Evans and Barbara Cartland," Catherine said as she set down the bags.

"Who?"

"James Bond and the Monkees?"

"James Bond and the Monkees?" Aly repeated. "Was that a rock group in the olden days?"

"Hey, hey, we're the mon-kees," Catherine sang, bopping her head as she did the Pony across the linoleum in the kitchen.

Her daughters looked at each other and rolled their eyes. She sighed. Her children had their father's sense of humor.

"Yes, the Monkees were a rock group and surely you know who James Bond is."

"Oh yeah. I forgot. Pierce Brosnan, huh?"

"Sean Connery."

"The old guy? Uh-uh," Aly shook her head. "He was Indiana Jones's dad."

Catherine felt ancient.

Aly dropped the grocery bags on a rag rug and plopped down on the cowboy sofa. She switched on the lamp. "I love lava lamps." She rested her chin in her hands and watched the lamp bubble.

Catherine watched her youngest daughter and was overcome with a sense of déjà vu. Aly was dressed in bell-bottomed jeans, a wide black belt, and a skinny turtleneck. She even had on a thick white headband and a flip hairdo like the Breck girl.

"Can we get one, Mom?"

"One what?"

"A lava lamp."

Catherine hadn't liked lava lamps back when they were

new. To her they were in the same category as Chia pets and diet tablets that helped you lose ten pounds overnight.

Aly was staring at her through the liquid of the lamp.

"We'll see."

"Where's the TV?" Dana looked at her and popped her gum.

Here it comes, Catherine thought. She opened the refrigerator and started putting things inside. When she had her head sufficiently hidden behind the door she said, "There is no TV."

It took a few minutes before she could get a word in between their melodramatic protests. Aly was going to miss "Nick at Night" and Dana just plain hated the island and wanted to go home, where "it was normal." And she wanted to go now.

"You need to give this place a chance. And even if I was willing to leave—which I'm not—there's no boat until Thursday."

Catherine crossed the room to the bookcase made of cinderblock and wood planks. "There's a whole wall of books here." She opened a huge cabinet. "Look in here. I see stacks of puzzles and games."

Dana shifted her gaze to the cabinet. "Oh yea!" She clapped her hands like a baby. "Candyland and Chutes and Ladders."

Catherine looked inside. "Don't be smart. There are adult games in here, too. And puzzles are always fun. We used to do those at home." She pulled out the top puzzle box. "Look at this one. It's a thousand-piece puzzle of a pepperoni pizza. You both like pizza."

Aly stood next to her and looked inside. She tilted her head sideways to read. "What's this? Two thousand pieces." She looked back at Catherine. "We've never done a puzzle with that many pieces. Have you?"

Catherine shook her head.

Aly read the puzzle label. "It says Classic Puzzle Series: Metal Rockers."

Catherine pictured a photograph made up of sleek, chrome and black leather Brancusi rocking chairs cut up into thousands of tiny pieces all shaped like Mickey Mouse. She smiled. It would be the kind of puzzle that was almost impossible to do in less than three days. "Take it out, Aly, and let's take a look."

Aly held up the box and they stared down at the lid. A whole group of chalk-white faces framed with wild black hairdos stared back at them.

Catherine felt her smile fade.

"Cool!" Dana said, taking the box from her sister. "It's Aerosmith and Kiss." Both girls moved over to the sofa as if they were chasing concert tickets, sat down and dumped out a huge pile of tiny puzzle pieces on the coffee table.

Dana looked up impatiently. "Come on, Mom."

"Let's get comfortable first." Catherine ran toward the downstairs bedroom. "Last one in their sweats has to make dinner!"

A few minutes later when she walked back into the room wearing old sweats, she found Dana already in her flannel pajamas and sprawled out on the sofa with Aly's cat asleep on her stomach.

"No Aly?"

Dana shook her head. "She couldn't find her boxers."

Catherine grinned. "Good. I don't have to cook."

A minute later Aly came running down the stairs wearing a pair of white cotton boxers patterned with bright red lips and a cropped T-shirt that said Smile and Kiss Me. She looked at Dana, then at Catherine. "I'm last, huh?"

They nodded.

Aly was a trooper. She just shrugged, walked over to the sofa and scooped up her cat. "I know exactly what I'm fixing for dinner."

"What?" Catherine asked.

She exchanged a sly look with Dana, then said, "It's a surprise."

Catherine didn't care what she made as long as the girls were reasonably happy for now. She'd take this one moment at a time. She walked toward the coffee table, then started to sit opposite it on the floor.

"Sit here, Mom." Aly tucked the cat onto her hip, shifted sides of the coffee table, then sank gracefully down to the rug. "You don't want to sit on the floor. Remember that time you couldn't get up?"

"I'd been skiing all day," Catherine said defensively.

Her daughters exchanged a look that said, "Yeah. Sure."

"I had." Catherine sat down on the Dale Evans sofa.

Dana laughed, a refreshing sound, then in a falsetto voice she said, "Help! Help! I've fallen down and I can't get up!"

Aly caught on and said, "We'll order you one of those clapper things, Mom."

"Funny. Real funny." Catherine tried to look serious and failed. Both her girls were grinning at her. For the first time in the last few days she thought that perhaps her plan just might work. The three of them were talking together and joking with each other. The girls were laughing instead of ignoring her.

"I found a corner piece!" Aly said, hunched over the puzzle with Harold purring in her lap. She sat up, her pert little nose in the air. "I was first."

A minute later, in the name of good old healthy female competition, they all lost themselves to the other one thousand, nine hundred and ninety-nine pieces of the jigsaw puzzle.

Six

Michael was outside cutting wood when the air began to fill with the smell of rain. Daylight had faded away and the wind was picking up, so he went inside. He hung his jacket on the old iron coat-rack, next to where his grandfather's tool belt still hung on the exact same hook as it had for almost forty years.

He'd kept that belt around long after his grandfather had died. The canvas was frayed, the edges were black with grease, and the leather was cracked. At first he'd told himself he kept it around because they didn't make tool belts like they used to, with a slot for a flashlight and for tools.

Hell. Now they made tool belts out of space-age, NASA-developed weave that was stronger than canvas and leather could ever be.

The truth was, he'd kept it for sentimental reasons. And he still used it. Maybe he wore it because he was trying to recapture his past. Maybe he was just old and needed something from his youth to cling to.

He turned away, not really giving a damn why he wore the thing. He just did.

He crossed the room and started a fire, then went into the kitchen where he made some soup. He stood at the stove and ate right from the pan. He ate most of his meals that way, when he was home alone and too lazy to dirty a plate or to bother with sitting down at a table.

Unless there was a football game on TV, then he sat down in front of his big screen while he ate from the pan.

Single people had singular habits. He drank milk and orange juice from the carton while standing at the open refrigerator, his arm resting on the door. He dipped his toast in the jam jar. He didn't pick up his socks or make his bed unless someone was going to join him in it. He usually left the cap off the toothpaste and squeezed the tube from the middle.

He knew himself pretty well, he thought as he crossed the room. He picked up the latest issue of *Money* magazine, then set down a glass of Jack Daniel's on a small table and sat in an old comfortable chair in front of the older rock fireplace that blazed and crackled with a fire.

He propped his feet up on a tired leather ottoman and relaxed—something he couldn't seem to do much of lately. At some point he had lost the ability to sleep on planes. Hell, sometimes he even lost the ability to sleep in a hotel room, and it didn't seem to matter how exhausted he was.

At this moment, though, he wasn't tired. But he knew he could easily fall asleep in the old chair if he just closed his eyes. There was a comfort in knowing he could do something easily, something that had until now eluded him.

He chose to sip his drink and look around him instead of escaping to sleep. He had a strong sense that he was where he belonged, in a place that seemed to fit him better than his sleek glass offices or his huge home.

He'd gotten so he only lived in three of the rooms in that enormous house on the water. Usually he came in through the garage, because when he walked in the front doors he felt as if he were walking into the Guggenheim.

Here he was surrounded by old things. He liked old things.

He took his glasses out of his flannel shirt pocket and slipped them on, then began to read the magazine. The Asian markets were on a downtrend and the Wall Street wizards expected the NASDAQ to drop. Some hotshot at Merrill Lynch predicted Letni stock to drop and profits to be down.

Michael had been reading about and hearing those rumors for over a year. But each quarter the company proved to be stronger than ever. This magazine issue was barely a week old, yet just yesterday, before he'd loaded the boat with supplies and motored to the island, Letni had released to the public the profit reports for the last quarter.

They were twice as high as he had expected.

He laughed and tossed the magazine into the fireplace, where it curled into dark flame that was as black as the magazine's predictions. He watched it burn, then picked up his drink and mockingly raised his glass to the jackass who'd written the article.

Michael toasted him with two extremely crude words.

* * *

By eight o'clock Catherine and the girls had polished off six cans of cream soda, a can of cheese Pringles, a box of Wheat Thins and two containers of Allouette spread, five apples, a slab of Tillamook cheese and two pints of Ben & Jerry's Wavy Gravy ice cream—Aly's idea of dinner.

"One more piece and we'll have the outside frame done." Catherine stuck her spoon in the empty ice cream carton and scanned the table for a piece that had a flat edge.

Dana was chewing on a handful of smoked almonds—a gift from Catherine's mother—and eyeing the small puzzle pieces with a determined look on her face. It seemed that Dana was driven to find that puzzle piece.

But not Aly. She had given up on the puzzle frame and was putting together Gene Simmons's chalky face. Even upside-down Catherine could see that in the photograph his tongue was sticking out.

She suddenly wished they were putting together a picture of Bambi, Thumper and Flower. She sighed in that quiet, tired way, when you knew time had slipped past far too quickly, then went back to the puzzle.

A few minutes later she had an awful thought. "If this puzzle is missing any pieces I'm going to scream."

Almost simultaneously she spotted the last outside end piece.

Aha!

She locked her eyes on it and casually set down the empty ice cream carton. Then she leaned forward and quickly reached across the table to snatch up the puzzle piece.

At that very same moment the lights went out.

* * *

It didn't take Catherine long to remember that whenever a storm hit Spruce Island, the power went out. The sudden and complete island darkness could jar your memory quickly.

There were no streetlights here. Just the stars and the moon, and on some rainy nights, not even that.

What she saw in the darkness was the remembered image of her father cursing at the old generator behind the rental house. She could remember her mother holding an umbrella and scolding her dad for cursing, and how Catherine always got to hold the flashlight so her dad could see inside the generator while he cursed at it.

So she and the girls went outside, loaded with one big old metal flashlight and a huge Mary Poppins-sized umbrella. Dana whipped the flashlight back and forth across the ground. She was on slug patrol.

Aly carried the umbrella. Catherine stumbled on a rock and almost fell on her face; she couldn't see because Dana, her slug-fearing daughter, had the flashlight shining near her own feet instead of the path that ran toward the north end of the yard.

Catherine stopped and turned around. "Dana."

"Huh?"

"Keep the flashlight ahead of us so I don't fall and kill myself."

Dana never even looked up at her.

Huddled under the umbrella with Aly, Catherine tapped Dana on the arm. "I promise no slugs are going to suddenly leap up from the ground and latch on to your face like that monster did in *Alien*."

"Oh, Mom."

Catherine stopped in front of a small wooden garden shed with a trap door. "Ah, here it is. Voila!" She paused and waved her hand dramatically. "This, my girls, is a generator…I think. Hold the flashlight up, Dana."

"Does it work?" Dana asked, glancing up for only one brief second before she turned her gaze back to the grass.

"I don't know. It used to drive your grandpa nuts, though. I'd come out here with him and hold the flashlight. Like you are, Dana. Aim it here, sweetie. That's right. I can still remember him banging on this metal thing when he couldn't get it to work. He made so much noise you could have heard him hammering on it all the way across the island. He used to say a generator is like a mule. It needs a swift kick to get going."

A few minutes later, the wind had picked up and the rain was coming down so hard it bounced back up from the ground. Over five times Catherine had read and followed the old instructions that were engraved on a metal plate attached to the lid, and still nothing happened.

"Who writes these things?" she muttered. "Probably the same people who write software manuals."

She took the flashlight from Dana and banged the generator a good one.

The motor gave a half-hearted start, then suddenly died.

"Oh Mom! It almost started!" Dana reached for the flashlight. "Let me try." She hit it a few times.

The generator started up with a loud coughing rev like a huge lawnmower.

She and the girls cheered, then she took the flashlight

from Dana and turned to trudge back to the porch. The clouds slipped by steadily and the moon cracked through with bright silver light. The wind blew in sudden, whipping gusts and caught the umbrella; it slipped from Aly's hands and tumbled across the yard like an shiny wet acrobat.

They chased after it, all of them yelling "I'll get it! I'll get it!" Dana made a grab for it at the same time as Aly. Both girls fell in the mud just as the umbrella danced away from their outstretched hands.

Catherine looked down at her muddy children and began to laugh. "First one to get the umbrella doesn't have to do any dishes for a week!" She ran after the umbrella while her girls scrambled after her.

"You're cheating, Mom! You had a head start!"

"That's because I'm old!" she shouted over her shoulder as she ran in front of them.

It became a game, one of them reaching for the umbrella just as the wind snatched it away, leaving behind nothing but their laughter. They were so wet the umbrella wouldn't have done them a bit of good, but it didn't matter. Between the stubborn and wild Winslow women, one of them was going to get that blasted umbrella.

Soaking wet and shouting, Catherine was now the closest to it. She gave a triumphant holler and launched after it like a missile.

One moment she was standing, the next she slipped in the mud and skidded on her stomach across the wet grass, all to the sound of her daughters' laughter being carried upward by that rascally wind.

Mud splashed up into her face and through her wet hair,

but she didn't care. She hadn't had this much fun since she was ten and her dad had brought home a bright yellow Slip 'n Slide he'd attached to the garden hose in the yard.

"Yahoo! I've got it!" She laughed and hooted, then scrambled up and chased the umbrella, until she realized she couldn't run fast enough to catch it. So she dove toward the wet ground on purpose and just slid after it on her belly.

Right into a large pair of Wellington boots.

A man's Wellington boots.

For a second she stared at the huge rubber tips, partially sunken in the new mud, then slowly raised her wet head to look up.

The moonlight was behind him and all she could see was a tall silhouette of a man holding the umbrella. He shined a flashlight in her face and held it there.

She squinted and held up her hand to block out the glare.

Without a word he turned the light away from her.

She stared up at him.

His features were blurred, so she swiped the mud and water from her face and slapped her wet hair out of her eyes. Just for good measure she pulled the flashlight out of her jacket and shone it upward, figuring she could either blind him or beat him with it if he meant them any harm.

The light shone on his face. Everything seemed to stop suddenly. The rain. The wind. Her heart. Her breath.

The whole world stopped.

She stared up at him and felt as if she were stepping into her most secret dreams. She whispered, "Michael?"

Seven

It took Michael a minute to realize just who he was looking at. Every emotion imaginable raced through him. Yet he didn't react; he had spent too much time in Vietnam, where he'd learned to never be surprised, and had developed nerves of steel that served him in his business and his personal life.

Until this very moment.

This was a face he had seen only in his memory for the last thirty years.

She was covered in mud and soaking wet. Her hair was dark and stringy from the rain, her mouth open in stunned surprise.

But that face was still uniquely Catherine.

"Hi, Squirt."

"Ohmygod… It is you." She buried her head in her arms the way she had when she was eleven. It was as if she still thought her embarrassing moments would just go away if she didn't look at him.

"How long have you been standing there?" she said into her arms.

"Long enough to be entertained."

She took a deep breath. "That's what I was afraid of."

"Who are you?" A young girl stuck her wet and muddy face in front of him. It was almost exactly the same face he had seen hanging upside-down from a tree.

Michael felt as if he were in an episode of "Star Trek," thrown back to a unique and significant time in his life just to teach him something.

The youngest girl looked exactly like Catherine did at eleven. Another Squirt.

For one brief moment—just a nanosecond of regret that had never hit him before—he was sorry he had never fathered a child.

While he stood there speechless and frozen in time, Catherine rolled over and sat up, resting her hands on her bent knees. She looked at the two girls. "This is Michael Packard, girls. An old friend."

"There are no houses around here," the older girl said after scanning the trees. She looked at him as if she expected him to grow horns. "Where'd you come from?"

He didn't take his eyes off Catherine when he answered her. "The stork dropped me down the chimney."

Catherine looked right into his eyes, half surprised and half amused. A moment later she began to laugh.

He could see she remembered that all those years ago he'd said those same words to her. A second later the older girl called him a weirdo under her breath, and Michael decided that time didn't change people very much.

"He was teasing you, Dana," Catherine said.

He stuck out a hand to help her up. "Here."

She sat there for a second, her gaze wandering over him. She paused to look at the tool belt hanging on his hips. He wondered what she was thinking when she looked at him like that.

She looked down quickly as if to hide her thoughts, like she was embarrassed. She wiped her muddy hand off on her even muddier pants, then put it into his hand.

He started to pull her to her feet.

"Michael is the handyman on the island," she told her daughters.

He had the sudden urge to drop her.

"Just like his grandfather was," she added not looking at him and in a tone that was all too bright and cheery to be real.

Damn it if he didn't just let go.

She plopped back down in the mud with a splat, and her daughters laughed.

"Sorry," he said through a slightly tight jaw.

She looked up at him with a stunned expression.

He shrugged. "My hand slipped." He stuck out his hand again.

"No, thanks. I can get up on my own." She stood then with her back to him so he couldn't see her face.

She thought he was a handyman. And from her voice he could tell she was disappointed.

He shouldn't have let go of her. It was vindictive.

He looked away quickly because he thought he might smile. He took a deep breath, shoved his hands into his pockets, and with a straight face he turned back around.

The older girl was looking at him suspiciously. He waited a moment, then gave her the same speculative look she was giving him.

She stared at him longer than most. He wasn't certain how to gauge that—as teenaged stubbornness or an innate strength of character he should respect.

She finally looked down and began to fiddle with her hand.

"These are my daughters. Dana and Aly."

He nodded to them. Daughters meant there was a father. A husband. He glanced at her hand. No ring.

The rain changed meter and began to pound down in sheets. They all looked up for a second, then Catherine touched his shoulder. "Come on to the house!"

She half-ran, half-trudged toward the house with the girls running ahead of her.

At the crooked porch, she pried off her wet tennis shoes by stepping on her heel with one foot, then did the same with the other foot. Her daughters pulled off their shoes and rushed inside, while he sat on an old bench and pulled off his mud boots.

Catherine waited for him, watching him until he stood and she had to look up. She opened the old screen door, which creaked on its hinges the way it used to.

"Come on in," she said in a rushed voice that was breathy and still too sexy for her own good.

He felt a little numb as he followed her inside and stood there while she took his wet jacket and hung it on a hook. They went into the big old living room where a red and yellow glow from an old lava lamp made the room seem warmer.

No husband on the sofa. No man's jacket on the hook or boots on the porch. No man.

She walked a few feet into the room and stopped so suddenly it was as if she had hit an invisible wall.

He followed her gaze to the sofa where empty soda cans and boxes and ice cream cartons littered the sofa and floor. A low table was covered with a jigsaw puzzle.

She mumbled something that sounded like a swear word, then rushed over and began to scoop together the mess.

"Girls, help me here." She jammed soda cans under her arms and he tried not to laugh.

"Don't mess up the puzzle, Mom," the youngest girl said as she bent down and picked up a spoon that had fallen on the rug next to a big gray cat that was sound asleep.

From the way Catherine darted all over the place snatching up empty food containers, he could see she was embarrassed.

Both girls stood there in front of him, soaking wet and staring at him as if they expected him to do something strange, like split and multiply.

He should just leave. Take his tool belt and go back to his cabin and forget Catherine was ever here.

Instead he squatted down and gave the cat a stroke on his back. "Hey, fella."

"He likes you."

Michael looked up at the kid called Aly and nodded. "You sound surprised."

"He doesn't usually let strangers touch him. His name is Harold."

Harold rolled over on his side and began to purr loudly.

"What would you like to drink?" Catherine called out from the kitchen where she was stuffing trash into a bag under the sink. "I don't have beer, but I have soft drinks and plenty of coffee."

Michael sat down on the sofa and flinched. He reached behind him and pulled out an empty aluminum can.

Cream soda.

The youngest girl giggled and took it from him. He gave her a quick wink and said to Catherine, "Coffee's fine."

Catherine looked at her daughters and said, "Go upstairs and change out of those wet clothes, girls. I'm not sure which one of you is the muddiest."

Dana gave him a look as if she were weighing whether he could be trusted to be left alone with her mom.

Aly jabbed her with an elbow. "Come on."

They went upstairs together arguing over who looked the worst.

At the top of the landing Aly stuck her head out over the stair rail and looked down just as Catherine came out of the kitchen with a tray.

"We're both wrong, Dana."

Catherine stopped in front of the coffee table and looked up at her daughter, who was grinning down at her.

"Mother's the muddiest!" she said, then disappeared after her sister.

He watched Catherine's face as she looked down at herself for the first time. He could read her expression perfectly.

Again his first thought was that he should be a gentleman and leave. Instead he stood and took the tray from her. "Go get into some dry clothes."

She nodded and muddy hair fell into her face and stuck to her lips. She looked at him rather helplessly, then raised her chin as if she wasn't soaked and covered in mud and she walked toward the back bedroom.

Catherine Wardwell and her stubborn pride; it was still there after all these years.

He watched her, because she was Catherine and because he didn't want to look away, even though he knew it would make her feel less conspicuous.

Just before she turned the corner of the hall, she flicked on the hall light and he caught the expression on her pale face. She looked like she wanted the ground to just open up and swallow her.

Catherine certainly had wanted the earth to open up and swallow her. The trouble was, she looked as if it already had and then spit her back out again.

She stood at the mirror in the bathroom and had trouble looking at herself without wincing. It was worse than she had imagined.

There was grass in her hair, which was glued to her head and plastered around her forehead and ears. Flecks of mud and slim green blades of grass were stuck to her cheeks and neck. Her sweatshirt was soaked and clung to her chest.

She stepped back and turned around. The muddy sweatpants were stuck to her butt, too. She continued to stare. Oh, why had she quit step-aerobics?

Shoot, shoot, shoot, shoot!

She shoved back the shower curtain, turned on the shower and stripped off her clothes, then hopped inside.

She soaped up, washed her hair and was out in about two minutes. She dried off, shrugged into a robe, brushed her teeth longer than necessary, then went into the bedroom.

She changed clothes seven times in under five minutes, until she finally decided her bra was the problem and put on a different one, then hiked the adjustment on the straps up a good inch. After that her green cotton sweater looked better.

She hopped around the room, shoving her legs into the pair of jeans that made them look the longest, then she laid down on the bed so she could zip them up.

She stood and jerked the sweater down over her butt and ran back to the bathroom, where she swiped on some deodorant, brushed her wet hair back and twisted it up, then stuck in a hair pick to hold it.

She slapped on some makeup. She didn't need any blush; her face was too flushed already. She was nervous, so she put on more deodorant, then stood back and looked at herself.

He had been attracted to her once, when they were young. But what would he see when he looked at her now?

When she looked at herself she saw her outside changing, growing older, while inside she still felt young. Aging was a strange thing—made you feel like you were wearing a striped shirt and plaid pants. Mismatched. Because you never felt as old inside as you looked on the outside.

There were those days now when she went to put on her eye shadow and little lines of it caked at the corners of her eyes. She had to smudge the eye shadow into her skin with a Q-tip.

And there were those little vertical lines along her lips

that her old lipstick had recently started bleeding into. She'd had to change types of lip liner and lipstick, something matte that wouldn't seep in the age cracks that were just beginning to show on her lips.

She put one finger at each end of her mouth and pulled her lips back. Collagen? A peel?

Neither appealed to her.

Bad pun.

She stood there for a long time, gripping the sides of the sink with her hands, hesitant to go out of the bathroom. Scared. Deep down inside, she wanted to still be young for him.

She stared at herself in the mirror. A moment later she pulled her bra straps out of the neckline of her sweater and tightened them another half an inch, then she bent over and grabbed the bottom of her bra and wiggled so she filled the cups differently. Higher. Younger?

She looked at the result in the mirror, then tugged down on her sweater. That was better. She wished she had packed perfume. She lifted her arm. She smelled like Camay soap and baby powder-scented deodorant.

Better than smelling like a garden slug.

Her hand closed over the glass door knob. She took a deep breath and finally mustered the courage to leave the bathroom.

Eight

Michael knew the exact moment she stepped into the room. It should have frightened him that he could be so attuned to another person that her mere presence could distract him. With anyone else he would have fought that awareness with a vengeance. Because it was a control thing, and he was a man who needed to be in control.

His awareness of Catherine was different; it didn't threaten him. It somehow felt right, as if the power between them, this thread of something that linked them together, was an innate part of him.

He glanced up at her from over the rim of a coffee mug. She stood framed in the hall doorway as if she were a painting that had just come alive.

She had been a knockout when she was a young woman. Fresh and tall and sleek. Now she was thirty years older, still beautiful, but added to her face was something better than youthful beauty.

She had character.

He had lived long enough to understand and respect that life did that to you, etched lines of experience on you that said to the world, "I've been there, done that, and lived through it."

On Catherine all that living only made her sexier.

"Hi," she said and walked calmly into the room, which suddenly felt smaller and warmer.

Aly and Dana had come back downstairs earlier and had been talking to him. Well, Aly had been talking to him. Dana was sitting on the sofa, pretending to work on the puzzle when she wasn't eyeing him like he was the Antichrist.

Catherine came over to the sofa in that same old long-legged walk of hers that after all these years could still get him hot and tight.

She poured herself a cup of coffee.

Aly scooted over and patted the spot next to him. "Sit here, Mom."

"No!" Dana said so suddenly Catherine looked up from her coffee with a startled expression.

The only sound for that split second was the rain on the roof, tapping tensely. It was the kind of constant monotonous warning sound that made you follow it with your hearing sharp and your breath held, waiting for the explosion.

Catherine cast a quick apologetic glance at him, then gave a small shrug.

So this wasn't Dana's normal behavior with men, he thought. It was him alone and not just any man that made her oldest daughter so protective.

Catherine sat down next to Dana at the opposite end of

the sofa. She looked up at him. "We were doing a jigsaw puzzle before the power went out."

He nodded. "So I see."

She looked at Dana, who was hunched over the table. "What piece are you looking for?"

"Steve Tyler's belly button," she said without looking up.

Catherine looked at him as if she didn't know what to say to that, which Michael knew was why Dana had said it. Shock value.

He reached out and picked up a puzzle piece and held it out to her. "Here, try this one."

Dana looked at it, then up at him, then took the piece.

It fit.

He winked at Catherine, who looked as if she wanted to strangle Dana. He shook his head slightly. It didn't matter. Catherine needed to ignore her daughter's behavior. It would work better than letting her teenager trap her into getting angry, which was Dana's objective, even if she didn't consciously know it.

The tension in the room was so taut you couldn't have broken through it with two hundred pounds of muscle and a timber ax.

Aly was quietly sitting cross-legged next to him. She had a huge book propped in her lap and seemed oblivious to what was going on with her sister.

Catherine looked at her and asked, "What are you reading?"

"An encyclopedia."

"Oh." Catherine frowned. "Why?"

"I was just curious about something."

"What?"

"Those slug things." She looked up and grinned. "Slugs are just like you, Mom. They don't have a mate."

Michael choked on his coffee and tried hard not to laugh. He had his answer. There was no man.

Catherine just sat there numbly looking like Christmas in her bright green sweater and her even brighter red face.

"It says here that they are mollusks."

He caught Catherine's eye and told her exactly what he had been thinking. "Not only does Aly look just like you did at that age, she is you."

Catherine sighed and gave him a weak smile. "I know."

Aly groaned and slammed the book shut. "Everyone says that." Then she stopped and looked back at her mother. "Not that you aren't pretty, Mom. It's just weird, you know?"

"I understand, kiddo. At eleven you want your own identity, not your mother's. I felt the same way. So did Dana."

"And at school everyone knows I'm Dana Winslow's younger sister. Mr. Johnson, the science teacher, even calls me Dana sometimes."

Dana looked up then. "Do you answer him?"

"I have to. If I don't he thinks I'm not participating." Aly got up and trounced over to the bookcase.

There was another lapse of awkward silence.

Catherine took a sip of coffee. "So. The island hasn't changed much, has it?" She didn't look at him.

He should tell her now, that he had changed, that he wasn't a handyman. He watched her and found himself staring at her hair. If she looks at me, he thought, I will tell her the truth.

She stared into her coffee cup as if she were searching inside of it for something to say.

Aly plopped back down next to him. "Mom says there's plenty to do here. Fishing and sailing and stuff."

Before he could answer Dana asked, "Do you have a boat?"

Michael nodded. "Yes."

The girl brightened suddenly. "Good, then you can take us back to the mainland."

"Dana!" Catherine looked at him then, clearly mortified. "I'm sorry. She seems to have forgotten her manners." She paused and took a deep breath, clearly exasperated. "Dana doesn't like it here."

"There's nothing to do here."

Michael was quiet. He looked away from Catherine and into Dana's sharp eyes. "The engine's not running right."

Dana looked like she didn't believe him. "What's wrong with it?"

Catherine groaned and buried her face in a hand, shaking her head.

But he answered her daughter. "The plugs are bad and the points need to be replaced." He stood up then. "I should leave."

Catherine stood up after him and followed him to the door as if she wanted to say something but didn't know what. He could feel Dana watching them intently and figured she would have been walking in between them if she thought she could have gotten away with it.

He took his jacket off the hook and put it on, then stepped out onto the porch, sat on the bench and pulled on his boots.

Catherine was leaning against the door jamb with her arms crossed, watching him. She had one of those wistful smiles he remembered, the kind she had just before he used to grab her and kiss the hell out of her.

"The rain's stopped," was all she said.

He stood and took two steps to stand near her. He looked down at her face. "I've got good timing."

"I'm sorry about Dana." She dropped her arms to her sides. "These teenage years aren't easy."

He nodded, thinking that she was a teenager the last time he'd seen her.

They stood there like that, not saying anything that mattered. It was as if they were both afraid to say what they were thinking.

He looked away. "Thanks for the coffee."

"Anytime."

Neither of them spoke again for a long stretch of seconds. He felt like he was twenty again, standing on the same porch and wanting to touch her so badly he hurt with it. But knowing he couldn't because her parents were right there on the other side of the door.

There were no parents this time; it was her children who were watching them, probably listening to them.

So he didn't do what he wanted to. He turned and went down the steps and across the lawn. He heard the screen door slam shut.

"Michael?"

He turned around.

She was standing on the porch gripping the wooden

railing in two hands and watching him. "I wrote you. Several letters." She waited, as if she wanted him to explain.

When he said nothing she added, "I never got any answer back from you."

"I never got any letters, Catherine." He turned then, and walked back into the woods.

Her father was shouting. They were in the boathouse, half-naked, their clothes askew, her hair tousled and her lips red and swollen. A foil Trojan wrapper was torn in two and carelessly thrown by their shoes.

Her father's flashlight beam was shining on it.

Then the light went out. It was dark. So dark. He was in a VC prison camp, locked in a box with two other prisoners. He couldn't move.

Something rattled the box. Opened it. Light pierced his eyes. His buddies rescued him. Suddenly they were half-dragging him through the jungle.

Go! Go….

Michael woke up fast and sat up in his bed in a cold sweat, panting like he'd been running from a sniper. Damn. He rubbed his face with his clammy hands. Those nightmares of Nam had stopped years ago.

Seeing Catherine tonight had brought it all back again—the scene with her father. Catherine and her mother disappearing from the island. Her father talking to his grandfather and to him.

He was not to call her. He couldn't write to her. He was to disappear from Catherine's life. Or he would go to jail for statutory rape.

Instead he'd gone into the Navy less than a week later and ended up in Special Forces, infiltrating into Laos or patrolling the Mekong Delta for weeks at a time. He'd been captured and spent three months in a dark box.

He drove his hand through his hair and took a few deep breaths, thinking for just a brief moment about a life he had left far behind him and never wanted to think of again, because it was like reliving hell.

He sat there for a minute, then threw back the damp sheet and pulled on his jeans. He shrugged into a jacket and shoes, grabbed a flashlight and left the cabin.

The moon had gone down and it was darker outside than his memory of the deepest jungle. There was silence, and a little rain, that misty kind that came on like soggy fog.

He walked down to the small dock where he moored his boat. He unsnapped the tarp and stepped inside, where he lifted the engine cover and shone the flashlight down into the engine compartment until he saw what he was looking for.

A few minutes later he was walking back down the dock and toward the cabin, the plugs and points jammed into his jeans pocket.

He went inside the cabin and headed straight to the refrigerator, took out a carton of juice and lifted it to his lips. He drank half of it, stuck it back inside without closing it, and took out a Mexican beer.

He grabbed something to eat from a cabinet and popped the cap off the beer as he crossed the room to sit down in front of the dwindling fire. He raised the beer bottle to his mouth, took a long drink and set the bottle down on the table next to him. The smooth flavor of the beer was on his tongue, but what he craved was egg-salad sandwiches.

There was nothing he could do about what he was feeling and wanting, so he did the only thing he could do—he ate a whole damn bag of barbecued potato chips.

Nine

At ten the next morning Catherine stood on Michael's front porch, rocking on her feet, her hands clenched behind her back while she waited for him to answer her knock. She could hear his footsteps clumping toward the door, so she licked her lips, brushed her hair back, and took a deep breath before he opened it.

He stared at her from eyes that looked awake but tired.

"The toilet is plugged and the boiler pilot won't light."

He seemed startled, like he didn't know why she was there. And he didn't exactly look happy to see her.

"I tried to light the boiler pilot again and again and we used the plunger on the toilet. No matter what I tried I couldn't get them to work."

He didn't say anything.

Perhaps she was speaking too fast. Her ex-husband used to chide her for babbling when she was nervous. And she was nervous. She tilted her head slightly and explained more slowly, "There's no hot water in the house without the boiler."

"I know what a boiler is, Catherine."

What a grump.

He turned without another sarcastic word and took a tool belt off a hook near the door. Besides an annoyed look, he was wearing a plaid shirt and jeans that were worn almost white in spots and that time and wear had molded to his body. He might be a grump in the morning but he sure looked good for fifty.

What would he look like in a suit? Catherine was a sucker for a man in a suit. And if a man wore a tux, well, she got all weak-kneed. Heck, Bill Gates probably looked sexy in a tux.

Life was unfair. Here she had to hike up her bra straps and slather on alpha hydroxy creams with a trowel. Some days she had to lie down on the bed to zip up her pants. He was three years older, wearing a plain old pair of jeans, and he looked stronger and sexier than he had when he was twenty.

The faces of all the men who had aged so well flashed through her mind: Sean Connery, Nick Nolte, Robert Redford, James Garner, James Brolin, Michael Packard.

She watched him strap and buckle the tool belt low on his hips the way Paul Newman had strapped on his guns in *Butch Cassidy and the Sundance Kid.*

It seemed like such an earthy, male thing—a man doing up his belt buckle; it was sexy and suggestive and made her mouth a little dry.

He stuck a pair of work gloves into his back pocket and turned back around. She quickly looked away.

"I need to find the toolbox. I'll be right back." He grabbed a key and walked past her.

She nodded without looking up, then decided to follow him. She didn't suppose luck would be on her side and there would be a tux in the shed, but heck, he might undo the belt buckle again.

She smiled a wicked little smile as she crossed over to a small shed he had already unlocked.

Heaven be praised if he didn't bend down to search through it. His jeans pulled tight over his thighs in a way that made her give thanks to Levi Strauss.

Then he knelt on one knee and leaned inside. If she stepped back just a foot or so she had a great shot of his backside. The work gloves stuck out of one back pocket and looked like fingers waving at her. It was almost as if they were calling to her, "Look here."

"Here it is." He stood up with a battered old red toolbox.

She quickly looked up at the sky. After a slight pause she said, "Nice day. No clouds."

He followed her gaze upward, then frowned. "The radio said it was supposed to rain today."

There was one thing different about this Michael Packard; he was no Mr. Sunshine in the morning.

She walked ahead of him on the gravel path between his place and hers. The silence just about drove her nuts.

Her mind was going a mile a minute, wondering what he was thinking, wondering if they could go the whole day without bringing up the past.

When they were about halfway there she braved the beast. "I wrote you five letters."

"I never got any letters from you."

She stopped, spun around and planted her hands on her

hips. She looked him straight in the eye. "Are you saying I'm lying?"

"No. I'm saying I never got any letters." He paused, looking squarely at her. His expression grew tighter. "What I did get was a promise from your father that he'd press charges of statutory rape if I tried to contact you."

"Oh God. Michael…" She sagged back against a tree, staring at the ground. "Did he really do that?"

"Yes."

"He was upset. I don't think he would have sent you to jail."

"Yes. He would have, Catherine."

There was nothing between them but a lapse of tense silence.

She looked at him again. "Did you really think I could just walk away after that summer together and never have any contact with you again? Didn't you know me better than that?"

"I could ask you the same thing."

"How do you figure that?"

"You thought I would ignore your letters."

"Give me a break, here," she snapped. "I was seventeen." She straightened and started to walk away.

He dropped the toolbox and touched her shoulder. "I know. And I was twenty, just drafted, and in love with a seventeen-year-old girl."

She stopped, but she didn't turn around. He had truly loved her then, all those years ago. Many times over the years she had wondered about that, if he had cared or if she had just wished he had.

His hand was still on her shoulder. She bit her lip because she thought she might do something silly like cry. "I'm sorry." She took a deep breath and turned around.

His hand fell away.

"When time passes by and you can't understand why something happened, I guess you make up excuses. You blame others." She looked at him then. "I was hurt and scared. I blamed you. After a while, when I didn't hear from you, I believed you were just lying to me about how you had felt so you could—" She stopped because she didn't need to say anything more.

"Get into your pants?"

"Thank you for sugar-coating it so nicely." She gave a laugh that wasn't amused. "But you're right. That was what I thought."

He only stared at her, not saying anything.

So she did. "It's stupid to stand here in the middle of the woods and argue over something that happened so long ago. We're different people now. It's 1997 not 1967." She looked back up into those blue eyes of his and stuck out her hand. "How about a truce?"

His gaze dropped to her outstretched hand.

"Friends," she said emphatically.

A moment later his hand closed over hers and she almost melted into the ground. It was like she was seventeen all over again. She stared at their hands so she could hide her eyes from him.

Just for good measure she gave his hand a firm shake.

When she looked up he was staring at her face not at their clasped hands.

He pulled her against him, clamped his free hand to the back of her head, and kissed her.

Oh God… She felt like Silly Putty. Her hand fell away from his and moved to his shoulder.

His other hand grabbed her and pulled her against him in one of those hot, eating kind of kisses you see in the movies, all wildness and heat, where an instant later they've unbuttoned half their clothes and they're doing it against a wall.

His hands ran over her back, pressed her closer. There were tools pressed against her belly. A hammer, a flashlight, screwdriver—lots of long, hard things.

One second his tongue was deep inside her mouth.

The next…the damn idiot let her go.

She stood there seeing stars and trying to keep her balance.

"Friends." He whacked her on the backside with one hand, picked up his toolbox and sauntered on down the path toward her place.

Ten

She caught him from behind, which surprised the hell out of him. The toolbox slipped from his hand and she shoved him back up against a tree with both hands.

"Catherine?"

One palm was flat against his chest; the other slid up to grip the back of his head.

"What the hell are you doing?"

A second later she was kissing him the way he'd just kissed her. Hard and fast and wild.

He bent his knees, hooked his arms under her butt and picked her up. Her hands drove through his hair, gripped his head and tilted it, then she thrust her small tongue into his mouth the same way he had done to her.

He pushed away from the tree, turned and pinned her against it, holding her there with his body so his hands were free. He slid one hand across her shoulder, pushed her sweater aside and tried to pull down her bra strap.

He couldn't get his finger under it. Damn. It was so tight you'd think it was made of iron.

He slid both hands to her waist and up under her sweater to cup her from beneath. She moaned against his mouth and their tongues switched places.

God, but she tasted so good. She felt so good. Her nipples grew hard from his fingers and her breasts were heavy and soft and felt just about as good as a woman could feel.

He slid his hands around and grabbed the back of her bra to unhook it.

"Harold!"

They both froze.

"Ohmygod! It's Aly!" Catherine wiggled out from between him and the tree trunk, jerking at her clothes and taking big gulps of air. She looked up at him. "Bend down. Quick!"

He did and she used her fingers to comb back his hair.

"Harrr-old!"

"Hurry!" she whispered, still straightening her clothes which looked fine. "Get your toolbox!"

When Aly came down the path a few seconds later, they were both walking casually with no signs of the passion that had burned between them just moments before. No outward signs.

"Mom!" Aly ran toward her mother with tears in her eyes. "Harold got out. I can't find him anywhere."

Catherine opened her arms and hugged her daughter to her. "Hey, sweetie, we'll find him. He won't go far. It's Harold. Remember? He never strays far from where we are."

"But this is a new place and remember when we moved that time and how the vet said animals can get lost because the smells are new and they get confused and can't find their way back."

Catherine pulled Aly away from her shoulder and held her head in two hands. "We'll find him. I promise you."

Aly sobbed.

"Tell you what. I'll cook some bacon. That ought to bring him running back home."

"You will?" Aly looked a little brighter.

"Of course I will." Catherine wiped the long strips of blond hair out of her daughter's eyes and smiled. "We'll look for Harold while Michael fixes the plumbing. Okay?"

Aly nodded, then cast a quick glance at him. "Hi, Mr. Packard."

"The island's small," he reassured her. "Your cat won't go far."

"Thanks." She sniffed again.

He walked past them and stopped. He wiped a tear from Aly's chin with one finger. "Don't worry there, Little Squirt. We'll find your cat."

Then before she could say anything about what he'd called her, he walked on down the pathway.

"Little Squirt?" he heard her whisper to her mother.

"I'll explain later," Catherine said.

He didn't look back but from behind him he could hear the two of them following at a slower pace, beating the ferns and woods and calling out for the cat.

He kept walking. He might make over a half a million dollars a year in salary and another mil in stock options, but hell, he had a toilet to fix.

He walked out of the woods and into the clearing near

the house. Dana was walking from the front door along the crooked porch.

She turned the corner to the side of the house and froze.

A second later she screamed so loud it sounded as if she had cracked the sky.

He ran toward her.

Harold was back, proudly sitting on the porch. He had a two foot long garter snake hanging from his mouth.

Eleven

"Dana!" Catherine came running toward the house just as she saw Michael hop over the porch railing and put his arm around Dana. She was huddled into a frightened stance, looking too scared to move.

Aly was about to run past her toward the porch, so Catherine grabbed her arm. "Stop."

"What's going on?" Aly frowned at her.

"I don't know, but don't move." Catherine looked up. "Michael?"

He was still talking to Dana, then he turned to her.

At that same moment Aly called out, "Is it Harold?" She already sounded like she was crying.

"It's Harold and he's fine so don't start crying. He brought home a present."

"Stay here," Catherine ordered Aly and she walked to the porch. It had been years, but she could smell the snake before she got there. She stopped where she was and peered over the porch railing, then up at him. "I forgot how much those things stink."

Aly was suddenly right next to her. "Oh, yuk! Harold! Get away from it!"

Catherine looked at her. "I told you to stay put."

"Is it poisonous?" Aly asked.

"No." Michael pulled his gloves out of his back pocket. "It's only a garter snake."

"Oh." She watched it a second. "Why do they smell?"

"Oh, who cares!" Dana snapped from around the corner. "Just get rid of it! Hurry! Please!"

The whole time Harold just sat there with the black snake hanging out of his mouth. He was waiting for praise.

Michael put on the work gloves, then he squatted down in front of Harold, who immediately dropped the snake.

Dana screamed again.

The snake slithered a few inches.

Harold ran off the porch.

Aly ran after him.

Michael picked up the snake.

So Catherine backed away into the middle of the yard. A good twenty feet away.

Michael walked down the porch stairs with the snake in his hands just as Aly came back to Catherine's side with Harold in her arms.

She stood by Catherine while she stroked Harold's purring head. After a second she started to follow Michael, but Catherine had a tight hold on her arm, so Aly stretched her neck toward them and asked, "Where are you taking it?"

"Away," he said over his shoulder as he walked toward the woods.

"Far away," Catherine added.

Michael was lying on his back on the bathroom floor with his head under the john. If his friends could see him now....

As Michael worked on the main pipe, he tried to decide how to go about telling Catherine he wasn't the island handyman. Sprawled underneath the toilet didn't feel like the right time for confessions. "Hand me the crescent wrench."

"Which one is the crescent wrench?" Catherine asked him.

"The one with the blue handle."

She handed it to him, then stepped back. After a stretch of silence she said, "You know all the tools by color." She made it sound like he was a kindergartner who had just picked the right crayon from the Crayola box.

Keep digging the hole deeper there, Squirt.

With narrowed eyes he watched her through the small space between the pipe and the bowl.

She was staring at his belt buckle.

He shot a quick glance to his fly, which wasn't open. He turned over on his side, then squirmed farther under the pipe and tried to get better leverage to loosen it. He kept cranking at it.

How the hell long were the threads on this pipe joint?

She shifted places, shoved the shower curtain back, and sat down on the rim of the tub. "So."

He cast her a quick glance over a shoulder.

She had her hands clasped in her lap and stared at his butt. "Do you get a lot of work on the island?"

He turned back to the pipes and didn't answer her. Instead, he kept on turning the wrench as hard as he could.

"I mean..." She paused. "...there are so many old houses on the island..."

He gripped the wrench harder and pulled.

"So I expect you keep busy." She stopped as if she were searching for the right words, then explained, "I mean, with you doing plumbing and all."

He twisted the wrench. "I make a good living."

"It must be a fascinating business."

Crissake, Catherine. That's stretching it.

"I mean working on old houses, watching them come to life again. It's like that TV show. What is the name of that show?" she muttered.

"'This Old House.'" He pulled so hard that the pipe almost came loose with one turn.

"That's it!" she said brightly.

"Yep, just fascinating." He adjusted the pipe. "Clogged drains rate right up there with snake catching and curing cancer."

She laughed. "That's funny, Michael. I bet you watch 'Home Improvement.'"

That hole she was digging herself into just got two feet deeper.

"My office in San Francisco is in a restored Victorian."

He grunted some kind of response and slid out from under the toilet, put a bucket under the pipe, then snaked it.

A balled up pair of white athletic socks fell into the bucket with a plop.

"There's your problem," he said.

"Good God, what moron would flush a pair of socks down the toilet?"

He shrugged, fixed the pipe, and checked the flushing mechanism. He finished up, put the tools back in the box, then washed his hands at the sink. He turned off the faucet and looked around for a hand towel.

"Oh, here." Catherine stood up and handed him a towel.

While he dried his hands they both stood in the small area of the bathroom between the pedestal sink and the high old tub. They were so close he could almost taste her breath in the air between them.

He looked at her.

She was staring at his mouth. It was an invitation if he ever saw one.

He started to lower his head.

She drew in a breath and ducked suddenly, as if she had been in a stupor, then grabbed the bucket and held it between them like a shield. "I'll just take this outside."

"Okay, that's it." He threw the towel down on the sink.

She blinked up at him.

"What the hell is going on in that head of yours?"

She frowned. "My head? Me?"

"Yes. You."

"Nothing's going on."

He waited for her to say more.

She didn't. She just hugged the bucket to her chest and gave him that same stubborn look she'd had when he'd pulled her from the water. "May I get by, please?"

He gave up and stepped aside.

She was gone an instant later.

He looked at the empty doorway in disbelief, then wondered if his instincts were off that much. All morning she had been giving him mixed signals.

Hell, with Catherine his instincts had always been screwed up. Thirty years later and it was the same thing—an overpowering attraction and complete confusion.

He ran a hand through his hair and sat down on the john. He stared at his grandfather's battered old toolbox like he was waiting for it to explain to him the workings of the female mind.

He shook his head.

He was fifty years old and he still didn't understand women.

Twelve

Catherine was forty-seven years old and she still didn't understand men.

For a brief moment she wondered if she had imagined what had happened between them in the woods. If so, she had one heck of an imagination. Perhaps, if she didn't get the Letni account, she should switch professions and try writing romance novels.

Dana and Aly came around the corner of the house. They were arguing until they spotted Catherine.

"Mom!" Dana came hobbling toward her dragging a rusty old bike with bent handle bars, a crooked seat, no tires and only one wheel. "Look at this!"

It was awful. She frowned at it. "Must I?"

"These are the only bikes in the basement."

"Are you sure?" She turned to Aly who hadn't yet reached the age where she needed to always be on the offensive.

Aly nodded. "That's the best bike of the bunch. It has a wheel."

Catherine tried to sound cheery. "Then we'll have to spend our time sailing instead."

Dana gave a bitter laugh. "In what?"

"There's a sailboat. I'm sure it's in the boathouse."

"Oh." Dana had that sassy look about her. "You mean that sailboat?" She waved a hand toward the beach.

"What sailboat?"

"That one. The one we pulled out while you were in the house." Dana pointed to a lump of green, algae-covered sticks and black boards.

If you really stretched your imagination—perhaps into another dimension—it could have once been a small boat.

"Mom, you can't make us stay here. It's sooooo awful." Dana was whining like she had when she was three.

Aly didn't look much happier. She was staring at the bicycle as if it were a broken doll.

"Catherine?" Michael came around the other side of the house.

Great, Catherine thought, rubbing her hands over her eyes for a moment. Just great.

Michael held out his hand. "Here's your problem."

No, she thought. My biggest problems—all three of them—are standing right in front of me. Then there were her inanimate problems—the broken bike and the sailboat from the River Styx.

She stared at the silver mechanism in his hand. Another problem? Probably. Her eyes almost glazed over. "What is it?"

"The sparking mechanism."

She nodded. "Okay."

He kept looking at her as if she should understand why he was holding that metal gadget in his big hand.

She shrugged and threw up her hands. "So?"

"Your ignitor is bad."

Not in the woods it wasn't, she thought. I could have lit the whole island. Which is why I'm staying a good distance away from you, Michael Packard.

"You won't have any hot water."

"Mo-ther!"

She held up a hand. "Not now, Dana."

"We have to leave. We just have to. You dragged me away from all my friends." Dana's voice cracked. "There's nothing to do on this dumb island but run from snakes." She shuddered and hugged herself. "The bikes are broken and that sailboat won't even float. You promised this would be fun. Now we can't even take a shower!" Dana burst into tears and ran into the house.

Catherine wanted to cry, too.

Aly looked at her. "She bragged to all her friends that she was going to learn how to sail."

Catherine nodded. Sailing was something she had promised Dana for years. Bad mothers don't keep their word. The phrase chanted through her mind as if there was a guilt devil on her shoulder reminding her over and over.

Would this failed vacation matter in five years? Maybe. Would they be able to laugh about this someday? That she didn't know.

She sighed because there wasn't much else she could

do. She slid her arm around her youngest daughter. "I'm sorry, sweetie. I guess this was all a big mistake."

"That's okay, Mom." Aly patted Catherine's hand. "I know you tried to make this trip fun even if it isn't."

Well, that about said it all. Her daughters were both miserable.

Aly hugged her back, then turned and walked toward the house with her small shoulders hunched and her head down.

"Don't beat yourself up about it, Catherine."

She looked up at Michael. "I had such high hopes." She sighed. "I wanted the island to be special to them, too. I'm a lousy parent."

"Looks like you're their only parent."

She nodded.

"Where's their father?"

"Dead."

He shoved his hands in his pockets. "I'm sorry."

She shook her head. "Don't be. We divorced eight years ago. He died a couple of years later."

Michael only stood there, looking at her as if he were searching for important answers that were hidden somewhere deep in her eyes.

"Okay, Catherine. What did he do to you?"

"What do you mean?"

"You know what I mean."

She was quiet for a long time. She stared at some spot over his shoulder because it was that hard for her. She couldn't even look at him as she said, "He walked out on us."

Michael swore under his breath.

"Aly was only three, so she doesn't remember much.

But Dana was seven. Even with counseling I don't think she ever understood why he left."

"Why did he leave?"

"Because we were too much for him to handle. Tom was different. A free spirit. He needed to chase his rainbows. Something I never saw in him until it was too late. He wanted a wife and children, until he had them." She shrugged. "Then we were a responsibility. It took me a while to admit and understand that he could never commit to anything. It wasn't just us. He had twelve different jobs in the ten years we were married, each one a bigger dream than the last."

Michael didn't say anything. Now that he had his answer, he looked as if he wanted to take back the question.

"But that was all a long time ago. Before he died I think I finally understood that he loved us. As much as it was in him to love someone other than himself.

"So." She waved her hand at the gadget he was holding. "There's no hot water without that…thing?"

He shook his head.

She gave him a weak smile and a shrug to cover up her disappointment. "Well, then. I guess we'll be leaving on Thursday."

He didn't say anything but seemed a million miles away.

She wondered what he thought of her and her past. She spoke openly because that was how she always dealt with her failed marriage, honestly. But it was a chink in her pride to admit that she had failed at something so very important.

She straightened, squared her shoulders back and held out her hand. "Thank you."

He tossed the gadget into his shirt pocket, wiped his hand on his jeans and took her hand. "Catherine."

It took every ounce of her pride and control to act natural. "Michael." Her voice came out in a raspy whisper, as if it knew this was the last time she would say his name, knew that there wouldn't be a bittersweet meeting in another thirty years.

She shook his hand, then quickly pulled hers away. She turned around, trying to hold on to a slim thread of dignity, and walked up the porch steps.

She could feel him watching her. His eyes could still do that, hold on to her as surely as if he'd used his hands to grip her shoulders.

She stopped and turned.

He hadn't moved. His hands were shoved into his pockets as if he didn't know what to do with them. She remembered that about him. The way he would hide his hands. She loved his hands.

He was still looking at her.

She gripped the porch railing because sometimes you just had to hold on to something to get through a certain kind of moment. "It was great to see you again."

She gave him a forced smile, one that covered up how she was really feeling.

It was great to have you look at me that way again. It was great to hear your voice again. It was great to kiss you again and feel your hands on me again.

It was great, but it wasn't enough.

And she walked into the old house.

* * *

"No, I haven't lost my mind. Have them bring it to the slip this afternoon. And make sure there's a towline." Michael crossed the cabin, his cellular phone cradled between his ear and his shoulder.

"They'll do it. Gladly. I spend enough money with them." Michael grabbed his running shoes and moved over to the chair.

"Then call Valiant Supply and have them deliver that part." He sat down and stuck his feet into his shoes, then tied the laces while his assistant wrote down the part number. "I'll be there by four. Meet me at the slip."

Michael flipped the phone closed and shrugged into his jacket, then slipped on a Mariners baseball cap. He went to the kitchen, opened a drawer and pulled out a bag.

A minute later he left the cabin at a half trot. He moved down to the dock, her words running over and over in his mind.

I wanted the island to be special to them, too.

All those years ago he had clung to the idea that she had run from him as fast as she could, young and scared and overwhelmed by that last summer. By him. Caught between him and her father's iron hand and all-too-real threats.

A month later boot camp had been a welcome escape. There, he'd been too tired to think for all those months. But it had been different when he got to Nam.

He saw her face on every tree in the jungle. In every muddy river or rice paddy. It was her face he saw whenever he closed his eyes, haunting him as surely as if her image had been tattooed there.

This time he wasn't going to let her go so easily. Not again.

Some fifteen minutes later he had the plugs and points back into his boat engine. He turned the key and fired it up, then he sped toward the mainland.

Thirteen

Catherine was standing on the dock the next morning when Michael sailed into the cove on a sleek white sailboat with wicked red sails.

He waved and called out her name.

She walked to the edge of the dock as he sailed toward her. Suddenly it was that last summer all over again, as if thirty years hadn't passed by, but time and life had just frozen in this one instant of déjà vu.

"Hey!"

She smiled.

He tossed her the line, which she tied onto one of the cleats.

"Thanks." He stood, then stepped on the dock, and the air around her grew thick and warm.

He was wearing a pair of cutoffs and a white cotton shirt with the sleeves shoved up his arms and the tails out and halfway unbuttoned. His dark hair was wind tousled, and he hadn't shaved. His beard was dark and scruffy and sexy as all get-out. He looked like an older more weathered version of JFK Jr.

She crossed her arms. "How did you manage to get that dark of a tan in the Northwest this time of year? It always rains until June or July."

"I didn't. I got it in Cabo." He stopped and added, "On a fishing trip."

Cabo San Lucas? Well, she thought, they said the dollar went pretty far in Mexico these days. And his financial status was none of her business, she told herself.

"Do you think your daughters would like to sail in this?"

"Oh, Michael. Anyone would like to sail in that!" She looked at the boat and got choked up. "It almost looks new."

"I take care of my things," was all he said, then he grabbed a sack, stuck of couple of colored tools in his back pockets and turned back to her. "I got to thinking last night about that ignitor."

"Oh my. What an exciting life you must have."

He looked down at her through narrowed eyes. "Now I see where your daughter gets her smart mouth."

Catherine rolled her eyes. "Every sassy thing I have ever said has come back to haunt me. Now what was so interesting about the ignitor?" She placed her hand on his arm. "And don't get too technical, okay? I don't sleep well standing up."

He laughed and held up the sack. "I think I've found the solution."

"You can fix it?"

"Let's just say that it might work now."

"If you can get the boiler working we won't have to leave."

"I know."

She looked up at him, at the pleased look on his face. He wanted them to stay. Ohmygod, but she was in trouble and she was so happy about it she almost shouted out loud.

"Go get your daughters ready for a day of sailing, Squirt, and I'll see if I can't get that boiler going." He winked, then a moment later disappeared around the corner of the house.

Laughing, Catherine sliced her fists through the air. "Yes!" Then she ran up the steps and called her girls.

The sailboat sliced through the water, leaving a stringy trail behind it. They had been on the boat all morning, during which time Michael had shown Dana and Aly how to work the lines and jib. To her daughters' surprise, Catherine had helped him coach them, then sat back watching them make their accomplishments and their mistakes. She never criticized them, but let them learn on their own.

She seemed relaxed and ready to just have fun, as if this kind of outing was a rare and unique moment in her life. It was one of the things he remembered about her, her ability to take the most joy from a moment no matter how trivial it might seem to everyone else.

Even now her arms were resting casually on the rim of the boat and her blond hair was flying back with the wind. She was laughing at something Aly said, and watching her made him smile.

She leaned forward, opened a cooler. "Here." She handed him a beer.

He leaned closer to take it and their bare knees touched. She looked startled, as if she'd just gotten a shock.

He smiled to himself and leaned back, then let the wind take them through the channel while he took a swig of beer.

She hadn't moved her knees.

Both her girls had been eager to watch and try to work the sails themselves. Dana was like a different person. No more playing the role of moody teen.

There was a strange kind of intensity about her. She had watched him, every single movement, as if he were a textbook on how to sail. Focused and serious, she took it all in. She wanted to do well. You could see the determination in her face. There was a drive in this girl that was different from both Aly and Catherine. He'd seen this same kind of drive in the men he did business with, the successful ones. This kid had potential.

Aly sat back after she had popped open a Coke. She looked at him. "Do you know why the water is blue?"

"No."

"It's blue because every color of the spectrum—like the colors in a rainbow—is inside each molecule of water. When light shines through it, the colors reflect back." She took a drink and swallowed. "Sometimes it's blue, sometimes it's green. The whole process all depends on the amount of light and depth of the water."

Michael looked at her. "I never learned that in school."

"I didn't learn it in school."

Catherine gave him a smile. "Aly's a walking fount of information."

"Mom."

Catherine laughed. "Well, you are. You learned to ask questions when you were two years old and you haven't stopped since." She looked at him. "She doesn't stop until she finds out an answer that satisfies her."

"She doesn't always find the answer to every question, though," Dana said. "Toss me something to drink, will you?"

Aly handed her a soda and sighed. "I still want to know why fingers aren't all the same size."

Michael looked down at his hands and wondered why that question had never crossed his mind. "She has a point."

"Aly's destined to be a scientist, I think." The look Catherine gave her younger daughter was filled with love and pride and all those things that he saw again and again in his friends who had children.

"I'm going to be an actress," Aly announced. "Someone truly wonderful like Winona Ryder."

"Okay, sweetie. You can be an actress. Dana can be something useful like a lawyer." Catherine smiled.

"You always say that, Mom." Dana obviously didn't want to be an attorney.

"But you argue so well, honey. Of course maybe you can be a political analyst instead."

Michael called, "Coming about!" And the boat swung into the wind.

Dana ducked under the boom so perfectly you'd have thought she'd been sailing all her life. "I don't know what I want to be." She looked at Michael, almost as if she were seeking approval, like she wanted to know that it was okay to be undecided.

He finished off his beer and set the bottle down. Then

he looked right at Dana. "I expect Dana will be anything she wants to be." He gave her a wink.

A moment later, for the very first time, she smiled at him.

Fourteen

Late that evening, Catherine walked him to the dock. The sun was beginning to go down in that golden way it had. "It stays light so much longer here. I can't believe it's seven o'clock."

"It's the Northwest. After all the gray and rainy days we have in the winter and spring, nature sort of evens things out. We've earned these long summer days."

She laughed, then about halfway down the hill she stumbled on a rock.

He grabbed her hand to steady her.

And he didn't let go.

They walked a few more steps to where the boat was tied to the cleat beside the boathouse. The water in the cove was bright gold and pink from the rich colors of the sky. And a flock of Canadian geese crossed overhead in a noisy arrow pattern that made the soft gull calls sound easy and far away.

She looked back at the house, which sat alone on the small grade above the rocks and glowed from the lights inside and the reflections of the setting sun. Behind it stood a wall of hills, jagged with tall green trees. A few soft-colored clouds moved slowly past, as though they were grazing the very tops of those same dark trees.

She leaned against the boathouse door and sighed. "I wonder if there is any place in the world right now, at this very moment, that is more beautiful than this."

"It's something to see." He was looking at her.

She didn't know who moved first, but suddenly she was in his arms. His mouth covered hers and he held her tightly, as if he couldn't let her go.

It was just like before, in the woods—a passion that flared and shook her senseless.

He pressed her against the door and one of his hands left her back. Then he was pushing her inside the boathouse. The door clicked closed behind them.

It had been so long. She wanted to crawl inside of him; she couldn't get close enough.

His hands were all over her, touching her in places that were private and had seemed lost and numb for so very long.

He slid his hand between her legs and she gave a small cry that didn't sound like her.

She came, right then, throbbing hard and fast.

He kept his hand there, hot against her jeans.

It took a few moments for her to come back down to earth. Then she realized what had happened. She'd had an orgasm when all he had done was touch her through her clothes.

This was not her. It was like some sensational article in a women's magazine, headlines plastered on the cover in bold red letters to sell more copies. She'd always thought a contact orgasm could never really happen. That it was no more than fantasy and fiction.

But it had just happened. To her.

"Oh God…." She groaned and turned away. "I'm so embarrassed."

"Why?" He laughed quietly. "I'm not."

She hid her face in his shoulder. He sounded like he had just saved the world.

He gently forced her head away from his shoulder with both hands.

Her nose was somewhere near his chin. She had no choice but to look at him.

That cocky male look he wore in the golden light made her laugh. She shook her head, still embarrassed. "It's been a long time."

"I guess that means I won't have to mentally recite the Greek alphabet backwards and conjugate Latin verbs while I'm waiting for you to get there."

Then she really laughed. "You don't actually do that."

He just looked at her. She couldn't tell if he was teasing her or not.

"Do you?"

"Some women take a while."

"Oh." She was quiet. She didn't know what to say so she blurted out, "I guess I don't. I mean…take long."

He rubbed his finger slowly over her lips, starting at the corner. Then he moistened that finger from inside her own mouth and traced her lip line. "I remember."

She looked into those eyes of his and she was lost.

He simply slid his hand behind her head and pulled her

mouth to his. His hand went to her jeans and an instant later he had them unbuttoned.

She pulled back. "Wait." Everything was going too fast. She didn't know what to say. She wasn't sure what she felt. She was just confused.

She could feel him looking at her. "I can't do this. My children are right up there, at the house. I…I'm sorry. I—"

He placed a finger against her lips. "It's okay, Catherine."

She tried to turn but he wouldn't let her. She looked away and shoved the hair out of her face. "I don't know how to do this."

He gave a sharp laugh. "You used to. I was there the first time."

She covered her mouth. "Oh God…"

He just kept holding her. "I was joking."

"I don't have sex," she said against his chest.

He laughed. "I thought I heard you say you don't have sex."

She looked up at him. "I did say that."

He stared down at her as if her words were just sinking in.

"At all," she added. "I don't have sex at all." There. She'd said it.

"You have two children. They're not adopted. They look just like you."

"But I haven't been with anyone since my husband," she explained. "That was eight years ago."

"Eight years," he repeated flatly.

She nodded.

"You haven't had sex for eight years."

"Uh-huh."

He was quiet for the longest time and she had no idea what he was thinking. Probably that she was a nutcase.

Then he reached down and rebuttoned her jeans.

She didn't know what to say. She wanted him, but not like this. She was so confused.

He tilted her chin up with one knuckle and gave her a strained smile. "I'll back off."

"But—"

"No. Let's give this some time, Catherine. We both need some time."

She nodded and they left the boathouse. She stood on the dock as he sailed away, hugging her arms and feeling antsy. She started to walk back to the house, but stopped. She opened the boathouse door and went inside for just a moment.

It was getting darker and the sunlight through the dirt on the windows was dull and lifeless. It smelled like damp wood and old canvas. She sat down on an old wooden bench that wobbled when she touched it.

They had made love here, that very first time.

Her mind went back all those years and she remembered something. She felt along the wood. Then she found the carved initials.

M P + C W.

She closed her eyes and just sat there. Her body was still taut and damp and ready. Her blood still raced through her, and her breath was not slow or even. She looked at those initials and wondered if she was nothing but a silly old fool.

* * *

Michael motored the sailboat back to his place. He tied off the line and jumped on the dock. The air had changed, grown lighter, cooler, and was turning blue with the nightfall.

He had always loved the island best at night, when he could stand there and watch the sky turn. It was that kind of night where the stars crawl above you in lazy patterns. The kind of night when the owl that lived in a nearby tree became silent, and you could make love all night long and still want more in the morning when the sun rose.

In his mind, the years that might have been slipped by. Waking up with Catherine, making love to her for days at a time, marriage and fighting and making up. And making children. If not for a cruel twist of fate Dana and Aly might have been his daughters.

Today had been something different for him. And he realized some things he hadn't understood before. That very first night he had stood there in the fringe of the woods and watched her with her girls, watched her sliding across the lawn in the rain, chasing that umbrella. He had watched their banter in the house afterward. That night had marked the first time in his life he had thought about the children he'd never had.

He knew now that it wasn't just children he had thought he missed. It wasn't some vague paternal instinct coming out in him when it was too late to do anything about it— not some kind of male emotional clock that was ticking away in his head.

What he had wanted, what he had truly missed, was having children with Catherine. He stuck his hands in his pockets and stood there for the longest time, then laughed at himself, at his thoughts. He had Catherine on the brain. He was in the same state he'd been in for days—hard and ready for something that would probably never happen.

"Eight years?" He shook his head. "Jesus…"

Then he stripped off his clothes and jumped into the icy cold water.

Fifteen

By Thursday, when the boat arrived, not one of the Winslow women wanted to leave the island. The same was true on the next Sunday. By the following Thursday when the boat had come and gone again, her girls were sailing by themselves in the cove.

Catherine and Michael had settled into an old routine, like the friends they found they still were. They talked about so much, and yet there was some part of him that he seemed to keep private.

She wasn't certain if he was ashamed of what he did for a living, but he always changed the subject, so she didn't bring it up anymore. As a safety net she didn't talk about her career either. They had plenty of other things to talk about. Sometimes it was almost as if there weren't enough hours in the day.

The noon day sunshine beat down on them, and it was warm and snug sitting on a huge rock at the water's edge. They shared a lunch basket between them, while they watched the girls sail in the cove.

"You're spoiling them," she said as he took a bite of fried chicken.

He waved the chicken leg in the air. "You're spoiling me. Lunch every day and dinner every night."

"Hmmm." She ate a potato chip and tried not to ogle.

He was sitting back on his elbows, a position that stretched his white polo shirt across his abdomen, which she knew from their second day out in the boat was still flat, and rippled and fit for a Calvin Klein ad.

The first time he'd taken off his shirt she'd almost fallen overboard. She'd spent the whole rest of the day trying to look everywhere except at his chest.

She sat there munching on another chip—just what her thighs needed—and looking at him. Half of her was still unable to believe they were sitting on this very rock, here and now, that it was real and not some wishful daydream.

His long legs were stretched out in front of him and crossed at the ankles. The breeze would bring his scent to her every so often.

"I feel seventeen again," she said, then laughed because it was a stupid thing to say. "I just wish I looked seventeen again."

He turned to her and cocked his head. "Why?"

"Only a man would ask that."

"Why this obsession with getting older?"

"It's not an obsession." She sat straighter and crossed her legs Indian-style.

"You sure make enough comments about it."

"I do not."

He laughed.

She chewed her lip. "Do I?"

He nodded.

She rested her chin on her fist and thought about it for a moment. "Don't you ever feel it?"

"What?"

"Old. As if life has passed you by?"

"I don't know, Catherine. With each year I find I feel more comfortable with who I am."

"Really? Hmmmm. And here I feel older and more uncomfortable with who I am."

"Women." He muttered in that foolish male way.

She was quiet for a moment, gathering control so she wouldn't haul off and punch him. "Women feel this way because men age so well."

"Women only think they don't age well."

She turned. "Do I look that stupid?"

"You don't agree."

"Society doesn't agree."

"Lauren Bacall, Goldie Hawn and Raquel Welch are all gorgeous."

"Clothing models are twelve." She sat up a little straighter and hugged her knees to her chest. "And look at all the older men with pretty young things on their arms." She gave a wry laugh. "All we women have on our arms is flabby skin."

When he didn't defend his sex, she looked at him.

"Suddenly you're not saying anything."

"I have a feeling this is a 'damned if I do, damned if I don't' discussion."

"Chicken."

"No thanks. I've had enough."

She gave him a look that said his tactic wouldn't work.

He sighed in that aggravating way men had. "I like you just the way you are, Catherine."

"You're changing the subject."

"I thought we were talking about you getting old."

"You think I'm old?"

"Hell no. You said you were old, not me."

"Don't tell me you've never dated someone a lot younger than you."

He was completely silent.

She laughed. "Ha! I got you on that one."

He looked at her while she crowed, then said, "I dated a woman for two years who was five years older than I was."

"I didn't ask you about older women."

He grinned. "I know."

She sat there while the sunshine beat down on them. After a moment of silence she said, "There must have been a lot of women in your life."

"Yes," he answered honestly, then looked at her and added quickly, "But they all looked like you."

She was horrified.

"Okay, then," he said in a rush. "None of them looked like you." He tried to look serious and failed.

She burst out laughing and shook her head. "You are awful."

"Yeah, but you love me," he said in a flippant and teasing way.

But it was so close to the truth she couldn't laugh. What would her life have been like if she had married Michael?

Her daughters could have been his had things been different, had he not gone to war, had she not let her father come between them. Had they been older.

Perhaps, she thought, being young wasn't such a good thing.

He slid his hand behind her head and before she knew it he had pulled her face toward his. Then he was kissing her deeply, but gently, as if he had all the time in the world to just savor her mouth. It was the first time he'd kissed her since that night in the boathouse. She gave herself up to that kiss, because she felt it clear through to her heart.

And it ended oh, so soon.

He pulled his mouth away from hers, but kept his hand on the back of her head. He searched her face and gave her a tender smile. "You are a beautiful woman, Catherine, and though it seems impossible, you are more beautiful now than you were at seventeen. I know you won't believe me, but those few lines on your face are the most beautiful part of you." He shook his head. "Sweetheart, don't regret even one of those forty-some-odd years."

And at that moment, Catherine wouldn't have wanted to be seventeen again for anything.

They had all gone on a hike that morning, even Catherine. And she hated every minute of it. But she never let on. Not one word of complaint, even when she lost her footing, smacked into a fir tree, and the needles poured down all over her.

She deserved a medal for valor, or at least tolerance.

They came home sweaty and muddy and all she wanted was a long shower and to never hear the word "trail" again.

She'd headed straight for the shower and Lord, did it ever feel good. She stood there and let the water beat on her, then she grabbed the shampoo and poured it all over her head.

"Mom?"

For heaven's sake! She couldn't even take a shower in peace. When you became a mother, you lost all your privacy.

Aly knocked on the door again. "Mom?"

"What?" She turned and let the water beat on her back while she scrubbed her hair into a nice foamy lather.

"Harold got out."

"He'll come back, Aly. Stop fretting about him." Silly cat.

"He's back."

"Fine. Now can I please finish this shower in peace?"

"Harold's in the bathroom with you."

"I don't care, Aly. He comes in the bathroom with me at home, too."

There was a long silence.

"Mom?"

She took a deep breath. She really didn't have much patience left. "Yes?"

"He's not alone."

Catherine stopped lathering her hair.

She heard Dana whisper, "Did you tell her?"

"Sort of," Aly whispered back. "Come here, Harold. Come here. I got him!"

Catherine pulled aside one small corner of the shower curtain and hollered, "There's a snake in here!"

"We know, Mom." Her girls had opened the door less

than an inch and she could see their eyes watching the snake through the crack.

"Well, don't just stand there! Do something!"

Sixteen

Her girls did something.

They got Michael.

"Catherine?" His voice came through the door.

The man of her dreams was on the other side of the door, ready to rescue her. She was naked, standing in the shower with a flimsy plastic curtain wrapped around her; it was the only thing between her and a long black snake.

She swore under her breath, one of those words her mother would have killed her for saying.

"Catherine," Michael called out. "Are you all right?"

"Just ducky." She pulled the shower curtain even tighter around her. "There's a snake in here!"

"I know. I don't want to open the door on it. Can you look and see where it is?"

She peered around the edge of the shower curtain. Oh God… She took a deep breath. "It's on the bath mat by the tub. You can open the door. Hurry. Please."

She hid inside the curtain the moment she heard him come in and close the door behind him. She waited, listening to the sounds on the other side. Finally she couldn't stand it any longer. "Did you get it?"

"Just a minute."

Oh God, oh God, oh God....

"I have it."

"Take it far, far away, Michael. Really far away."

"I'm putting it in a cooler."

"That's not far enough."

"It's the Igloo cooler that locks."

She heard a sharp snap.

"There. You're safe now."

"Is it still in here?"

"Yes, but it's locked up tight."

"Do you want a cat?"

He laughed.

"This isn't funny." She peered out from behind the curtain.

"It kind of is, Catherine. How can you be afraid of something so harmless? You're a thousand times bigger than that snake is."

She stared at him over the edge of the curtain. "I think there are two snakes in this bathroom."

"Look, I didn't mean to insult you. That's not what I meant."

"Using the word 'big' to a forty-seven year old woman who is naked and wrapped in a shower curtain isn't smart, Michael."

The fool was still grinning at her.

"It's not funny."

"Yes. It is."

"Would you just leave, please?"

He shook his head. "I don't think so."

"What are you doing?"

"Taking advantage of a great opportunity."

"Michael. Stay back!"

Then he was kissing her again and whispering to her and running his hands all over her wet body. Who knew where the shower curtain went? And she didn't care.

His kisses were slow and deep and wonderful.

"Come to my place tonight. Just you." He ran his lips over her ear. "Only you."

She whispered his name.

"Mike? Mom? Did you get it?"

He pulled away from her mouth, his finger against her lips. "Just about!"

Then he kissed her some more. "Say yes, Catherine. Say yes."

"Yes," she murmured against his lips.

He gave her one more soul-eating kiss, then said, "I'd better get rid of the snake."

She almost asked "What snake?"

"Seven o'clock?"

"I'll be there," she said and watched him leave the bathroom.

Through the door she heard Dana ask, "Is Mom okay?"

"I'm fine," she called out. But she wasn't. She was in love all over again.

Catherine showed up on his door step at ten after seven. She had been standing in the woods for fifteen minutes so she wouldn't look too eager. When it had started to rain lightly, she'd come out of her hiding place and walked up his front steps, scared and excited and just a mess of emotions.

She took a deep breath, knocked once, and the door flew open so quickly she jumped.

"Hey, Squirt." He stepped aside for her and took her jacket, then hung it on a coat-rack made of ancient moose antlers. "There wasn't a problem with your girls, was there?"

"No. When I mentioned coming here for dinner they exchanged some rather pointed looks. Then Aly informed me that they saw us kissing and if I was going to be doing anymore of that sort of thing, especially at my age, she would prefer it if I did so in private."

"She's a piece of work."

"They both are, but I wouldn't trade them for the most perfect children in the world."

"You shouldn't. They're good kids. Smart and funny. You've done a great job, Catherine."

"You think so?"

He nodded.

"Sometimes I think I'm the worst mother in the world."

"If you were a bad mother you wouldn't be worrying about what kind of mother you were."

"I guess you're right." She smiled. "Thank you."

"So what can I get you to drink?"

"Something potent." The second she'd said it, she wanted to sew her lips shut. Potent? Good God...

"Strong," she added in a rush. "I meant strong."

He looked like he wanted to laugh, but he was a smart man. "I have Jack Daniel's on the rocks."

"Not that strong. Wine. I'd like wine." And a new mouth,

she thought. She turned away. *You're here for sex and you say "something potent."* She wanted to kick herself. She looked around the cabin to keep from saying another stupid thing.

The place was rustic and woodsy, the way she remembered. There were dark wood floors that time and wear had given character. A couple of wool rugs in reds and blacks were scattered around, and a fire in a huge rock fireplace gave the room a warm glow.

He was bent over the refrigerator when she turned around.

"I'm disappointed. You don't have a Dale Evans sofa."

He straightened with a bottle of white wine in his hand, then looked at her and laughed. "Just old leather like Buttermilk's saddle."

"You can remember the name of Dale Evans's horse?"

"Only from a Trivial Pursuit marathon."

"Good." She moved to the kitchen. "I'd hate to think your memory was that good. Most days I can't find my keys. Aly says there's too much aluminum in my cookware."

He laughed.

"Speaking of cooking, something smells great."

A wonderful looking salad of spring greens was in the bowl on the counter, and a golden loaf of warm bread cooled on a chopping block.

"You made fresh bread?"

"No. I made frozen bread."

They laughed.

A steaming pot sat on the stove top and gave off the scent of shellfish mixed with sherry and cream.

She leaned over the pot and breathed it in. "Ohhhh." She looked up at him. "It's clam chowder."

He nodded and opened the wine.

Without thinking she picked up the spoon, skimmed some off the top of the pot and tasted it. "Hmmmm. This is so good." She looked up.

He was frozen, the wine bottle in one hand and a wine glass in the other. His expression was unreadable.

The spoon was still near her mouth and she realized she had just walked into his kitchen and eaten right from the soup pot.

"I'm sorry." All flustered, she waved the spoon around, then quickly turned to the sink. "I'll wash it for you. I do this at my place all the time. The girls aren't home for dinner a couple of nights a week and usually I'm so lazy I just stand there and eat from the stove. It's a bad habit." She was babbling. She stood there feeling stiff and awkward while she vigorously scrubbed the spoon with an orange and red plastic scrubber.

"Catherine," he said from behind her. "It's okay."

"No, it's not."

"This afternoon I had my tongue in your mouth and you're upset about rinsing off the spoon?"

He was right.

She dropped the scrubber and turned off the water.

"Turn around." His voice was soft and deep and near her ear.

She turned slowly.

He reached around her, picked up a piece of red lettuce from the salad and held it above her mouth. "Taste it."

She opened her mouth and he fed her. It was one of the most sensual moments she could ever remember.

"Good?"

She nodded and chewed and tried not to be a huge fool and throw herself at him.

He lifted the wine glass to her mouth as she watched him over the rim of the glass. She was leaning against the counter in the small kitchen for support.

His body was only inches away. She could feel the heat from him and something else, something so primitive she felt it clear to her toes.

She took a small sip.

"You're nervous."

She took the glass from him and set it down. "Yes."

"Don't be."

"I can't help it. I feel so naive."

"This from the same person who once informed me that she knew all about sex?"

"I was eleven and pretty full of myself. Besides, I wanted to get your attention."

"You got my attention all right." He laughed. "That's the first time you've ever admitted it."

"Is it?"

"Still nervous?"

"Yes."

"You know you can ask me anything."

She just looked at him and threw up her hands. "How is this whole thing done nowadays?"

"The same way it's been done for thousands of years."

She shook her head and looked down.

He reached out and touched her cheek. "You used to know how."

"How ungallant of you to remind me."

"You realize that to answer your question we have to decide which one of us wants to be on top." He looked to be having a great time with this conversation.

She crossed her arms and raised her chin a notch. "That's not what I meant and you know it."

"Then tell me what you mean, sweetheart, in plain English."

"AIDS." That was all she could say.

His face grew serious and his manner was no longer teasing. "I've lived with two women in thirty years, both were for long term monogamous relationships. Since then, I've chosen my partners carefully. I've been tested. They've been tested."

"Oh," she said, unable to find another word. He had spoken so matter-of-factly, and she knew how important this was, but felt as if she had been living on another planet. "I haven't been tested."

"Why would you? You've been celibate for years. Was you husband unfaithful?"

She shook her head. "Just irresponsible."

He tilted her chin up with his knuckle so she had to look at him. "You have nothing to worry about. I don't have sex, sweetheart, without protection. For you and for me."

"The way we're talking about this, openly. It seems so cold and clinical. So planned."

He was quiet for the longest time and she had no idea what he was thinking. Finally he placed his hands gently on her shoulders. "Are you certain you want to do this?"

She nodded, but she was still hugging her arms, a nervous habit she could not even think of breaking at this moment.

"I'm not cold. Are you?"

"No." She was on fire. He could do that to her. Just burn her up with a look or a touch.

She felt as if she had been waiting for this for longer than eight years. For thirty years. "Kiss me, Michael. Just kiss me now."

And he did, kissing her deeply and tenderly, until things got too hot, then his hands began to move over her. To her breasts, her waist, and between her legs.

Minutes later their clothes fell away, and she didn't even care. With Michael she couldn't seem to get close enough. His mouth was moving over hers. His tongue was inside her mouth and driving her nuts. His fingers moved inside of her, then moved slowly up and down her body.

One minute she was standing there, the next he swung her up into his arms and carried her to the bedroom. He set her on the bed, and for one long, awkward moment she lay there while he slid on protection.

Then he was crawling over her on the bed, between her legs, his lips exploring her breasts and her belly. Her hands threaded through his thick hair. He raised up on his forearms and just looked at her, as if he needed to.

He entered her slowly, easily, kissing her with those quick, nipping kisses she adored, watching her in that intense way he had, loving her as she hadn't been loved in so long.

They spoke in half-finished phrases, because a hot intense passion stole away their words, their thoughts, their breath. It went on forever, this loving, an eternity with him inside of her.

Soon they weren't doing it slowly, but rolling together—her on top, moving with him, then him driving her forward, their legs tangled at first, then changing positions again.

She could feel her release coming on. He gripped her hips, held her still and thrust into her hard and fast because she begged him to.

His name was on her lips when she came. He held onto her, said her name, too, in a long, drawn-out breath and came hard and fast.

Then they lay there, each lost in a world of dreams that come true. His chest was heaving, his heart pounding against her own. He rolled off her, then pulled her against his shoulder and stroked her head with a hand.

She sighed, then curled into him, her cheek resting on his chest.

"Catherine?"

She felt his lips on her forehead. "Hmmm?"

He shifted and his mouth closed over hers. Then the whole thing started all over again and again and again, as if in this one single night they had to make up for thirty lost years.

Seventeen

The rain was coming down so hard it sounded as if there was thunder right on the roof. Michael stood at the kitchen stove with Catherine, eating clam chowder from serving spoons. When he noticed the clean bowls and flatware still sitting atop fresh placemats on the dining table, he smiled to himself.

She dipped the spoon in the pot and held it up to his mouth, so he ate it. She was wearing his flannel shirt and nothing else. He slid his hands down over her bottom and pulled her closer.

She leaned back and looked up at him. "I can't believe I'm standing here like this."

"Like what?"

"Half-naked in your kitchen."

He laughed. "You could always take off my shirt."

"No way. The lights are on."

He paused, then began to unbutton the shirt.

She grabbed his hands. "What are you doing?"

"Taking back my shirt."

"You have on jeans. You don't need this shirt as badly as I do."

He slid his hands to her wrists and pulled her fingers away. When she tried to pull free, he wouldn't let go.

"Michael," she said with a warning in her voice.

He switched tactics and started at her neck, moving his mouth over her soft skin. He couldn't remember when he'd felt skin so soft. He used his mouth to taste her, to skim over her neck, along the solid bones of her shoulders.

He breathed in her scent. She smelled like Catherine, light and musky and female, like his dreams and memories and youth.

And all over her was the scent of the sex they'd shared. The scent of himself on her, the mixture of them, together. It made him hard and made him want her again. He wanted to hear that little cry she gave when he entered her, wanted to feel the way her breath would pick up when she was close to coming.

There were five empty Trojan wrappers next to his bed. That hadn't happened in over twenty years.

He nudged the shirt over her shoulder with his chin while he was kissing her. Her head drifted back and he dragged his mouth along the vee in the neckline, then nipped at her through the fabric.

He pulled a button through with his teeth, then quickly moved to her mouth to distract her.

She kissed him back the same way she had all night, with her mouth and lips and tongue. God, but she tasted of everything he remembered.

He moaned her name and slid his arms under her, lifting

her and letting her head fall back over his other arm. He buried his face in her breasts, licking and kissing, and every so often, unbuttoning his way down the shirt.

He walked around the kitchen and carried her to the fire, where he bent slightly and set her feet down on the rug. "Stand up for a second, sweetheart."

She did stand up, and his shirt fell right off her. He snatched it away before she could cover herself.

"You rat!" She reached for the shirt. "Give that back!"

He grinned at her and shook his head.

So instead of trying to cover her body, she buried her face in her hands. "I hate you."

"No, you don't."

"I'm embarrassed."

"Tell me why."

She didn't say anything for a moment, then admitted, "Because I'm old."

Old, my ass, he thought. God, but she was a beautiful woman. The firelight cast her skin in a golden glow. Her figure was curved and lush and womanly. Her breasts were full, not a young woman's breasts, but ones that had fed her daughters when they were babies. He regretted the fact that he hadn't been there to see it. He wished he could have tasted her afterward. "Catherine."

"What?" Her voice was still muffled by her hands.

He pulled out foil pack number six, opened it with his teeth, slipped off his jeans and kicked them away. "Come here."

She spread her fingers a bit and peeked out at him.

He was sitting on the arm of the chair, ready and just watching her.

Her shoulders sagged with regret or defeat, he wasn't sure which, and she let her hands fall away.

He leaned toward her and grabbed a hand, then pulled her to him.

She looked down at him as he pulled her into his arms. "Why did you do that?"

"What?"

"Take the shirt. Make me stand there in front of the fire. Naked."

"Because you're a beautiful woman."

"No, I'm not."

"I believe you are beautiful."

"Then you must be blind."

He stood and turned her around, then leaned her back against the chair and slipped easily inside of her. "Okay, then, I'm blind," he said against her lips. "And I like old things."

A cell phone was ringing in her ear.

Catherine opened her eyes and stared at a strange ceiling above her. Then she remembered where she was. She turned toward Michael, who was sound asleep next to her.

The phone rang again, muffled, but nearby. She turned toward the sound, opened a drawer next to the bed and pulled out the ringing phone.

She flipped it open. "Hello?" She listened. "Just a minute, he's right here." She turned to Michael and nudged him awake. "You have a phone call."

He shot up, scowling, then blinked at her and reached for the phone, his eyes suddenly sharp.

She turned away while he answered the man on the other end in brisk, one-word answers. In the open drawer where the cell phone had been, there was a DayTimer, a palm pilot and laptop, a key ring and a leather portfolio.

The rental agent had told her that the island telephone lines weren't at this side of the island yet, which was why she'd brought her own cell phone. She supposed it was the only way anyone on the island could reach him if they needed to. She stared at the contents in the drawer— business items. Then she shrugged into his shirt again and went to the bathroom.

She stood at the sink, washing her face and hands while something bothered her. He had a business. Why shouldn't he have those things in his drawer? He must have regular clients and pay tax bills and such. She was being silly.

And suffering from a definite lack of sleep, she thought, then smiled an evil, little satisfied smile.

If you were going to go without sex for so long this certainly was the way to end those celibate years. Well, Catherine, you ended them with a bang! she thought, then giggled.

"A bad pun," she told the mirror. She drove her fingers through her hair, grabbed a bottle of mouthwash and took a swig, then swished it around her mouth.

When she went back to the bedroom, he was off the phone and sitting on the bed in a pair of worn jeans. The pillows were wadded up behind his back and head, and his feet were crossed at the ankles. He watched her with an unreadable expression. He was drinking a beer. "You want one?"

She shook her head, "No, thanks. Do you have to leave?"

"No." He frowned, "Why?"

"Oh, I thought perhaps the call was because someone needed you."

"I can take care of it tomorrow morning."

She stood there. "I should leave, now. It's almost midnight."

He didn't say anything.

"I have a big project I was supposed to be working on this month." She turned around and smiled. "We've been having too much fun. I've hardly opened a file and I have an important presentation with Letni Corporation early next month."

He started to choke on his beer.

"Are you okay?" She rushed toward him, but he stood and raised a hand to ward her off.

"I'm all right." His voice was strained and hoarse. His face and neck were red. He set the beer down, his back to her. "Who do you work for, Catherine?"

"Carlyle Relocations. We specialize in handling the relocation and moving of companies and their employees. I've been trying to get the Letni account for years. They have huge expansion plans into other states. It will really put Carlyle on the map if I can land this account." She looked around the room, then turned back to him. "Where are my clothes?"

"In the kitchen." He stood up and followed her out of the room.

She picked up her clothes, feeling awkward and anxious, but well-loved. She could feel him watching her as she switched his shirt for her sweater.

"I need to talk to you about something."

She pulled her sweater down over her head and shook out her jeans. "What?"

He looked serious.

Suddenly her mind flashed with all the things he could say to her. Goodbye. Thanks for the sex. It was fun, but a fling. I don't love you. I do love you.

"I've made a mistake," he said.

She froze. *Oh Michael, don't do this to me.*

"I should have told you before."

She stiffened. "Are you married?"

"No," he said sharply. "What do you think I am?"

"I don't know. Why don't you tell me what you're talking about."

He ran a hand over his eyes and then looked at her. "I'm not a handyman, Catherine."

She let his words sink in. She stared at the fire for a moment, her mind racing a mile a minute. "That's what was wrong," she muttered to herself.

"What?"

She ignored him and went into the bedroom. She pulled open the drawer and looked inside. She picked up the keys and stared at them, then turned around.

He was standing in the doorway watching her.

"You drive a Porsche?" She held up the keys with the car emblem.

He nodded.

She felt like an ass. "I suppose it's a red Porsche."

"A black Carrera."

"You drive a hundred thousand dollar car?"

He nodded.

She threw the keys on the nightstand. "Just where is this car, Michael?"

"At my house."

"Where?"

"On Carillion Point."

She knew the area. It was exclusive and ungodly expensive. She crossed the room, but he was blocking the doorway. "Move."

He stepped aside.

She marched over, grabbed her shoes, then stuck them on her feet. She hopped in a circle, so angry she couldn't tie her shoelaces fast enough.

"That would be easier if you would just sit down."

"I don't want to sit down." She glared up at him. "I want to leave."

"I'm telling you the truth and you're angry."

"Because you lied to me!"

"I never said I was a handyman. You jumped to that conclusion all by yourself."

"Well, you didn't correct me, now, did you?" She walked to the door.

"No. I was too busy watching you try to liken a handyman's job to that of the Surgeon General."

"Oh, for Pete's sake. I did no such thing."

"I bet you watch 'Home Improvement,'" he threw back at her.

"What the hell was I supposed to do? You wouldn't answer my questions. All you did was grunt. I felt like Jane Goodall."

His eyes narrowed dangerously.

"Or Fay Wray."

"Sit down."

"Don't talk to me as if I'm a child."

"You're acting like one."

"Oh? And lying is so adult. For heaven sakes, you fixed my toilet and you couldn't say, Catherine, I'm not a handyman?"

She spun around and jerked the door open. "Stay there, Michael. Just stay far away from me." She could hardly look at him, but forced herself. "I'm sorry I came here. Sorry I saw you again. And I'm really sorry I flushed those socks down the toilet!"

Then she slammed the door and ran into the woods before he could see her cry.

It only took her two hours to get packed up and ready. Then she sat on the sofa for hours, watching the sun rise and the clock tick away like a counter, adding up every stupid thing she'd ever done or said or believed in.

She told the girls to pack, made up some lame excuse. It was the longest day of her life; she felt like such a fool.

By the time the boat arrived, she and the girls were standing on the dock. Within minutes they were loaded up and motoring away.

"I wish we didn't have to leave, Mom." Aly sat Indian-style on one of the molded seats as the boat moved away from the island.

Catherine faced her. "I know, sweetie. I know." But the truth was that Catherine couldn't have gotten out of there soon enough. Her girls would never know it, though.

"Do you think Mike will call sometime, since he had to leave so suddenly?"

Not if he's smart.

"We didn't even get to thank him."

"Mom! Quick! Look!" Dana said, saving her from having to answer that question with another lie.

Catherine turned toward Dana, who was sitting in the aft of the boat, pointing at the western sky where the sun was beginning to go down through a thick wall of oncoming rain clouds. The sky turned rich and bold— purple and red and as orange as Myrtle's hair color.

Dana turned back to Catherine, her eyes as bright as the sunset. "Isn't that the most beautiful sight you've ever seen?"

Catherine found a smile from somewhere and slid her arm around Dana. "Yes, honey, it sure is." She just stood there with her girls on either side of her and watched the island shrink and fade away like yesterday's dreams.

Michael watched the boat take off toward the mainland. He turned and walked back to the cabin, went inside and slammed the door. He swore viciously.

Then he began to pace the room, thinking. He stopped and looked at the moose antlers on the wall. Her jacket was still hanging there. "I'm not waiting another thirty years," he said, as if her jacket could understand him.

He crossed the room in three long strides and picked up his cell phone off a bookcase. He called his office, his fingers tapping impatiently on the bookshelf.

His assistant answered.

"Jim? This is Mike. I'm coming back. No, just some unfinished business I need to take care of. Right. When is that presentation meeting with Carlyle Relocation?" He paused, then said, "Move it up a week. That's right. Call them immediately. I'll be in the office tomorrow morning."

And Michael flipped the phone closed.

Catherine would be seeing him again in four days. Only she didn't know it.

Eighteen

The Letni building in the Silicon Valley was tall, slim, and coolly modern, exactly the kind of place that impressed California. It had an expansive view of the other sleek glass office buildings and complexes that housed Sun Microsystems, IBM, Xerox, and the other techno-conglomerate companies that surrounded a small green on the north side of a sprawling business park.

There was an all-natural whole food deli on the first floor plaza, where they served sandwiches on seven grain pita bread layered with sprouts and avocado, along with warm crocks of specialty soups garnished with floating squares of tofu instead of chunks of meat.

Trendy coffee carts and frozen yogurt stands flanked a wide bank of elevators with glass doors and electronic eyes that spotted you on the lobby level so you never even had to press the call buttons.

On the fourth floor was a mirrored gym with the latest weight equipment and muscular blond trainers who had all-over suntans compliments of the corner tanning booth.

You could get a massage or a manicure, even a shave and a haircut on the third floor spa located next to a travel agency that offered deals to Mexico or the Virgin Islands.

And deep in the ground, well below the limestone-tiled lobby, there were rollers under the foundation to make the building flexible during earthquakes. The Letni building had everything to ensure you would look healthy inside and out when the "big one" hit and you died under a pile of steel and glass.

Catherine tossed her empty latte cup into a shiny, bullet trash can made of chrome. She hadn't been in this building for four years—the last time she'd called on this account. She had forgotten how intimidating it was, so stark and hard and steely, as if it housed weapons of mass destruction instead of offices filled with people.

The elevator doors slid open and people filed out. She stepped inside and watched the doors close. She hadn't slept well last night and had been working fourteen-hour days ever since she came home.

There was dampness on her forehead as she stared up at the lit numbers above her.

Floor three…four…five….

She took a deep breath to calm herself and looked up again.

Floor fifteen, sixteen…twenty.

So fast, she thought. That was how quickly time could get away from you. One single breath and you were past ten whole floors. You could wake up one morning and find out that suddenly most of your life had passed you by.

The floor numbers blurred together into the image of a man she had loved for what seemed like forever.

She was miserable. So very miserable.

Since she'd left the island and her anger had faded into something painful, she had done some soul-searching, while lying awake at night. And she discovered she had been lying to herself. Letting herself believe that she didn't need to be loved or in love.

She was so wrong.

For over the past eight years she'd had a stronger relationship with her dreams than she had in her real life. The truth was plain and simple; she was scared to death to trust a man again. Because of Tom, and perhaps because of Michael, too.

She was like a small child who was afraid of the monster under the bed. She had spent all this time being frightened of something that might not even exist.

The elevator doors opened. She tightened her grip on her briefcase and checked the floor number. Thirty-three. She walked through the doors.

Come on, silly. This is the biggest presentation of your career. Get focused.

She stood there for a moment, feeling scared and nervous and human, then she took a deep breath, told herself she could do this and walked toward the reception desk.

Jim Edmonds opened the conference room door for her. Catherine stepped inside with a bright smile plastered on her face. Her gaze flew to the man at the head of the table.

Her smile died.

Michael didn't say a word to her. He just sat there at the head of the conference table while he studied her face. He was wearing a gorgeous silver-gray suit that made him look better than any man had a right to look. And she wanted to kill him.

She said nothing, but the longer she stood there, the more she felt like a butterfly about to get stuck with pins.

Jim gestured to a seat at the conference table. Catherine put her briefcase down, then opened it and took out the presentation folders, wondering what would happen if she just reached across the table and slapped Michael with them.

Jim said, "This is Catherine Winslow, executive vice president of Carlyle Relocation."

Michael stood up. "Catherine." He extended his hand to her.

She wanted to cut it off.

"Michael Packard," he said as if they had never met before.

"Michael is our president and CEO," Jim added.

No, she thought. He's not the president; he's a dead man. She looked right at Michael, hoping he could read her mind.

He had a death grip on her hand. "I understand you were bidding for our business about four years ago, when Rainy was president."

She gave him a look that should have burned a hole in him. "Yes." Her voice was more clipped than she meant it to be. "We were bidding against Westwood."

He wouldn't let go of her hand. He just pulled her closer until she was standing next to him. Then he introduced her to the two vice presidents, the general manager and the corporate relocation team.

She smiled and shook hands with each of them, the whole time aware of his other hand on her lower back, aware that the smile he wore for the room was strained.

She stepped away as soon as she could, then picked up the presentation folders and gave them to Jim to pass out.

Michael never took his eyes off her. He just sat there casually playing with a gold letter opener, tapping it against the table and being just obnoxious enough for only her to notice.

He could tap that thing all day; she refused to look at him. She stood there waiting for Jim to finish.

When he was done, she snapped open her folder, looked at the other three executives and smiled.

Ignore him and do this proudly. Don't let him know you feel a thing.

She took in an easy breath and let the anticipation of plain old silence work for her for a second, then she began, "Gentlemen…"

She was good. Damn good. And this proposal and bid were more comprehensive and thorough than any he'd ever seen. He could see the impression she was making on the other executives. They were enthralled with her plans.

He stopped watching her, looked down at the table while he fiddled with a letter opener and just listened. He wanted her to show her stuff.

For the next half an hour she went over her company's eight-year plan for relocating Letni's personnel and offices to new sites in five Western states.

She finished, then scanned the faces at the table. "Any questions?" Her chin shot up, her shoulders went back, and she looked right at him.

He wanted to stand up and applaud. Instead, he listened to each question raised and to her quick and knowledgeable answers.

When there was a small lapse of silence he stood. "Well, it looks as if there are no more questions. I think everyone is pleased."

There was a murmur of agreement and some positive nods.

She started to move, but he clamped his hand on her arm.

"Excuse us, gentlemen. I'll handle the rest of these negotiations in private." Then he steered her toward the door to his office, opened it and almost had to shove her inside.

Nineteen

Catherine was mad as hell. "I'm going to make your life so miserable, Michael Packard."

"You already have."

She tried to squirm away from him.

His other hand was gripping her hip. He guided her toward the sofa across from a huge desk. "Sit down."

"I don't think so." She stiffened and crossed her arms.

He picked her up and set her down, then placed his hands flat on either side of her and leaned down. "We have to talk."

"You knew I worked for Carlyle, didn't you?"

"Not until you mentioned it that night."

"You expect me to believe you?"

"I'm telling you the truth."

"Since when?"

"Since I fell in love with you all over again."

She pretended he hadn't spoken because she didn't want to crumble, not when she was hurting and vulnerable and angry.

"You don't have anything to say to me." He was waiting.

"Yes." She looked him squarely in the eyes. "Do I have the account?"

He looked as if that was the last thing he'd expected her to say.

"Answer me, Michael. Does Carlyle have Letni's relocation business?"

"Yes." His voice was clipped.

She gave him a look that said he had better be telling the truth. "Does Carlyle have this account because of me?"

"Yes. That bid and presentation you just gave earned you and Carlyle our business. You're good at your job, Catherine." He leaned closer. "But that isn't what I want to talk about."

"It's the only thing I want to talk about with you."

"Dammit! Will you give me five minutes?"

"Put it in writing, Michael."

He just looked at her, clearly confused.

"I want a written agreement right now that Carlyle has the Letni account."

"Fine." He grabbed her hand and pulled her over to his desk, then let go and wrote out the agreement. "Here. Sign it."

"You first."

He signed the agreement, then handed her the pen.

She signed it and snatched it off the desk.

"Now will you listen to me?"

She just looked at him, then waved a hand as if she didn't care what he said. "Fine. Speak away."

"Explain to me how allowing you to believe I was a

handyman is any different from you flushing those socks down the toilet."

"It's not," she shot back. "And once I realized we'd both been wrong, I was pretty much ready to contact you and try to work things out between us. But first I had to get this presentation done." She paused. "You moved up the date."

He swore under his breath.

"Why didn't you tell me you worked for Letni?"

"Because you ran out the door before I could."

"Not good enough. You could have followed me. You could have told me, Michael. But you didn't want to tell me, did you?"

He was silent.

"Nothing to say? Can't you think of a good enough lie?"

He just stared at her, his jaw tight.

She had the agreement in her hand, and she had a break in her heart that was so big it could echo. She looked at him, then looked down at the paper she was holding.

"I'm not lying."

"Go straight to hell." She shoved a desk chair between them and ran out the door.

"Catherine!" He pushed the chair aside and came toward her.

She slammed the door closed, quickly wedged a nearby chair under the doorknob and ran for the elevators.

Michael tried to open the door. It wouldn't budge. He swore and crossed to the conference room door, ran through, ignoring the startled looks of his employees, and made straight for the elevators.

She was standing there frantically punching the call button. An instant later the doors opened and she went inside.

"Catherine! Wait!" He ran toward her.

The doors closed in his face.

He made for the stairs, playing a hunch and hoping luck was on his side. He flew down four flights, half-flying over the stair railings, then out the door to the twenty-ninth floor.

He ran to the elevator bank. His gaze shot to the floor numbers above the doors.

She was stopped on the thirtieth floor.

He hit the call button and waited, his breath coming fast, his chest heaving.

The doors finally opened. He rushed around some people who were getting off and stepped inside.

She was in the corner glaring at him.

He moved toward her, his hands out. "Don't do this."

She ducked under his arm and slipped out just as the doors were closing.

"Catherine…please." He stuck his arm out to hit the electronic eye, but he wasn't fast enough. The door slipped closed.

He punched the open door button, but the elevator started moving down.

"Shit!" He punched number twenty-eight, then sagged against the wall for a couple of seconds.

The doors opened on the next floor. He jumped out and looked up at the numbers above all the doors. Every elevator was on a lower level except the one he'd just gotten off and one on the thirty-first floor, which meant she had to still be waiting on the twenty-ninth.

He ran back to the stairs, then up one flight, loosening his tie and throwing off his jacket. He burst through the door and ran toward her, just as she got on another elevator.

"Dammit, Catherine!" He was shouting. "I didn't tell you who I was because I was afraid of losing you!" He skidded across the floor.

The doors were closing.

He threw out his hands. "Don't make me wait another thirty years!"

The doors slipped closed.

Don't make me wait another thirty years. Those words played again in Catherine's head.

They could go their separate ways, never speaking again; never loving again. And years from now they would think of the other one and wonder at what might have been.

Catherine hit the Open button.

The stupid elevator paused for just a second, then started downward.

Oh, God. She had waited an instant too long.

Panicked, she looked at the line of buttons, then slammed her fist down on the one marked Emergency.

A bell blared through the air as if there were a fire.

The elevator jolted to a stop.

Catherine chewed on her lip. She didn't hate him; she loved him. She wasn't really hurt; her pride was just hurt.

Pride could be a funny thing. It could make something completely worthless seem like the most important thing in the world, could keep you from reaching out and grabbing the most precious moments in life. She didn't have a whole lifetime ahead of her, but whatever time she had left, she was going to spend with the man she loved.

The red phone in the elevator rang. She picked it up. It was Security checking to see if everything was okay.

"I need to go up to the twenty-ninth floor."

The man began to yell at her for hitting the red button.

"I hit it by mistake," she lied.

A moment later the bell stopped ringing and he told her to punch the button she wanted. The elevator began to move, then stopped on twenty-nine.

The doors opened. And there was Michael, standing there and looking as if he'd lost his best friend. He ran a hand over his eyes for a second and he said her name. When his hand fell away, his eyes were misty with emotion.

At that moment she loved him more than she thought was possible. She gave him a small smile, because she was afraid she might cry. She stepped toward him. "I don't want to wait another thirty years either."

His face was beet-red and sweaty, his tie askew and his shirt half pulled from his slacks. He looked down at his clothes. "It's a damn good thing I work out or I'd have died on the thirtieth floor."

She stepped closer, taking his hands and wrapping his arms around her. "I love you," she said against his lips.

He took the hint and kissed her slowly and deeply, in that special way he had.

Someone gave a cat call.

Someone else whistled.

He broke off the kiss and grabbed her hand, then took her through the stairwell door and closed it behind them.

He pressed her back against the door and kissed her again, for a long, long time, then just held her against his chest, rubbing his chin against her head. "How are the girls?"

"Mad at me because I won't let them call you."

"I knew I liked those kids of yours."

She could hear the laughter in his voice.

"So. How do you think they'd feel about us getting married?"

"I don't know. I don't remember you asking me to marry you."

"Will you?"

"What?"

"You're going to make me do this the hard way, aren't you?"

She nodded. "You bet I am. I've been waiting thirty years for this."

"Catherine," he began to propose.

She raised her hand and cut him off. "You're standing."

He looked at her as if he thought she was kidding, then shook his head in defeat and sank to one knee. "Do I need a rose between my teeth, too?"

"No. It wouldn't fit. Your foot's already there."

He laughed, but she just crossed her arms and waited.

Finally he held his arms out like Al Jolson. "Catherine Winslow. Will you marry me?"

She didn't answer him right away, but counted to ten slowly, then asked, "Why?"

"Why?" he repeated, surprised. He stood up and towered over her for a second. Then his expression changed. "Do you want me to tattoo the words on my forearm?"

"No. Just say them, Michael."

"I love you, Squirt." He slid his knuckle under her chin and tilted her head back so she had to look into his eyes. "I think I have always loved you."

She smiled.

He slid his hands slowly down her arms. "I want to marry you because you have two great daughters, and I'd like to be part of their lives, too."

"They adore you."

"Smart girls." He winked at her, then said, "I want to marry you, because you make me crazy, Catherine." He pulled her against him, trapping her arms at her sides and kissing her neck. His lips drifted over to her ear. "And especially because I like old things."

After she stopped laughing, she said yes.

Epilogue

Spruce Island, 1998

"**D**id you know that if you don't close your eyes when you sneeze, you can blow your eyeballs out?" Aly reached for a Coke from the cooler aboard the sailboat, then leaned back against the side and stretched her long legs out in front of her. After a second of silence she turned and looked at all of them.

"No. I didn't know that." Michael cast a quick glance down at Catherine, who was sitting between his legs in the bow of the boat, her head tilted back, her amused face looking up at him.

"It's true." Aly took a swig of her Coke. "You sneeze at speeds up to two hundred miles per hour."

Dana turned around. "Good, then why don't you sit here behind the sails and sneeze for a while. There's hardly any wind."

"Funny." Aly made a face at her.

Michael was used to this kind of bickering from his new daughters. It had been almost a year since he and Catherine got married, with both girls' blessing, something that meant a lot to him. They liked him. Trusted him.

The move from San Francisco hadn't been easy for Aly and Dana, having to up and leave behind everything that was familiar to them. But Michael had flown some of their friends up for visits that first summer, and once school started the girls had adjusted pretty well.

Dana made the sailing team and had her own Laser she sailed whenever she could. She was sixteen and dating the captain of the sailing team—a tall boy that Michael kept an eye on because the kid reminded him of what he was like at seventeen.

He and Catherine had bought Aly a horse, a little Arab mare that she rode almost every day at the stable not far from their new house.

He'd gladly sold the Guggenheim and bought another waterfront home closer to the girls' schools and better suited to his new family, which now included three cats, a dog, a parrot and a tank of tropical fish.

He'd kept the Porsche. But Catherine drove it most of the time. She was still with Carlyle, but employed as account coordinator based out of the Letni offices in Seattle. She had to travel about once a month, but he usually tagged along, claiming he had business there, too, even if he didn't.

They sailed past the cove and Aly sat up, pointing. "Hey! Look what they've done to the old house."

Michael turned at the same time as Catherine. He'd

heard that someone had bought the old place shortly after they'd gotten married.

Catherine leaned forward, her hand raised over her eyes to block out the bright June sunshine. "What does that sign say?"

"Rainshadow Lodge." Dana turned the boat toward the inlet. "Wow. What a change. It looks so different. Nicer."

She was right. Someone had put plenty of money and work into restoring the old Victorian. It sported a new shingled roof without a sign of green algae. A large bay window had been added to the western side of the house, which had been painted gray.

But the biggest change was the wrap-around porch, which stood straight, perfectly level and painted the same crisp white as all of the Victorian trimwork. The lawn was a lush green and closely cropped, framed by new plants that edged stone-paved walkways and a new set of steps that led down to the dock.

"Oh, no…" Catherine's voice sounded lost. "Michael look. They're building a new boathouse."

She was right. At the end of the dock was a pile of new lumber and roofing materials, sitting where the boat-house had been.

"Pull up to the dock, Dana." Michael spotted a pile of old wood on the other side of the new lumber.

Catherine shifted out of the way and Michael stood up, then stepped onto the dock.

He moved over to the junked wood and looked through it, tossing each plank into another pile behind him.

"What's he doing, Mom?"

"Looking for something we left there. You girls stay here." Catherine stood and followed him. She touched his shoulder while he was bent over. "Any luck?"

"No." He kept looking. Almost at the bottom, he found it—the splintered plank that still carried their old initials.

He exhaled a breath he hadn't known he'd been holding and held up the broken plank of wood. "Here it is. All in one piece."

"I'm so glad." Catherine slid her arm through his.

He was as relieved as she sounded. They walked back to the boat still arm in arm, and he helped her inside, then jumped in after her and unwrapped the tie line.

"Let us see," the girls said, shifting closer to sneak a look.

He handed the board to Catherine, who held it up.

The girls looked at both of them as if they were nuts, then shook their heads and wisely said absolutely nothing.

Catherine looked back at him and asked, "Where shall we put it?"

"I have just the place."

"Where?"

He leaned over and whispered, "I'll add it to my collection of old things."

* * * * *

PRIVATE PARADISE

Debbie Macomber

Dearest Friends,

There's no place more beautiful than the Pacific Northwest during the summer. When Susan Wiggs, Jill Barnett and I were asked to contribute to this anthology, we knew exactly where we wanted to set it—our own backyard.

The three of us had great fun planning our stories. We met for lunch at a local Thai restaurant, removed our shoes and crawled into the booth. Between sampling the exotic dishes and sipping wine, we shared our ideas. We were three women on a mission, and that mission was to let everyone know what a fantastic state we live in.

Be sure to pay close attention to the scene in *Private Paradise* that involves kayaking. You guessed it— I took a kayaking class. Once I got over my initial fear (that my hips were too wide to climb out of the kayak and I'd end up wearing it home), it was one of the most incredible adventures of my life.

I hope Susan, Jill and I convince you to come and visit scenic Puget Sound…especially in summer! And I hope these stories are as much fun to read as they were to write.

Warmest regards,

Debbie Macomber
P.O. Box 1458
Port Orchard, WA 98366

For Stephanie Cordall, who's fifty
and so much
older than me.

One

Mary Jane: I'm telling you, Beth, a month in the San Juan Islands will be heaven. We'll sit up and talk all night the way we did in high school, lounge around the beach and eat fabulous meals....

Beth: Fabulous meals?

Mary Jane: You're cooking, aren't you?

July 1998

"Hey, Mom, this place is way cool."

Standing in front of the three-story summer home with its elaborate gingerbread trim, Beth Graham had to agree. She set her suitcase down, still staring at Rainshadow Lodge. A wide welcoming porch wrapped its way around the front, and huge picture windows granted an unrestricted view of Puget Sound. The sun shimmered on the gentle waters lapping the shore. Mary Jane had been right—a month's vacation on Spruce Island was exactly what she needed.

"Can you imagine what a place like this rents for?" Paul said in awe.

More than they ever could've afforded on their own, that was for sure. It really was a lovely house, and just knowing she'd be able to enjoy the luxury of this island paradise for the next thirty-one days made Beth feel almost lighthearted. Better yet, she'd be sharing it with her longtime friend Mary Jane Reynolds. All thanks to Schumacher and Company, a consulting firm based in Southern California. Schumacher had actually rented the house. Not for Beth and her son, but for Dave Reynolds and his family. Mary Jane was the one who'd invited Beth to join them while Dave did consulting work for Boeing, the airplane-manufacturing company. No fool she, Beth had leaped at the chance to escape St. Louis in July. Leaped at the chance to escape, period!

The past two years had been difficult ones as she adjusted to widowhood and being a single mother. She knew it was time to pick up the threads of her life. Time to resume her catering career and get back into the swing of a daily routine.

Past time, really, or so her friends had said. Beth couldn't understand that attitude. She didn't know where it was written that a woman had six months or twelve, or whatever preordained number of months to recover from the death of a loved one. Some of her friends—although Mary Jane wasn't among them—seemed to imply that her allotted time for grieving had now expired. Life wasn't quite that simple in Beth's experience. But ready or not, she'd decided to return to work in September. She'd accepted a good position with a five-star hotel and had agreed to start right after Labor Day.

Which meant she had all of July and August to spend with her fifteen-year-old son. Plus this whole month with Mary Jane. The summer would be a transition between what remained of her old life and her new one.

"When will they get here?" Paul asked.

He knew that as well as she did. They'd gone over the details a hundred times in the past twenty-four hours. Beth and Paul would arrive first, picking up the keys from the rental agency. From there they'd go directly to the house and unpack. Mary Jane, Dave and their three teenage boys would arrive around seven that evening. By then Beth would have dinner prepared. The months of planning, the countless phone calls would all pay off and the fun would begin.

"Seven o'clock, right?" Paul answered his own question. He reached for his suitcase and one of hers.

She could have carried it herself, but he insisted. She nodded solemnly, observing not for the first time how much her son had matured in the past couple of years. Good heavens, he'd gotten his learner's permit the week before they left and would start a driving course in September. That alone seemed unbelievable.

Since Jim's death, Paul had taken on quite a few household chores, but more than that, he seemed to want to protect her. To shield her emotions, perhaps, and fill the hole Jim's passing had left in her life. It was because of Paul that Beth had agreed to return to work, to give the impression that she'd recovered from her husband's death. For Paul's sake more than her own. He'd taken his father's death hard and rarely spoke of him. Beth suspected it was too painful even now. She hoped that when *she* showed signs of healing, of growing, of moving forward, her son would, too.

With a dramatic flourish, Paul inserted the key into the lock and threw open the front door. The summer house was impressive from the outside, but little could have prepared her for the charm that awaited her when she stepped over the threshold. The hardwood entry brought them to a living room filled with large overstuffed chairs and a sofa. There was a stone fireplace against one wall. A sweeping staircase led to the second floor. Paul carried their bags up the stairs, eager to explore the bedrooms, while Beth headed for the kitchen. That was where the heart of a home existed, she believed.

She wasn't disappointed. The big bright country kitchen had a cooking island, more than adequate counter space, all the modern appliances, including an espresso machine and a second oven. Only a woman who loved to cook as much as Beth did would appreciate the convenience of two ovens.

Tucked in a corner was a breakfast nook with benches built below a bay window. It could have comfortably seated eight, Beth figured, loving it.

"Mom!" Paul shouted from halfway down the stairs. "I counted six bedrooms."

"Six!" The brochure Mary Jane had mailed her said five. It also explained that the house had been renovated within the last year. They were only the second group of summer tenants.

"All right, five and a television room. One of the bedrooms is on the third floor—there's a Jacuzzi, too."

Although she'd read about the Jacuzzi in the brochure, this was something Beth longed to see for herself. She hurried out of the kitchen, leaving the door to swing in her wake, and raced up the stairs. Breathless, she followed her son down the long narrow hallway, glancing in each room along the way. Sure enough, there were four spacious bedrooms, with the largest room at the far end. Just as Paul had said, it was a television room. Bulky mismatched sofa and chairs were haphazardly arranged in front of a big-screen television. They hurried up the narrow flight of stairs to the third story, which had been converted into a bedroom with an adjoining bath. This was where the Jacuzzi resided.

"There's a library, too," Paul said.

"Up here?"

"Downstairs. It's off the living room. It's got a huge fireplace and big double doors that slide open. You'll love it."

Beth could see herself quickly falling in love with this house.

Eager to explore the rest of it, they raced down both sets of stairs. Paul reached the bottom first just as the telephone rang. "I'll get it," he yelled as if he were back home in St. Louis.

"Hi, Mary Jane," he said, turning to look at Beth. "Shouldn't you be on the plane by now?" He checked his wristwatch.

Beth's actions mimicked her son's.

"She's right here," Beth heard him say before he handed her the receiver.

"Where are you?" Beth asked, hoping it was the airport

and somehow knowing it wasn't. The laughter and excitement that had filled the air only seconds earlier evaporated with the knowledge that something had gone wrong.

"Beth," Mary Jane said urgently. "I'm so sorry."

"Sorry?"

"I've been trying to reach you since late yesterday afternoon."

"We spent the night with my mother-in-law," Beth explained. "She lives close to the airport." But that wasn't important just now. "What's wrong?"

"It's Dave. He fell off the roof yesterday. While he was trying to fix the skylight."

Beth gasped. "Is he all right?"

"Yes…and no. He broke his leg in two places. He was in surgery for three hours this morning, and he's still too groggy to understand what's happening."

"Oh, my." She glanced at Paul. "Everything's all right," she whispered, placing her hand over the mouthpiece.

"Dave's doing much better than we expected," Mary Jane went on.

"Is she coming?" Paul mouthed.

Beth shrugged, unable to answer, although that question was on her mind, too. With luck, they'd only be delayed a few days.

"Dave's going to be in hospital in traction for the next week or so."

The hope that had briefly flared to life died a quick and sudden death. After months of planning, of excited anticipation, Mary Jane wouldn't be coming.

"The company's sending another consultant."

"Oh." It went without saying that this new consultant wasn't ready to share the house with Dave Reynolds's wife's best friend from high school and her fifteen-year-old son.

"His name's John Livingstone. Dr. John Livingstone."

"How long do we have?" Beth asked, hoping they could at least spend the night. They'd come a long way to be heading back to St. Louis this soon.

"Have?"

"Before John and his family arrive?"

"There's only him and his daughter," Mary Jane said. "He's divorced."

Not that his marital status had anything to do with the problem at hand.

"You might strike up some kind of arrangement with him," her friend suggested.

"What kind of arrangement?" Beth's disappointment was sharp. Too sharp to see past the discouragement and sense of loss she felt at being cheated out of this vacation, this time with her best friend. They'd spent hours on the phone discussing all the things they were going to do. All the sights they intended to see, the adventures they planned with their children. The nonstop conversations they'd have…. Now none of that was going to happen.

"John's a reasonable man."

"I'm sure he is."

"He wasn't expecting to fly up to Seattle, and he's got a twelve-year-old daughter who isn't that keen to come with him. I don't know much about him other than he's brilliant."

Beth's mind was working fast. If Dr. John Livingstone
let them spend tonight here, surely she could find something else tomorrow. Surely there was some cheap place
they could rent for a week or two. If she watched her
pennies, there might be a way for her and Paul to stay in
the area, after all. It seemed a shame to turn around and go
home, especially when they'd been looking forward to this
respite for so long.

"I can't remember the girl's name, but I do recall that
he's got custody of her. You'd be great with her, a positive
female influence. Besides that, John's nice-looking."

"What's that got to do with anything?" Beth demanded irritably.

"Not a single thing," Mary Jane responded, but Beth
could almost see her friend's mind working. "It's just that…"

"Just what?"

"It seems to me that you're both adults and you could
come up with a compromise."

"Such as?" Beth didn't mean to be obtuse, but she
needed to know precisely what Mary Jane was thinking.

"Sharing the house. You were our class valedictorian,"
Mary Jane reminded her. "*You* figure it out."

Beth brushed the frothy row of bangs from her
forehead. While she had all the book smarts she'd ever
needed in life, that hardly qualified her to deal with a
situation like this. Sharing a house with a stranger, a
man… No, it couldn't be done.

Beth didn't get the opportunity to tell Mary Jane that her
idea was out of the question. The words died on her lips at
the sound of the front door opening.

"When's this John Livingstone supposed to arrive?" Beth asked, whirling around as though to confront an assailant. She stiffened and glanced at Paul. Like her, he was concentrating on the entryway.

"He's due anytime," Mary Jane told her.

"I think he's here now," she said. "I'll call you back later." She set the phone in its cradle, placed her hand on Paul's shoulder and prepared to confront Dave Reynolds's replacement. *Just let us stay here tonight,* she breathed. *Please. Just tonight.*

The daughter entered the house first, and one look at her dashed all Beth's hopes. She might be twelve but she looked much older. The ends of her hair were green and everything else was black, including her lips and her fingernails. She had on a black T-shirt, black jeans and a black backpack.

"Who are you?" the girl demanded, glaring at Beth.

The man who stepped in after her looked tired and irritated.

Beth forced herself to smile and stepped forward to offer her hand. "Dr. Livingstone, I presume?"

Two

Mary Jane: I've always believed that things happen for a reason. God doesn't close a door without opening a window.

Beth: Unfortunately a seagull just flew in that open window and pooped right on the carpet.

"Just exactly who *are* you?" Nikki snapped, narrowing her eyes at the woman and the boy as if she worked for the FBI.

"Nikki," John muttered, "I'll ask the questions." This wasn't his day. Or his month. Or his year, for that matter. He looked at the woman and asked, "Just exactly who are you?"

"I'm Beth Graham and this is my son, Paul." Her voice shook with nerves, but she met his gaze squarely. "We're friends of the Reynolds family."

"Ah."

"Who?" Nikki frowned, glancing up at him.

"Perhaps I could put on a pot of coffee and we could talk this out," Beth suggested, pushing her bangs away from her forehead. "We just arrived ourselves and...oh, dear, this is something of a mess."

"You were planning to share the house with Dave Reynolds and his family?" John asked, thinking the situation was becoming far too complicated. He'd gotten a call around eight the night before from the company president, who'd asked him to fill in on this assignment. John had agreed, but really, what choice did he have when it was coming from Schumacher himself?

Then there was Nikki, who made spending a month away from her friends sound as if he was dragging her off to boot camp.

Now this.

"They aren't staying here, are they, Dad?" If it was up to his daughter, she'd throw them out on their ear without giving the matter a second thought. He found himself annoyed with her lack of patience, her lack of compassion. Then again, if he was going to complain about Nikki's failings, he should look to his own. He'd been a rotten husband, and now it seemed he wasn't much of a father.

"Yes, why don't we all sit down and talk this out," John said, wondering just how uncomfortable this was likely to get. Dave's accident was unfortunate, but it wasn't John's fault the man had taken a tumble from his roof. Frankly he wasn't interested in playing host to a couple of strangers just because Dave had decided to play handyman by repairing a broken skylight.

The four of them moved into the kitchen, and Nikki threw herself into a seat at the breakfast nook as if sitting down in a civilized manner required too much effort. Paul slipped in across from her and the two eyed each other warily.

Beth and her son might have arrived only a few minutes ahead of him, but John was impressed with how quickly she located everything they needed for coffee.

With her back to him, she explained the situation. "Mary Jane and I are friends from high school."

"Mary Jane is Dave's wife?" he asked. "I think I met her at the company Christmas party."

Beth nodded. "When Mary Jane learned Dave would be spending a month in Seattle, she researched rental houses and found this one. It was cheaper to rent Rainshadow Lodge than for Dave to stay alone in a hotel room for the month. Seeing that there are five bedrooms—"

"And a huge TV room," Paul inserted.

"—she asked Paul and me to join them."

"We've been planning it since last March," Paul added, his voice betraying his disappointment. "It's the first time we've gotten away since my dad died."

John watched as Beth gave her son a gentle look that said she'd do the explaining.

"But, Mom, he needs to know how much we've been looking forward to this! I must've read five books about Seattle and the San Juans and—"

"Paul, please."

"It's a really big house," her son said. "They wouldn't even know we were here." He turned to John. "We've got trips planned for practically every day, and Mom signed us up for kayaking lessons this week, and then there's the Sol Duk Hot Springs and a trip to Victoria, British

Columbia—I've never been to Canada. And...and we're gonna visit the Seattle Aquarium and the Pike Place Market and ride the ferry. We were even going to take a drive up to Hurricane Ridge. Did you know there are mountains in Washington State that have never even been explored?"

John watched as Beth's cheeks flushed pink. Clearly her son's outburst had embarrassed her. She was around his own age, he guessed, and attractive. The realization caught him by surprise. It'd been a long while since he thought of a woman in those terms. For the past three years he'd done his best to ignore the opposite sex altogether. His own wife had left him for a man she'd met on the Internet. Even now, just thinking about Lorraine and her cyberspace boyfriend tightened his jaw. The fact that she'd actually divorce him for a man she'd never met face-to-face had deeply scored his pride. But apparently it was a match made in cyberheaven, because the two of them appeared blissfully content. Within a month of exchanging their first e-mail messages, Lorraine had left her husband and daughter—lover boy didn't like kids—and moved to Philadelphia. Once the divorce was final, Lorraine had remarried within a week.

"My mom's a really wonderful cook and she could fix all the meals."

"Paul!" She cast John an apologetic look. The color in her cheeks had splotched her neck now. "I'm sorry. Paul's disappointed and, well, I can see it'd be best if we found other accommodations."

The teenager wasn't the only one who felt disappointed, John suspected. Beth's shoulders sagged slightly and the luster was gone from her eyes. This was one hell of a predicament.

"Is there someplace else you can stay?" he asked, and immediately wanted to grab back the question. He already knew the answer. He'd been told that the island's population doubled in the summer months. A drive through town hadn't revealed a single vacancy sign.

"I'm sure there is," she said bravely, reassuring him with a smile. "We'll call for a taxi and be out of your hair within the hour."

It would have helped if she wasn't so damned gallant about it. Only moments earlier he'd been irritated with Nikki for her lack of understanding, and now he found himself behaving without charity. A widow and her kid, no less.

"Hold on," John said. Sighing, he buried his hands in his pants pockets. There was only one decent thing to do, not that he liked it. He didn't, no way, but he couldn't see any other alternative.

Paul's eyes widened with gratitude. "You mean we can stay?"

"Ah…" John hesitated. All he'd intended to offer was the night.

"You won't be sorry," the boy insisted. "We can earn our keep. Mom can cook and I'll clean up around the place, mow the lawn and—"

"Paul," Beth said, raising her voice slightly. "I think it'd be best if Dr. Livingstone and I discussed this privately."

Her son accepted her words with good grace, turned to Nikki and said, "You wanna see the upstairs?"

"Sure," Nikki replied, showing the first signs of life since they'd arrived.

The two kids left the room, and Beth waited until they were out of earshot. "I am so sorry," she murmured, handing him a mug of freshly brewed coffee.

"Sorry?" He didn't understand why she felt the need to apologize.

"Paul makes it sound like we're…"

He watched her as she searched for the right word.

"…desperate," she said finally.

"You cook?" He walked to the table and claimed a chair, and she sat down on the bench.

"I'm a caterer, or I was until two years ago. I quit work after my husband was killed, but I have a job now, or I will starting in September."

John took a restorative sip of coffee while he mulled things over. It boded well that Nikki and Paul seemed to get along, although it was too early to know for sure. He'd never been comfortable with the idea of leaving his daughter alone every day while he went to work. He'd be taking the new direct-to-Seattle ferry, which meant an hour's commute each way. Then there was all the time he'd actually be spending in the city.

"Listen," Beth said, smiling brightly, "this has been a shock, but once Paul and I get our bearings, we'll be out of your hair. I apologize for any inconvenience we might have caused you."

John stared into the dark rich coffee before he spoke. "Let's not be hasty. Perhaps we can work something out, after all."

* * *

The phone pealed like a fire alarm at nine o'clock, just before Beth was ready to head upstairs. The west coast was two hours behind St. Louis, but she didn't feel two hours younger or two hours more refreshed.

"It's for you," Nikki announced, then handed her the telephone and walked out the front door. The kitchen had the latest in modern conveniences, but as far as Beth could tell, there was only one phone in the entire house.

"Me?" It had taken Beth a moment to realize the twelve-year-old was speaking to her. Other than that first direct question, Nikki Livingstone hadn't said a word to her, almost as if she thought that ignoring Beth would make her disappear. It was clear to Beth, if not to John, that his daughter wasn't the least bit pleased with this unexpected turn of events.

"Hello, Mary Jane," Beth said.

"How'd you know it was me?"

"Who else could it be?"

"I've decided to forgive you for not calling me back right away. I'm going to tell you what I learned about John Livingstone and his daughter. I take it you two worked out some kind of living arrangement?"

"Yes, but—"

"Then listen up, because this is important. Like I said, he's divorced, but from what I understand, it wasn't a friendly divorce."

"Is there such a thing as a friendly divorce?" Beth asked. She'd witnessed the emotional agony her friends had endured during the breakup of their marriages. It might start out friendly, but then declined to merely civil, followed by out-and-out anger and bitterness. Divorce ravaged lives.

"His wife left him and the girl high and dry," Mary Jane continued. "Apparently the daughter's a handful. Age twelve with attitude."

Beth had already noticed.

"Also, John's got a reputation as something of a curmudgeon."

Seeing how generous he'd been to her and Paul, Beth had trouble believing it. "Curmudgeon or not, he's been very kind. We were able to come up with a compromise."

"I told you it'd work out." Mary Jane sounded downright gleeful. "Details! I want details."

"I'm staying at the house in exchange for cooking meals and entertaining Nikki." Provided she could find a way to communicate with the kid.

"This is *ideal*."

"Ideal?" Beth echoed. "I'm glad you think so."

"Sure. Throw together two lonely people, raising their children alone. It's perfect! You'll be in love before you know what hit you."

"Mary Jane!" In high school MJ had been the world's most incorrigible—and least successful—matchmaker. Now it seemed she was up to her old tricks.

"Mark my words!"

Beth groaned and glanced over her shoulder, making sure no one was eavesdropping on their conversation. "Shouldn't you be sitting by Dave's bedside holding his hand?"

"I always said things happen for a purpose," Mary Jane said. "Unfortunately Dave had to break his leg so you could finally meet a decent guy. Ah, well," she finished good-naturedly, "he should never have gone up on that roof in the first place. I *told* him to call a repairman."

Three

Beth: Mary Jane, the most incredible thing happened today! I saw an eagle.

Mary Jane: Did this one poop on your carpet, too?

This had to be the worst summer of her life, Nikki thought, sitting on the porch steps after dinner—which she'd barely touched. She was stuck here with Martha Stewart and the Boy Wonder because her dad was going to desert her every morning.

It hadn't taken long, she thought darkly, for the intruder to sucker her dad into letting them stay.

Nikki couldn't believe he'd actually agreed to this. What bothered her most was his saying this was for her benefit. Yeah, right! She didn't want company, and the last thing she cared about was seeing the sights. As for kayaking classes, she had news for them. They could forget it. She wasn't remotely interested in anything to do with water.

Nikki didn't know what her father was thinking. The last thing she wanted—or needed—was a baby-sitter. As for

Beth seeing to their meals, big deal. Up until now, her dad had been eating the dinners *she* made without complaining.

The screen door creaked behind her, but Nikki didn't turn around to see who it was. She already knew.

Her dad sat down on the step next to her. "Tired?" he asked.

"No."

"You don't look very happy."

"Give the man a prize," she said with an exaggerated sigh.

"It isn't my fault Dave Reynolds broke his leg."

That wasn't the point. "She manipulated you into letting her live here rent free and I'm supposed to be happy?" Nikki blurted. No use beating around the bush. The one thing she'd learned in the three years she'd been living exclusively with her dad was that he didn't take hints.

"You think I should have kicked her out?" He sounded incredulous.

"Damn straight I do. We don't need her."

Her dad didn't say anything for a couple of minutes. "You're right, we don't need her."

"Then why'd you let her stay?"

He took his own sweet time answering. "She needs us."

"Oh, puh-leeze."

"There're no vacancies on the island."

"How do you know that?" Nikki demanded. He hadn't made any phone calls; neither had Beth. They hadn't even tried.

"Don't you remember what the ticket agent said when I mentioned Spruce Island?"

Nikki didn't.

"He said it was one of the most popular of the San Juans. Spruce Island is a great summer escape. You didn't notice any vacancy signs while we were driving in, did you?"

She shrugged. Truth be known, she hadn't looked.

"I don't need a baby-sitter." Her vehemence surprised even her.

"Of course you don't."

"Then why—"

"I suggested Beth include you so she'd think she was earning her keep. People have their pride, you know."

"Well, then, what about mine? You make it *sound* like she's my baby-sitter."

"She isn't."

"So I can do what I want, right?"

He hesitated. "Right, but—"

Nikki groaned. "There's always a but!"

"You can do what you want," he continued, "*but* it has to be within reason."

"This is going to be a real fun month," she said sarcastically. Nikki heard someone move up behind her. She twisted around and glared over her shoulder. Sure enough, Beth Graham stood on the other side of the screen door, watching them.

"What are you doing sneaking up on my dad and me?" Nikki shouted, vaulting to her feet. "Let's get something straight right now. My dad said you could live here, but I don't have to like it. Just because you—"

"I'm sorry, I—"

"That's enough, Nikki."

It was her dad's tone of voice that stopped her. When

he was annoyed, he raised his voice, but when he was angry, *really* angry with her, he kept it level. Only someone who knew him as well as she did would realize that.

"I apologize for intruding," Beth said softly.

Nikki crossed her arms and rolled her eyes. She'd just bet Beth was sorry. Yeah, sure.

"I wanted to tell you I was going up to bed and tell Nikki I'd see her in the morning."

Nikki couldn't contain a snicker. See her in the morning? Not if she had anything to say about it.

Tired though she was, Beth barely slept that first night. It wasn't the bed or even the circumstances. Well, that was probably *part* of the problem, but what seemed strangest of all was the silence. She lay awake half the night straining to hear something, anything. She wasn't accustomed to the lack of sound and found it downright…eerie.

She supposed that in time it would strike her as peaceful, rather than unsettling

With her window open, the scent of the sea wafted lazily into her room. Once, in the early-morning hours, she heard the cry of a gull and smiled to herself, remembering her earlier exchange with Mary Jane. She felt relieved to know that life went on outside her bedroom window.

When the sun rose, it was so bright it woke her. She opened one eye and looked at the clock, shocked to discover it was only five-forty-five. The sun, however, refused to go away. Actually she had to admit this was a pleasant way to wake, and she sat up in the feather bed, stretched her arms and yawned.

A gull screeched once more, followed by a chorus of frantic cries. Beth slid out of bed and hurried to the window to see several birds in flight, along with a flock of crows excitedly beating their wings. Obviously they'd been disturbed by someone or something.

As she turned away from the window, Beth caught sight of an eagle. It soared elegantly in the distance, circling the beach. For once, the word "awesome" seemed apt. This was the first time she'd seen an eagle in the wild, and its beauty and grace were stunning. Hypnotic to watch.

It didn't take her long to realize there was no love lost between the eagle and the other birds.

After she'd spent several minutes studying the eagle, it flew off and Beth reached for her robe and headed down the stairs. Not wanting to wake anyone else, she made as little sound as possible.

Her plans were to brew a pot of coffee and take a mug outside to the porch swing. Enjoy the luxury of early morning. She hadn't done much of that, even with a two-year break from her career. During quiet times, when she allowed her mind to wander, it invariably went searching for memories of Jim. She could think of him now without the crushing burden of grief. Remember the good times and smile, grateful for the life they'd shared. Thank him for the incredible gift of her son. She'd loved her husband, and his death had badly shaken her world and her sense of self. Yet she'd known then and knew now that she had everything she needed to be happy.

She was halfway into the kitchen before she realized

John was up and dressed. He sat at the table in a business suit, reading the Seattle morning paper.

"Oh," she said before she could stop herself.

He lowered the newspaper and frowned. "Morning."

"Good morning." Self-consciously she brought her hand to her neckline and clutched the edges of her robe together. "I…I didn't realize anyone was up." Since she'd slept so lightly, it surprised her that she hadn't heard him.

"There's coffee," he said, and gestured toward the pot.

"You're going into work? So early?" She regretted the question as soon as she'd asked.

"I'll be back late this afternoon."

"Would you care for breakfast?" she asked, thinking he might want her to cook him something. That was their agreement, after all, and she fully intended to keep her end of the bargain.

"Nothing, thanks." His gaze didn't waver from the newspaper. He seemed to resent her intrusion.

"Have a good day, then," she said, pouring herself a cup of coffee. She was almost out of the kitchen when he stopped her.

"I'll leave a phone number where I can be reached if you need to get hold of me," he said.

"Thanks." But she stayed where she was, suspecting he intended to say something else.

"About Nikki…"

"Yes?" she encouraged. Beth could see she was going to need all the help and advice he had to offer.

He hesitated. "She's got a chip on her shoulder about all of this."

Beth smiled despite her effort to suppress any reaction. "You might have noticed."

"I did."

"My daughter hasn't adjusted very well to the divorce."

"I'll be patient with her," Beth promised. "I won't force her into anything she doesn't want to do."

His eyes revealed his gratitude. "She's a little difficult."

"Teenagers can be," she said, forgetting that Nikki was only twelve and technically not a teenager. Then, because there didn't seem to be anything left to say, she carried her coffee outside.

The morning was lovely beyond description. Beth sat on the porch swing and gazed out over Puget Sound. A green-and-white Washington State ferry could be seen in the distance. It intrigued her that this island, which seemed so remote, could be only an hour away from a huge metropolitan area like Seattle. Spruce Island was quiet and charming, almost untouched by the busy world bustling around it. That was, no doubt, due to the fact that the only access was by ferry—or, she supposed, by private boat or seaplane. It felt as though she'd stepped back ten or fifteen years the moment she'd walked onto the island.

The screen door opened and Beth turned, expecting John. Instead, it was Paul.

"What are you doing up so early?" she asked.

He rubbed both eyes with his fists and sat down on the porch step. "I woke up and it was morning."

He sounded none too pleased by the discovery.

Beth leaned back and savored her coffee. If it wasn't for Paul, she would have left on the first available ferry the minute she learned Mary Jane's plans had fallen through. But Paul had been looking forward to this trip for months. She could accept the disappointment for herself, but not for her son. Not when he'd already experienced so many.

A part of her still said she should pack her bags and go. John was only being kind in letting her stay. If it was up to Nikki, they would've been booted off the property within the first ten minutes.

"What would you like to do today?" Beth asked, figuring he'd reel off a list of suggestions.

"You know what I think, Mom?"

"You'll have to tell me, since my mind-reading skills aren't up to par these days."

He grinned. "I think we should spend the day getting to know Nikki. She isn't so bad, you know, if you give her a chance."

Four

Beth: This situation with Nikki just isn't working out.
I want to be her friend, but she won't let me.
Mary Jane: Then don't act like a friend—act like a
mom.

"**P**aul and I are going to explore the island," Beth told
Nikki when the girl wandered downstairs shortly after ten
o'clock. She wore bulky coveralls and combat boots and
her green-tinted hair was pulled away from her face in a
spiky ponytail. "Would you like to come?"

Nikki tossed her a defiant look. "Not on your life."

"We found a tandem and a couple of old bikes in the
carriage house," Paul said with unbounded enthusiasm.

Nikki made a couple of lazy circles with her index
finger. "Yippee-skippee."

"Would you like some breakfast before we go?" Beth
asked, wishing she knew how to reach this child. Otherwise, the month would be next to impossible. Beth had
expected John's daughter to turn down the invitation to

explore the island. Nevertheless, she'd hoped the girl would warm to them a little—accept her offer of breakfast, maybe even agree to tag along. But she could see it was a lost cause.

"I'll fix my own breakfast," Nikki muttered, heading for the kitchen. "If there's anything to eat in this place." She cast a disparaging look around. "If I want salmon for dinner, I'll probably have to catch it myself. Can't expect much when…" She went on mumbling half under her breath.

Beth felt completely inadequate in dealing with this kid.

"Sure you don't want to come?" Paul asked.

"Positive." Nikki dumped cereal in a bowl, then hid behind the refrigerator door as she rummaged for the milk.

"Come on, Mom," Paul said. "I'll meet you outside."

Beth badly wanted to make peace, but she could see it wasn't going to be easy. Nikki had no incentive.

"I don't know how long we'll be," Beth told her as she walked toward the kitchen door. "Probably not long."

"Yeah, whatever."

"Would you like me to pick something up for you while I'm in town?"

"Yeah, would you?"

Beth brightened. This was her first opportunity to prove she wasn't the enemy. "Sure, what do you need?"

"How about a new life?"

"Oh, Nikki." Beth stepped toward her, aching to give her a hug. She might have followed the impulse if Nikki hadn't read her intention, stiffened and abruptly spun around.

"Mom," Paul called impatiently from the yard. "Come

on, let's go." He had the tandem out of the garage and was obviously excited about trying it out.

Still Beth hesitated, torn between making peace with John's daughter and exploring the island with her son.

"Mom!"

"We won't be long," Beth said again as she headed out the door.

Paul frowned when he saw her. "Just leave Nikki alone for now," he advised.

"I wish she'd come."

"Why?" he asked with all the wisdom of his fifteen years. "She'd go out of her way to make us both miserable. Give her time. She'll come around." He hopped onto the front of the bicycle as if it was understood that he should be the "driver."

Beth had never ridden on a tandem before and wasn't convinced it was such a good idea. She might have suggested they ride the other bikes if Paul hadn't been so keen on trying this. Besides, she wasn't sure how well she'd do. The last time she'd sat on a bike, it'd been stationary and inside a gym. And *that* was at least a decade ago.

Paul stood astride the tandem while she climbed on. "You ready?" he asked glancing over his shoulder.

"I...don't know." Now that she was actually in the seat, she *knew* this was a mistake.

"Here we go."

Before she realized it, the bike was in motion. It wobbled a couple of times before Paul's feet pumped the pedals, but then they were moving. Well, sort of moving.

"Mom," Paul grunted. "Are you helping?"

Hard as she tried, her feet kept missing the pedals. "Not yet."

Paul strained to carry both of them up the short incline in the driveway. Beth couldn't help it; she found herself giggling. Here was her son, working up a sweat, while she was still struggling to get her feet in place in order to help him.

The bike swayed, and before either of them could react, it toppled onto its side. Luckily the grass cushioned their landing. Beth lay there for a moment, stunned, and then she started to laugh. Really laugh. What a sight they must have made.

"Mom, this isn't funny," Paul said, but she could tell from his voice that he was smiling.

Soon they were both sitting up on the lawn, laughing until Beth thought they'd never stop. Paul helped her back to her feet, and as she stood, Beth caught a flash of green. Sure enough, Nikki was staring at them from the window above the kitchen sink. It was the first time she'd seen the girl smile, and the transformation was miraculous.

"You aren't giving up, are you?" Paul asked.

"Are you kidding?" Beth made a face at him. "I was just beginning to get the hang of this." There were other things she was beginning to understand, as well.

John arrived back at Rainshadow Lodge at four o'clock. He wasn't actually supposed to begin work until the following day, but he figured the sooner he got started on this project the better. Maybe he could even finish ahead of schedule and get out of here a week early. His temporary home was hardly going to be a haven of peace and quiet. If Nikki's attitude wasn't bad enough, he was stuck playing host to a widow and her teenage son.

He didn't need the aggravation. Already he could see that he wouldn't have a moment to himself. Mornings were his, and he liked it that way. Some people woke up cheerful and eager; not John. He eased into the day, accepted it gradually, without rushing. By habit he awoke early, showered, shaved, made coffee and took his time reading the paper.

One thing he didn't want or need in the morning was a lot of chatter. Nor did he appreciate company. This was his hour alone and he preferred not to share it with anyone else. Including Beth. Yet not ten minutes after he sat down, she'd come into the kitchen, asking questions and making a general nuisance of herself. Well, to be fair, not exactly a nuisance. But he'd have to make sure she understood he didn't want to be disturbed. If she was awake, fine, but she should stay in some other part of the house. He planned to tell her that at the first opportunity.

To John's surprise the house was empty. The back door was open and the screen unlatched when he entered the kitchen. A salmon filet was marinating on the island inside a glass baking dish covered with clear wrap.

"Nikki?"

His daughter didn't respond. Setting aside his briefcase, he worked his tie loose and wandered into the living room.

"Nikki?" he called again, and noticed the front door was wide-open. No one with a shred of self-preservation left a door unlocked in California. Unlocked was one thing, but unlocked and open was beyond comprehension.

He stepped onto the porch and saw his daughter sitting on a large rock that overlooked the beach.

"There you are," he said, walking toward her.

"Hi, Dad," she said, smiling at him.

He wasn't accustomed to a warm greeting from her. "What did you do today?"

"Nothing."

"I thought Beth and Paul were riding bikes into town."

"They did."

"You didn't join them?"

She rolled her eyes, implying that was a stupid question. "No way."

He wondered at her mood, which seemed to have improved vastly in the time he'd been away. Perhaps it was wishful thinking on his part. She'd been brooding for so long that anything even resembling a smile encouraged him.

"Where are Beth and Paul now?" he asked, certain he'd noticed the tandem and the two regular bikes when he pulled into the garage.

"There," she said, and pointed toward the beach.

His gaze followed her gesture and he found mother and son walking along the beach side by side. The tide was out and they appeared to be beachcombing, stopping now and then to lean over and examine something the tide had left behind. Already Beth had a number of seashells cradled in her hands.

Then he heard her laugh. It'd been so long since he'd heard a woman laugh with such sheer pleasure that the sound took him aback for a moment, almost as though he had to identify its source. A brisk wind blew off the water, buffeting the pair.

Paul seemed to be enjoying himself, too. Every little while he'd race ahead of his mother, pick up a rock, stand back and hurl it into the water with all his might.

Beth removed her shoes and left them on the sand. She ventured toward the water and let it lap at her feet, then jumped back the instant the cold surf touched her toes. Her legs were long and white and slender. She really had lovely legs, although that wasn't something he generally noticed in a woman.

Paul said something that made his mother laugh. Even without knowing what it was, John almost laughed, too. Watching Beth with her son had affected him the same way it had Nikki. That was what her small tentative smile had been about.

"Did you know Paul has his driver's permit?" Nikki commented as though she found it hard to believe. "He's *fifteen*."

John's only response was to arch his eyebrows. He wasn't sure if Nikki's tone meant the boy was that old or that young.

"Boys don't mature as fast as girls," she said, sounding like an expert on the subject of child development.

"Is that right?" he said, playing along. It was unusual to have a conversation with Nikki for more than a few minutes without some kind of conflict arising. He envied the camaraderie between Beth and her son. He would've given anything to share that kind of experience with Nikki—to explore the beach, to laugh with his daughter, to tease her and not have her react in anger.

When he first learned he'd been granted sole custody of Nikki, he'd felt relieved. Not for the important reasons; he understood that now. He simply hadn't wanted to be alone. It'd been difficult enough to lose his wife, to have his marriage jerked out from under him. He hadn't wanted to lose his daughter, too. Yet in many ways he *had* lost her.

"I don't think Paul's going to be much of a driver," Nikki said.

"What makes you say that?"

"You should have seen him and his mom on the tandem. I'm telling you, Dad, it was one of the funniest things I've ever seen. I laughed so hard I had to hold my stomach."

She relayed the scene for him, and John soon found himself grinning.

"Did they pick up the salmon while they were in town?" he asked casually.

"Yeah."

"Did you ask her to?"

"Nope."

Salmon was his daughter's favorite dinner; she'd eat it seven nights a week if she could. If she *had* made some remark, it was considerate of Beth to notice.

Beth and Paul turned back toward the house and must have seen him and Nikki. With a smile as bright as a lighthouse beam, Beth raised her free hand above her head and waved.

Even from this distance, John was warmed by her welcome.

Five

Mary Jane: So how's it going with you and John?
Beth: Going?
Mary Jane: Has he kissed you yet?
Beth: Good grief, no! It isn't like that with us.
Mary Jane: Listen, girlfriend, this guy is wonderful.
He's smart, gainfully employed and decent. You two
have a lot in common. He's about as high on the
food chain as you're going to get.

"At least come down to the dock with us," Paul urged
Nikki the morning of their scheduled kayaking lesson.
The first few days with Nikki had been rough, but
Beth soon realized her most powerful ally was her own
son. When Paul did the inviting, the chance that Nikki
would tag along immediately increased. She'd joined
them for a couple of outings, and while she laughed
and goofed around with Paul, she kept a protective
distance from Beth.

Beth acted as if it was understood that Nikki would be

joining them in all their activities. As if this was how things had been planned from the very beginning.

"I'm not getting inside any boat that rolls over in the water," Nikki protested.

"The least you can do is come down to the dock with us," Paul said. "It's better than sitting around the house all day by yourself."

Nikki hesitated. "Oh, all right," she muttered with ill grace. "But don't expect me to change my mind."

Beth tossed her son a triumphant smile, marveling anew at what an asset he'd turned out to be in this situation. It didn't hurt any that Nikki and Paul were becoming friends.

Nikki raced upstairs and returned in shorts and tennis shoes—black, of course—with a backpack slung over one shoulder. Once she was ready, they headed toward the carriage house for the bicycles. Up to this point Beth had ridden on the tandem with Paul, but she'd seen Nikki glance enviously at the two of them.

"Nikki," she whispered conspiratorially, "would you mind riding the tandem with Paul? I don't seem to be able to get the knack of it and…well, frankly I'm a bit afraid to try it again. I'll take one of the regular bikes."

She wondered briefly if Nikki had seen through her ploy; if so, the girl chose to overlook it.

"Yeah, sure," Nikki said.

For just an instant Beth thought she might have seen the girl smile. It astonished her how gratified an almost-smile made her feel. While no longer openly hostile, Nikki wasn't exactly friendly, either. But thanks to Paul, Beth felt she was making progress, bit by bit, day by day.

As soon as they got down to the dock and met their instructor, Nikki decided—with a little persuasion from Paul—to try kayaking herself. Beth's reaction to the girl's change in attitude was a blend of relief and unreserved delight. So what if she couldn't expect that change to last? Needless to say, Nikki grumbled and complained until she was in the water and paddling on her own. A smile teetered on her lips, then gave way to a full-blown laugh as the three of them practiced maneuvers in the protected waters of the marina.

Concentrating on her own kayak, Beth was shocked at how low she sat in the water. She felt every ripple, every wave. Had they arrived a week or so earlier, she learned, they could have actually gone whale-watching by kayak. Normally, more than eighty whales lived in the Puget Sound area. Beth could only imagine what an experience that would have been.

High on their adventure, they rode home. Naturally Nikki and Paul were well ahead of her, two pairs of legs pedaling to her one. It surprised her that they waited at the top of the hill for her, but again she attributed that to Paul. When they biked into the yard, Beth noticed John's car parked in the carriage house.

Nikki couldn't get off the tandem fast enough. "Dad, Dad!" she shouted as she ran toward the house.

John must have been standing at the kitchen window because the next thing Beth knew he was on the back porch.

"I saw an eagle!" Nikki called out to him, breathless with excitement. "I mean, I really saw an eagle."

"I thought it was going to claw me," Paul said, and

shaped both hands into giant hooks. He dove at Nikki, who ducked and raced to her father's side.

Laughing, Nikki glanced at Beth. "You should've seen Beth. She screamed for us to cover our heads and—"

John frowned. "Perhaps you'd better start from the beginning."

"We were kayaking…"

"You went kayaking?" John asked, his look incredulous. He glanced to Beth for confirmation.

She nodded, still breathless from the effort of keeping pace with the kids.

"We were about a hundred yards off the island when an eagle started circling overhead."

"I saw him first," Paul announced proudly.

"Paul pointed him out," Nikki added, "and it was as if the bird saw him, because he swooped down to the water with his claws open."

"That was when my mom started screaming."

John's mouth quivered with a smile.

"But he wasn't after us," Nikki said. "He dipped his claws in the water and grabbed a fish. Dad, Dad, it was so close I saw the gills of the fish move."

"He dripped water all over me," Paul said as though it were a matter of pride.

John's smile widened. "That must have been an incredible sight."

"The most awesome experience of my entire life," Nikki said solemnly, pushing her way into the kitchen. "I need something to drink. Anyone else want lemonade?"

"Me," Paul called, and hurried in after her.

John remained on the porch with Beth. Their eyes met for the briefest of moments, then she glanced away.

Feeling the need to say something, she brushed back her bangs with one hand and said, "We had a great time."

"So it seems."

"Here," Nikki said, shoving open the door from the kitchen. She thrust a tall glass of lemonade into Beth's hand. "I'm glad I went kayaking," she whispered.

"I'm glad you did, too."

"But it doesn't mean anything," she said as if warning her not to expect more.

"I wouldn't think of assuming that it did," Beth said, not sure whether to laugh at Nikki's stubbornness or feel discouraged. She supposed she was leaning toward discouraged. Just when she seemed to be making progress with the girl, Nikki went out of her way to prove otherwise.

It really was beautiful here, John had to admit. The water was a deep blue-green. The surrounding fir trees had a delightfully pungent scent. The air, which retained the day's warmth, was fresh and clean. He sighed with complete satisfaction as he stood on the front porch, hands in his pockets. Beth sat in a wicker chair no more than five feet from him. He'd been wanting to talk to her for some time now, to thank her for the subtle softening he saw in his daughter. But he felt awkward and wasn't sure how to go about it.

This had been his problem with Lorraine, as well. He could analyze a business's computer system, see its mistakes and offer suggestions on how to correct them, but he couldn't seem to apply those same analytical skills to his own life. Somehow words just got in the way.

"It's a lovely evening, isn't it?" Beth asked.

John nodded, grateful she'd taken the initiative in starting the conversation. "I didn't expect it to be this beautiful here. I've always pictured the Seattle area as having lots of rain, fog, gloom, that sort of thing."

"Not according to what Paul read," she said, gazing out over the water. "He checked out a number of library books about the Pacific Northwest and discovered that New York City has a higher annual rainfall than Seattle."

"You're kidding!"

"In Seattle there are more days that it rains," she clarified, "but often it doesn't amount to much. Apparently the Northwest isn't nearly as wet as people have been led to believe."

On days as sunny and gorgeous as this one, it was difficult to believe it ever rained here. This was the kind of weather he expected living in Southern California, but Puget Sound had the advantage of lush greenery in addition to sun and sea. A short ferry ride away was an actual rain forest.

"The weather doesn't surprise me as much as Nikki and Paul volunteering to put the dishes in the dishwasher," John said, sitting down in the empty chair beside her.

"That really was very sweet." She relaxed in the wicker chair and sipped her coffee.

"Well, it was fair exchange after that wonderful dinner." The halibut had been simply prepared, broiled and served with fluffy rice and crisp green beans. There'd been a salad, too, and a strawberry pie for dessert. One thing about living in Rainshadow Lodge—these were the best meals he and Nikki had eaten in years.

"This compromise of ours is working out rather well," he said. Better than he'd ever imagined. Like Nikki, his attitude hadn't been the greatest when he discovered he'd be sharing the house with a school chum of Mary Jane Reynolds. Yet within a week, Beth and Paul had influenced Nikki's attitude for the better. He felt confident that it wouldn't be long before Nikki was her old self again, laughing, running, being a kid. She'd been forced to grow up too fast since the divorce, taking on extra responsibilities. She seemed to want to make it up to him for Lorraine's leaving when *he* should be the one making it up to her.

"If I haven't told you before—thank you for letting us stay." Beth's voice was low and mellow, as though she was half-asleep. John was sure she had no idea how sensual she sounded.

"This afternoon…" He hesitated, finding it difficult to speak because of the emotion crowding his heart. "I can't remember Nikki ever being that excited about anything."

Beth took another sip of her coffee. "Well, you have to admit it was a pretty incredible sight. Oh, John, I wish you'd been there. The entire afternoon was fantastic—the kayaking, biking with the kids, everything. I'm so grateful to be here, to experience this."

"Even without Mary Jane?" He wasn't sure why he'd asked, possibly because he needed to know she enjoyed his company. Without realizing it, he'd come to look forward to the few hours they spent together in the evenings. It wasn't a lot of time, but each instance left him wishing he knew her better.

"I miss Mary Jane," she admitted. John knew as much, although they spoke by phone nearly every day. "But I'm enjoying my vacation nonetheless—more than I expected."

"Mom." Paul burst onto the porch, Nikki at his heels. "Can we have a fire on the beach tonight?"

"Ah…" Beth glanced at John.

"Why not?" John asked lightly. If ever he'd had a reason to celebrate, he did today. His daughter was happy, and just hearing her laugh again was cause enough.

"Come on," Nikki said to Paul. "Let's go collect the wood." She leaped off the top step and raced toward the beach with Paul right behind.

The two of them ran along the shoreline, shouting instructions at each other.

"Such energy," Beth murmured.

The silence seemed even louder once the children had come and gone. "I haven't been much of a father," he confessed.

"Oh, John, that's what every parent believes."

"But you…"

"I suffer my own doubts."

"Paul didn't dye his hair green."

"No," she agreed, "but he sucked his thumb until he was six. I was convinced I hadn't nursed him long enough, that I'd failed him as a mother. It's obvious how much you love Nikki, and really, that's all she needs, all any child needs."

Hearing her tell him that was just the balm his heart

craved. Gratitude filled him, but he could think of no way to tell her how he felt. He stood. "You ready for this fire?" he asked.

She groaned. "If you had any idea how sore I am after today, you'd never have agreed to this."

He held out his hand to help her up. "Do you want to beg off?"

"And let Paul and Nikki think I'm out of shape?" She groaned again. "No way." She placed her hand in his and let him pull her to her feet.

They stood with only a few inches separating them. In any other circumstances John would have stepped back, but neither of them moved. Their eyes met and he studied her, looking for some indication of what she was thinking, what she was feeling.

He read the question on her face and knew it was a reflection of his own doubts. He hadn't kissed another woman since Lorraine, hadn't even been tempted. But he was now. More than he'd dreamed possible. It required every ounce of restraint he possessed not to ease her into his arms and taste her lips. The need pulsed through him.

Something was happening. His heart pounded like a teenager's, an odd staccato that echoed in his ears.

He cleared his throat. "I guess we'd better see how the kids are doing."

She nodded and lowered her gaze. "I'll put my cup in the kitchen and join you in a couple of minutes."

"Sure," he said.

As she entered the house, John exhaled a deep breath while he tried to reason out what had just happened.

"Dad," Nikki shouted, running up from the beach. She stopped short of the house and stared at him.

"What?" he asked, certain that his attraction to Beth showed in his face. Another minute and he would have kissed her, and he strongly suspected she would've let him. In another minute…hell, he didn't know *what* he would have done. Thank goodness he'd regained his wits when he had, otherwise he might have made a first-class fool of himself.

"Are you all right?" Nikki gave him an odd look.

"Of course I'm all right," he snapped, and then instantly apologized.

Nikki readily forgave him. "We're going to need matches," she said.

"I'll take care of it," he told her, but as far as he was concerned he didn't need anything to light a fire. A lovely widow had already set one under him.

Six

Beth: First you, and now the kids.

Mary Jane: What do you mean?

Beth: They're plotting to throw John and me together. I'm here to tell you it isn't going to happen. A relationship is impossible.

Mary Jane: Methinks thou dost protest too much.

Beth: Given the circumstances you would, too. Mary Jane, honestly, would you stop laughing? This is no laughing matter. Mary Jane? Mary Jane?

Troubled, Nikki returned to the beach and sank onto a log.

"What's wrong?" Paul asked.

"My dad," she muttered, not sure how she felt just yet. Seeing him like this had come as a shock. "I'm afraid he's got the hots for your mom."

"He's got what?"

"The hots. You should've seen him just now. He looked like he was about to throw up and then…he snapped at me." That was rare enough, but she'd known for a while that something was amiss. Clearly he'd been emotionally shaken, and it didn't take Nikki long to realize what was wrong, either. She frowned just thinking about her dad and Paul's mother.

"What's wrong with him liking my mom?" Paul demanded.

"I didn't say there was anything wrong," she returned, just as defensively. "But…" She was confused about this situation. Definitely confused. Beth was all right, Nikki decided; actually she was a lot of fun. Spending time with Beth and Paul while her dad went into Seattle every day had turned out a whole lot better than she'd imagined. Paul might be fifteen, but in some ways he was more of a kid than she was. Not that it bothered Nikki.

"But what?" he asked.

"My mother was a real ditz," she said, wanting him to understand.

"Your parents are divorced, right?"

"Right. My mom ran off to meet another man. I saw it happen. I mean, she was always on the computer sending this weird guy e-mail messages. My dad didn't have a clue what was going on. He just couldn't believe it when she told him she was leaving."

"My mom didn't know, either," Paul murmured, lowering himself onto the beach beside her.

He hung his head and his voice dipped so low she had trouble hearing him.

"I thought your dad died."

"He did," Paul said, and his mouth thinned. "But he had a girlfriend. He didn't think I knew, but I did."

"Your mom didn't know?"

"Of course not. She never even suspected. She really, really loved my dad. When we found out he'd been killed, I thought my mom was going to die herself, just from the way she was afterward. It wasn't like she cried or carried on all the time, but she wasn't the same. Even now…" He let his words fade as he became involved in his thoughts.

"How'd he die?" Nikki didn't mean to pry, but she couldn't help being curious. "Car accident?"

"He was a contractor, and a bunch of bricks fell on him."

Nikki gave an involuntary grimace.

"Don't you want your dad to remarry?" Paul asked, studying her.

Nikki didn't, not when he'd been so hurt by one woman, even if that woman happened to be her own mother. But before she could tell him, Paul continued.

"I don't want my mom to be alone, especially after I leave for college."

"But that won't be for years." Nikki hadn't thought about her father being alone. Once she did, she understood Paul's concern. Without her around, her dad would be helpless. "But don't you worry about the man she might marry? He could turn out just like your dad, with a girl-friend on the side."

"This time will be different."

"How do you mean?"

"Because I'm here to help her decide. I won't let her marry someone like my dad. Someone who'd cheat on her. If she ever found out, it would just kill her. A new husband would have to pass *my* scrutiny."

"Same with me," Nikki said. Paul made more sense than she'd first thought. If her dad ever did remarry, she'd be around to make sure the new woman was worthy of his love. A woman who understood and appreciated him—unlike her mother.

"My mom's going to need help, though," Paul said, interrupting Nikki's musings.

"Help?"

"Well, just look at her," Paul muttered. "She isn't even *trying* to meet anyone. It's been two years, and her friends all tell her to date again, but she won't listen. I told her once that I thought she should start meeting other guys, but she just shook her head and walked away."

"My dad doesn't date much, either." Until she'd talked with Paul, Nikki hadn't considered the matter too deeply. The only thing she'd worried about was protecting her dad against other women like her fickle-hearted mother. "If my dad did remarry…" she began thoughtfully.

"Yeah?" Paul encouraged her to continue.

"I'd want him to choose someone like your mother," she said, thinking out loud. Once she'd said the words, she realized how much she really did like Beth. She hadn't wanted to; it'd just sort of happened, one day at a time. Paul's mom hadn't ever tried to change her or suggest she do something about her hair. She'd known Nikki wanted to ride the tandem, too, and had found a way to let her try without making a big deal of it. She was willing to laugh at herself, and while Nikki hated to admit it, Beth was a fabulous cook. She'd picked up on her comment about salmon that first morning and had made this wonderful marinade for it. Nikki knew about things like marinades because she studied cookbooks. Beth did incredible things with salmon and shrimp and even oysters. Not only that, she didn't pressure Nikki to be her friend or to confide in her. Beth was just there, the way her mother had never been.

"I like your dad," Paul murmured, his face a study in concentration. "He's quiet and intense. My dad was always cracking jokes and goofing off."

"He's brilliant, you know." She was proud of her father's brains; unfortunately she'd inherited them and had to struggle to get poor grades. It was a curse.

"You think he might be interested in my mom?" Paul asked, then sat back and slowly smiled. His smile started small, but quickly grew until it dominated his entire face and he looked downright silly.

"Interested?" she repeated. "I'm telling you, Paul, he's got it bad. He *wants* her."

"Think about it, Nikki," he said cheerfully. "My mom and your dad."

For someone who'd inherited her father's genius, she'd been exceptionally slow to see the obvious benefits of such a union. She turned and stared at Paul. "Do you really think they might get together?"

"With a little help, like I already said," Paul answered. "They're adults, which means they're obtuse, plus they're both gun-shy."

"We've got three weeks to make it happen," she said.

Still grinning, Paul stuck out his palm and she slapped it with hers. All of a sudden this vacation held *lots* of promise.

* * *

The small fire on the beach crackled and snapped. Beth sat in the sand between Paul and Nikki. John sat on his daughter's other side and they sang boisterous camp songs. It amazed her how many she knew and how easily she recalled the words once they got started.

Beth liked the sound of John's voice, which was surprisingly deep. She found it almost impossible not to turn in his direction and stare at him. Something had happened between them earlier, but she was hard-pressed to say exactly what. She *thought* he'd been about to kiss her. He hadn't, but she wondered how she would have reacted if he had.

It'd been so long since any man had looked at her like this. She wasn't sure she could trust herself to judge his intent. She recalled how quiet he'd grown and how their eyes had met. Her heart had started beating hard and seemed to want to pulse its way out of her chest. It was either anticipation of the kiss or she was suffering a terrible case of indigestion.

Beth laughed out loud at that thought right in the middle of the song.

Paul cast her a curious look and she placed her arm around him and squeezed his shoulder. She felt almost giddy with happiness.

"Anything wrong?" he asked in low tones as John and Nikki continued singing.

"I'm just happy, that's all."

Happy. Beth could barely remember the last time she'd allowed herself to experience joy. It was almost as though she'd felt it was wrong to let happiness back into her life.

Her husband, the man she'd sworn to love, was dead. Her once-secure world had been turned upside down, and for two years it was all she could do to hold on.

When the song ended, they sat silently around the fire. Beth drew her knees up under her chin and gazed at the stars that sparkled and winked at her conspiratorially, as if to say they liked the new Beth, the one who smiled and laughed and sang silly songs.

"I invited Nikki and her dad to visit the rain forest with us tomorrow," Paul informed her. "'Cause it's Saturday."

"Good idea," she said, not giving his suggestion a second thought until she saw Nikki and Paul exchange a knowing look. Those two were up to something. She just wasn't sure what…and she didn't like the suspicions that quickly presented themselves.

"I'm tired," Nikki announced, and made a show of stretching her arms high above her head and yawning loudly.

"Me, too." Paul mimicked her actions, releasing an exaggerated yawn, then leaping to his feet. "We have a big day tomorrow," he said, covering his mouth as he yawned a second time. "Come on, Nikki, I think we should make an early night of it."

"I don't think I can hold my head up much longer," Nikki added, as though stumbling the great distance to the house was beyond her limited endurance.

Before Beth could so much as wish them good-night, the kids had disappeared. She couldn't help reacting a little cynically, because for the past week both Paul and Nikki had been up half the night playing Nintendo. After they left, she glanced at her watch and discovered it was just past ten.

"They couldn't have been any more obvious, could they?" John asked, a smile in his voice. "I think they have plans for us."

"I think so," she whispered, embarrassed that Paul would agree to this blatant form of matchmaking. "I apologize, John. I...I don't know what got into my son. He knows better."

"Your son and my daughter have got to be the world's worst matchmakers," he said. He moved to lean back against a log the size of a telephone pole that had washed onto the beach. "Although I have to admit I'm kind of touched they'd come up with such an idea."

He was right. So far, Beth had assumed Nikki tolerated her more than actually liked her. "It is sweet, but..." She faltered, wishing he'd fill in the blanks.

"But?" he pressed.

"Well, it's rather embarrassing. I have no intention of becoming involved in another relationship and I don't appreciate having two children attempt to manipulate my life. I'm sure you feel the same way."

"Well...it is rather funny."

"You mean us?" she asked, then answered her own question. "It's hilarious." She gave a short laugh for effect. Unfortunately it sounded more like nerves than amusement. Paul had never done anything like this before, and she wasn't about to let his scheme continue. Come morning, she planned on having a heart-to-heart with her son. She'd set the record straight and make sure he understood how embarrassing this was for her. And John.

"What about you?" she asked when she could stand the silence no longer. "Are you...have you considered remarrying?"

"Hardly."

"Me, neither." Her voice grew strong with the strength of her conviction. Anyway, what else could she say? Certainly not that she found him attractive, especially when he'd just made sure she understood he wasn't interested in a relationship. Any more than she was. She'd repeatedly said this to Mary Jane and she meant it. She liked John—there was a great deal to like—but he wasn't interested and neither was she. No, there was really nothing else to say.

The silence stretched between them. Finally John said, "You must have loved him very much."

"I...did love my husband," she whispered. Then, rather than endure any more of this uncomfortable conversation, she hurriedly stood and brushed the sand from her backside. "Shall we put out the fire?"

"It seems a shame to let it go to waste, don't you think? Stay awhile. Enjoy the night with me."

Beth couldn't believe the way her heart reacted to his request. "The fire has been fun," she said when she found her voice. Slowly she sank back onto the sand. She wasn't sure which of them moved closer, but before she knew how it had happened, they were sitting side by side.

"You don't need to include Nikki and me in your trip to the rain forest if you don't want," John told her.

"Oh, please, do come. It's going to be great. Paul picked out a hiking path that's about five miles long. He said it's ranked easy enough even for me."

"You're sure you don't mind if we intrude?"

"Positive." Including him and Nikki in her outings was a small thing after everything he'd done for her.

They listened to the sound of the waves gently stroking the beach for a few moments before John spoke again. "You don't really think they've gone upstairs to bed, do you?"

"I…couldn't say."

"My guess is they've got a pair of binoculars and they're watching us from the porch."

"They wouldn't dare…would they?" Although she asked the question, she knew there was every likelihood he was right. "What should we do about this?" she asked. Like John said, this matchmaking nonsense was flattering and rather sweet, but unchecked, it could become downright troublesome.

"Do?" he echoed. "I think we should give them something worth seeing."

And with that, he wrapped his arm around her shoulders and bent his head toward hers. There was ample time to resist, but for the life of her, Beth couldn't deny herself his kiss.

Seven

Mary Jane: How'd the five-mile hike go?
Beth: Fine…
Mary Jane: You're not telling me something. Come on, Beth, give. I'm living this holiday vicariously.
Beth: It's sort of like the time I decided to take up cross-country skiing. I thought I was in better shape and…well, I should've picked a smaller country.
Mary Jane: Five miles was that far?
Beth: Farther than you'll ever know.

"Come on, Mom," Paul called, hopping like a jackrabbit from one spot on the hiking trail to another. Nikki bounded behind him, matching him step for step, and John followed his daughter. Only Beth lagged behind.

"Is there any reason to rush?" she shouted ahead to them, sinking to her knees to study a patch of columbines. A hike through the rain forest was a feast for the senses. Moss draped from trees that formed a canopy overhead, and parts of the trail meandered through meadows filled with wildflowers. The snowcapped Olympic Mountains stood guard to the west, the Cascade Mountains to the east. There were glaciers, lakes, rivers and waterfalls, all within a few miles, waiting to be explored. Beth had never seen anything like it, and the last thing she wanted to do was hurry the experience.

They'd spent the morning at Sol Duk Hot Springs, soaking in the warm water and then swimming in the huge concrete pool. The pool water had seemed impossibly cold after a dip in the hot springs and both Nikki and Paul had complained about the sulfur smell. After a quick lunch they'd ventured out on their five-mile hike.

She hated to admit it, but Beth wasn't as physically fit as John and the two kids. Stopping to admire the wildflowers had been a convenient excuse to catch her breath. She was perfectly content to ramble at her own pace, taking in the ferns and flowers beside the path, gazing up at the trees, trying to identify birds. This time alone had another advantage. It gave her the opportunity to consider what had happened on the beach between her and John.

The kiss had been for show, she was sure of it. John hadn't *meant* anything by it and yet…and yet it had been wonderful. She hadn't been able to stop thinking about it. She couldn't resist the hope that it'd had the same effect on him; somehow she doubted it.

On the other hand, John didn't seem the type to treat relationships casually. Beth wished now that she'd paid closer attention to the information Mary Jane had taken such pains to unearth. Instead, she'd blotted out her friend's words and refused to listen to any suggestion that there might be a romance developing between her and John. Of course, she could ask Mary Jane to repeat what she'd found out. God knew she had plenty of opportunity. During her first week on Spruce Island, they'd had almost daily telephone conversations, and there was every indication that would continue. Beth told Mary Jane about their latest adventures and reassured her everything was going just fine. She did her best to sidestep any questions about her involvement with John. Not that there'd been much to say—until recently.

Other women, women with more experience and more confidence, might have been able to deal gracefully with the embarrassing questions Mary Jane persisted in asking. Beth had married young, too young it seemed now. Even before her marriage, she'd dated only a handful of boys. Jim had been her only lover.

The mere thought of romance terrified her. Although John hadn't said or done anything—outside their solitary kiss—that led her to believe he was interested. In fact, he'd categorically denied any romantic intentions, toward her or any other woman. And yet, without the least bit of hesitation or reserve, he'd kissed her.

It wasn't like any kiss she'd ever experienced, either. She'd felt it all the way to the tips of her toes. But then, it'd been a long time…and maybe that was why she'd reacted the way she had. Certainly leaping up from the sand and running to the house must have left him with serious doubts about her mental condition. This morning, neither of them had mentioned the kiss, which was just as well.

The three hiking ahead of her had disappeared from

sight. Reluctantly Beth decided she'd better catch up. She followed the twisting trail and discovered Nikki sitting on a rock, waiting for her.

"I was afraid you'd get lost," the girl said, jumping down from her perch with an agility Beth envied.

"You guys are in better shape than I am," Beth confessed.

"You're doing all right."

"I'm glad you think so." Apparently she was in even worse shape than she'd thought, because Nikki placed her arm around her waist as though to guide her the rest of the way. If she hadn't been so surprised by the friendly gesture, she might have commented. Overnight, it seemed, the kid's attitude had done a decided about-face.

"I saw my dad kissing you."

The words shocked Beth so much that her steps faltered and she nearly stumbled. "You did?"

"Paul and I were watching."

So John had been right—and their kiss *had* all been for show.

"How was it?" Nikki asked, studying her.

"How was what?" she asked, although she understood the question.

"Dad's kiss. I probably shouldn't ask, but he hasn't had a lot of practice lately and…you know, if it wasn't as good as it should've been, I hope you'll give him another chance."

"I don't think this is something you and I should be discussing." Beth said in as quelling a voice as she could muster. She could feel the embarrassment flooding her cheeks.

"That's what Dad said when I asked him," Nikki said, sounding discouraged. "Are adults always like this?"

"Yes," Beth returned, leaving no room for doubt. "Always."

Nikki's sigh was expressive. "That's what I thought."

"Are you ready?" John asked Paul, who sat in the driver's seat of the Ford Explorer. He was fairly sure the car-rental people wouldn't approve of him giving driving lessons to a nervous fifteen-year-old boy in their vehicle. Not that John planned to tell them.

"Ready," Paul muttered, sounding anything but. He white-knuckled the steering wheel.

"Relax."

"I…I don't think I can."

"You're going to be a wonderful driver," John said in what he hoped was a reassuring voice. Actually the role of instructor was new to him, but he figured he'd better get some practice in. Before he knew it, Nikki would be ready to drive. The thought wasn't a comforting one.

"You don't know what kind of driver I'm gonna be," Paul challenged.

"Ah, but I do," John said. "Because I was just as nervous as you when I was fifteen, and I'm an excellent driver."

"Driving school starts in September," he said, and John realized the boy was casting about for conversation to delay backing out of the garage.

Time to get down to business. "Put your foot on the brake and slowly put the gear into reverse," he said. "No need to have your foot on the accelerator just yet." He was extra-patient because he knew any signs of anxiety or brusqueness would intimidate the boy.

When they'd returned from the hike, Beth and Nikki had gone upstairs to shower. John had unloaded the Explorer only to discover Paul sitting in the driver's seat, pretending to drive and looking pleased with himself. The kid had been embarrassed and started stuttering excuses in an effort to explain. That was when John had impulsively offered to give him a lesson. Although John was well into his thirties, he understood the boy's eagerness. He could still remember the burning anticipation he'd felt after receiving his own learner's permit.

"Okay," Paul said, his hand on the gearshift. Once the vehicle had been put into reverse, he glanced at John for instructions. "Do you want me to back it out of the garage?"

"That sounds like a plan." John hid a grin.

Slowly, so slowly it was almost impossible to detect that the car was moving, Paul eased the Explorer out of the carriage house. Once he'd cleared the sides of the building, he stepped on the gas and roared backward. Almost immediately he hit the brakes, sending both of them flying forward. The seat belts locked, halting their progress, then dashed them back against the seat.

Paul forcefully expelled his breath and said, "I told you I wasn't any good at this."

"Hey, you're doing fine. Don't be so hard on yourself."

"What if I wreck the car?"

"You aren't going to have an accident in the driveway."

It took three trips around the circular driveway for the boy to loosen up. By the time Beth appeared on the back porch, Paul had relaxed enough to roll down the window and shout, "Hey, Mom! Watch me!"

Even from a distance John recognized the look of sheer horror that came over her when she saw her son actually driving. She continued to stand there for the longest time, one arm wrapped around her middle. She held her free hand to her face as if to shield her eyes.

It was all John could do not to stare back at her. Her hair was wet and curly from the shower, and she'd put on a pair of shorts and a sleeveless yellow top. He wasn't the kind of man who paid a lot of attention to clothes, but he'd noticed just about everything Beth wore. She had beauty and grace and somehow managed to make even the most mundane outfit look elegant.

Her clothes weren't the only thing John noticed about Beth. She'd been on his mind day and night almost from the moment they'd decided to share the house. He found himself observing little things, like the way she sliced tomatoes or set fresh-cut flowers on the table. Everything she did, everywhere she went, she added small touches of charm.

"Hey, Nikki, look!" Paul yelled out the driver's window. "I'm driving."

Nikki stood next to Beth and waved excitedly.

Paul eased the car into the garage with a little more finesse than he'd used to back it out. He turned off the ignition and handed the car keys to John with a triumphant smile. "Thanks," he said.

"Anytime."

As they headed for the house, Nikki came down the back steps onto the lawn and, in an awkward duck-like walk, hurried toward them. She appeared to be trying to keep her weight on her heels.

"Beth and I painted our toenails," she announced. A smile radiated from her, unlike anything John had seen in months. Years. Since the divorce.

Lorraine phoned Nikki once a month, but his daughter had been rude and unreceptive. John hadn't encouraged or discouraged her regarding these conversations. He figured Nikki had to make her own peace with her mother—but he didn't plan on smoothing the road for his ex-wife. In fact, he'd secretly been pleased that Nikki continued to reject Lorraine's overtures.

In that moment he realized how wrong he'd been. How selfish and vindictive. Nikki needed her mother, needed Lorraine's love, and instead of helping her, he'd focused solely on his own anger and sense of abandonment.

He'd been thinking of himself, not his daughter. He'd been wallowing in his misery, collecting petty victories against Lorraine, when he should have put all that aside and concentrated on Nikki.

The realization hit him like a physical blow.

"Dad?" Nikki hesitated. "Are you okay? You're wearing a funny look."

"You're beautiful," he said, and meant it. His daughter, green hair and all, strongly resembled Lorraine. In his pain he'd tried to ignore the similarities between them; doing that, he'd hurt Nikki. No wonder the girl did outrageous things to her hair. While he'd never openly said anything about her looks, Nikki knew. It was her mother's face she saw in the mirror every morning.

Somehow, he knew he had to hug her right then. Without warning he pulled her into his arms and squeezed hard.

"Dad," she protested, "you're going psycho on me."

"I love you, Nikki."

"Because I painted my toenails with Beth?"

"No." He chuckled. "Because you're so damn beautiful."

She hugged his waist tight and said in a whisper, "I look just like Mom."

"No." He lifted her face so she could see into his eyes when he spoke. "You look like Nikki Lynn Livingstone, my beautiful, beautiful daughter."

A hesitant smile appeared on her lips. "You're acting pretty weird, Dad."

Laughing, he swung her up in his arms the way he had when she was a little girl and whirled around while she screamed with delight.

The next time Lorraine phoned, John decided, he'd urge Nikki to speak to her. Whether Lorraine loved him or not wasn't the issue; it never had been. Nikki needed both her parents.

"Nikki," Paul yelled, "are we playing Nintendo or not?"

"Playing," she yelled, and broke out of John's embrace, but not before she'd thrown him a wide jubilant smile.

The two kids raced upstairs and John returned to the Explorer for the picnic basket. He carried it into the kitchen and found Beth at the sink with her back to him.

"Anyplace special you want me to put this?" he asked.

"Anywhere's fine," she said, but she didn't sound like herself.

"Beth?" he asked. "Is everything all right?"

She reached for a tissue and loudly blew her nose. "It's nothing."

A part of John yearned to accept her explanation and leave it at that, but he'd been married long enough to know better. "Obviously something's troubling you," he coaxed in gentle tones.

She shrugged. "I'm sorry. It's foolish, I know."

"It's okay."

"Just now…when Paul was driving…" She turned toward him and wiped the tears from her cheeks. "He's growing up, John. My little boy isn't a little boy anymore."

This seemed to be the day for insights, John mused.

"Soon he'll be a man. An adult. He starts high school next month. He's going to have his driver's license next year." She walked over to the breakfast nook, sat down and buried her face in her hands.

Feeling completely at a loss, John opted for the practical. He brought her a box of tissues and sat down across from her.

Beth sniffled a couple of times and he stretched across the table and patted her hand. He wished he knew how to comfort her.

After a couple of minutes, she offered him a watery smile. "I'm sorry."

"For what? Being human?"

"It's just that…" She grew silent as if she regretted having said anything.

"Just what?"

Abruptly she stood, walked to the kitchen island and leaned against it. "His dad would never have driven around the driveway with Paul. Thank you for that."

Her look held his and he watched as fresh tears filled her eyes and spilled onto her cheeks.

"Beth?" Something was going on inside her, some deep emotional pain. He recognized the look, the hurt. "What is it?" he asked softly.

"My husband…" She paused and drew in a stabilizing breath, and when she spoke her voice was low and hoarse. "I know how you felt when your wife left you. I've experienced that kind of pain, too—all the doubts, the questions. I know, because Jim was having an affair at the time of his death."

John frowned, unable to believe that any man married to Beth would do such a thing.

"I've never told anyone—not even Mary Jane. I couldn't, not when Paul idolized his father. I refuse to destroy his memories of Jim, so I've kept this secret to myself." She covered her mouth with her hand, obviously struggling with her pain. "I loved him, I swear I did, so very much. Deep down I knew about…her. But I chose to look the other way for fear of what would happen if I confronted him. I…I didn't want to face the truth, because if I did, I'd have to make a decision, and I couldn't. I just couldn't. I didn't know what to do. His betrayal turned me into a woman I didn't know I could be. Blind and stupid and angry, so incredibly angry…"

Her pain was like his own. It felt impossible not to hold her. He wanted to take her into his arms the way he had on the beach; he'd ignored that desire as best he could, but now the effort was futile. As always, any words of comfort abandoned him, so all he could do was act.

He stood and pulled her to him. They clung to each other for long minutes. A deep sigh lifted his chest, and John felt as though his own pain, his own disappointment, had eased.

Strange as it sounded, hearing of her pain had somehow diminished the sharpness of his. Still, his thoughts were muddled and confused; there was nothing logical about any of this. He didn't know whether he'd released himself from his grief because Beth, in her agony, needed him. Or because his feelings for her allowed him to put past hurts and betrayals aside, to see them from a new perspective.

When she finally looked up at him, he did what he'd promised himself he'd never do again. He took her face between his hands and kissed her.

She moaned a welcome and her lips parted as her arms crept up and around his neck.

His kiss turned hungry, urgent. He didn't court or coax her lips, nor was he gentle with her. The need in him was too great to restrain. After more years than he wanted to remember, he was greedy for a woman's tenderness. Greedy for her warmth and passion. Eager to show her how she'd touched his heart, eager to ease the ache from hers if he could.

Then it came to him. The understanding that he couldn't continue with his life, couldn't trust and love again, until he'd forgiven Lorraine. Knowing Beth had made that clear. Slowly, gradually, that awareness had grown in him. He needed to forgive Lorraine, for his own sake and for Nikki's. He needed to build bridges to the past—and to the future.

It cost him everything to break off the kiss. His eyes remained closed and he rubbed his lips against her temple. "I told myself I wouldn't do that."

"I…I didn't mean to run away last night, but I was afraid."

"Of me?"

He felt her smile. "No, of me. Of what would happen if you saw how much I enjoyed your touch."

At the sound of the kids racing down the stairs, they instantly broke apart. Beth turned away and shakily swept back her hair. John thrust his hands into his pockets.

Nikki burst into the room first and stopped dead in her tracks. She stared at him and then at Beth.

John was sure he looked guilty as sin. Beth, too.

Paul joined Nikki, skidded to a stop and did a double take. "We didn't interrupt anything, did we?"

Eight

Beth: How's Dave these days?
Mary Jane: He's doing well. How about you?
Beth: Better than I have in a long while.
Mary Jane: Something's happened! Come on, Beth, tell me.
Beth: You're right, something's happened. Something wonderful…

The message light on the answering machine was blinking when Beth walked into the house Thursday afternoon. A good part of the day had been spent kayaking on Puget Sound with Paul and Nikki. They were continuing with their lessons and grew more and more adventurous in their outings. Nikki had taken to the sport with a skill and dexterity that drew unlimited praise from their instructor. Paul was more than capable, too. Beth felt she provided comic relief.

She glanced at her watch and then the phone. John usually caught the four-o'clock ferry from Seattle, so they generally ate dinner at six. Beth could either respond to the phone message or get dinner going. She chose the latter.

After a full afternoon Nikki bounced upstairs to shower, and the ever-energetic Paul went outside to shoot a few baskets. Beth ignored the blinking light and went into the kitchen instead.

Once she had the oysters shelled and a fresh broccoli salad prepared, she headed for the telephone. But she already knew the call had come from Mary Jane. She switched off the answering machine and punched in the number from memory.

"Where have you been all afternoon?" Mary Jane asked immediately.

"We were kayaking," Beth said. Pressing the portable telephone to her ear, she returned to the kitchen and started to peel potatoes. "We didn't see any eagles this afternoon, but there was a harbor seal at the marina. I don't know if I'll ever get accustomed to seeing wildlife up close and personal," she said, chatting easily. "If it hadn't been for the kids, I would've stayed in the marina all afternoon so I could study that seal. I'm telling you, Mary Jane, he was huge and—" She stopped when she realized she was rambling, and all because she was trying to avoid the one topic that interested Mary Jane the most. Her and John.

"How's Dave?" she asked, fending off her friend's questions before she had a chance to ask them.

"Physically he's doing great, but he hates this inactivity. To be perfectly frank, the man is driving me crazy. At least he's able to do some work from his bed. Thank God for laptops."

"This is hard on you, isn't it?" Beth said, sympathizing with her. Jim hadn't been a good patient, either. Whenever he was ill, he'd demanded constant attention. Beth smiled as she remembered how she'd loved to tease him. Men were all big babies when they had the flu. Jim had enjoyed being pampered and had often exaggerated his symptoms to the point of being comic. He'd request she make all his favorite comfort foods, rub his temples and read to him. She'd done it, too, often spending hour after hour waiting on him, seeing to his every desire.

"Having Dave underfoot is driving me nuts," Mary Jane admitted, "but it's kind of nice, too. At least now his curiosity is satisfied. For years he's wondered exactly what I do every day. I think in the back of his mind, he assumed I lounge around the house, watch soap operas and nibble on chocolates. He didn't have a clue how much effort it takes to keep up with three teenage boys, work part-time and volunteer with two different charity organizations."

Little had changed about her friend since they were in high school. Even then Mary Jane had been involved in half a dozen projects and clubs at a time. Outgoing and personable, she was a natural choice when it came to heading up committees and organizing study groups. She quickly got bored if there weren't five or six items constantly on her agenda.

"So?" Mary Jane prodded. "Are you going to volunteer the information or are you going to make me ask?"

Beth sighed. "About John and me?" She might be forthright about the question, but she sure didn't know how to answer it. Telling Mary Jane they'd kissed was one thing;

telling her she'd wept in John's arms was another. And confessing she'd revealed her deepest sorrows to him—well, that was something else again.

The kisses they'd shared after their trip to the rain forest were unlike any she'd experienced before. Physically, they'd been exciting. Passionate. Sensuous. But no words could describe their emotional effect. Beth didn't even want to *try* explaining it—not to Mary Jane and not even to herself.

"We've kissed," she said quietly, hoping that would satisfy her friend's curiosity. She should have known better.

"And?"

"And what?"

"What did you *think?*" Mary Jane demanded. "What was it like?"

Beth closed her eyes, remembering. "It was… wonderful."

Mary Jane emitted a gleeful sound. "There's a lot you're not saying, isn't there?"

"Yes," Beth admitted reluctantly.

"This whole fiasco—Dave's accident, you guys sharing the house and everything—is working out magnificently." Anyone might think that having a bedridden and miserable husband was the best thing to happen since the invention of the bread machine.

"I need to get off the phone," Beth said, wanting to cut this inquisition short. "John'll be home soon and everyone's starving."

"You sound just like a wife."

"I've got dinner started," Beth said. She knew she sounded defensive, but couldn't help herself. "Cooking dinner is the least I can do under the circumstances."

"Hey, you don't need to get testy with me."

"I wasn't testy."

Mary Jane actually chortled. "Oh, yes, you were. And you know what else? You're disclosing more by what you *don't* say."

"How?" Beth wasn't sure why she felt compelled to pursue this, especially since it guaranteed delving into a subject that left her confused and uncertain.

"You like this guy, *really* like him, otherwise you wouldn't care what I thought or said, but you *do* care." Her friend sounded absolutely delighted. "Think about it. John Livingstone is the first man you've had any interest in since Jim died, and all I can say is it's about time."

"John's a friend."

"And more," Mary Jane added knowingly.

"With the potential for more," Beth felt obliged to add, although even that was probably being too optimistic. "We've been thrown together for a month. It's only natural that we'd be attracted to each other. But we're different kinds of people." That wasn't all, either. Any romance between them was complicated by a number of factors. She lived in Missouri, while he was from California, and that was only for starters. The problems of maintaining a long-distance relationship seemed overwhelming. Especially with kids involved.

"I've got to go," Beth said. "I'll call you soon."

"Promise?"

"Promise." But when she did phone, Beth was determined to steer the subject away from John.

She carried the phone back into the hallway. It wasn't

until she set it back in its cradle that Beth realized how much she did want to talk to someone about John. She just wasn't sure she could trust Mary Jane to be objective.

John and Beth had kissed on two occasions now, and both times had been incredible. Both had left her head reeling and her heart pounding for hours afterward. She'd felt shaken and frighteningly vulnerable. Not a comfortable sensation. And yet she found herself wanting to be close to him. It made no sense that she should hunger for his touch—but she did.

Beth suspected their attraction was fueled by the hurt they each carried from their failed marriages. Jim wouldn't have turned to another woman if he'd been happy in their relationship, Beth believed.

The fact that he'd loved this other woman was painfully obvious. Beth had found a love letter in the glove compartment of his truck, along with a stack of credit-card slips from a cheap hotel. What hurt most was the receipt from the high-priced downtown jeweler for a diamond bracelet. Her husband had taken money from his business, from his family, and spent it on a lover. Finding that receipt had felt like swallowing acid. It burned even now, the anger fresh and searing.

Beth closed her eyes against the memory, the pain, the humiliation.

"Beth?"

Her eyes flew open. Nikki stood in front of her, dressed in shorts and a T-shirt, wet hair combed away from her face.

"Are you feeling sick?" the girl asked with a worried frown.

"I'm okay," Beth said, and hoped Nikki believed her.

"What can I do for you, kiddo?" she asked, forcing a lightness into her voice she didn't feel.

"Can I talk to you a minute?" the girl asked, her eyes round, her voice suddenly uncertain.

"Of course." Beth slipped her arm around Nikki's slim waist and together they walked back into the kitchen. Without asking, Beth poured them each a tall glass of iced tea. They sat at the table directly across from each other. Nikki didn't speak for a long moment, but Beth was content to wait, realizing that whatever was on Nikki's mind must be difficult to express.

"My dad said I'm beautiful," Nikki whispered at last. She didn't look at Beth, only gazed down at her drink.

"You are."

The girl's eyes shot up to Beth. "Are you just saying that because you think you're supposed to? Because you think that's what I want to hear?" Every syllable was a challenge. An angry fire leaped into her eyes, reminiscent of those first few awkward days. It was almost as if she was trying to start an argument.

Beth took her time answering, instinctively knowing the seriousness of the question. "What you have, Nikki, is the promise of beauty." She reached across the table and ran her finger down the side of the girl's face. "You have classic lines and—"

"I look like my *mother*," she spat out. "People think she's beautiful, but she isn't. Not after what she did. I hate her." Her voice rose until she was shouting. "I hate her. I don't want to look like her. I don't want anything to do with her." Nikki's face reddened and tears ran from her eyes.

Beth's heart ached at the pain she saw and heard. She longed to hug Nikki, but before she could get up, the girl slid out of her seat and raced for the kitchen door. It slammed behind her.

Beth followed, shouting, "Nikki, wait! Please…"

Nikki ignored her plea, flew down the steps and across the yard, heading for the beach.

Paul stopped playing basketball and tucked the ball under his arm as he watched Nikki scramble to the water.

"What was that about?" he asked when Beth joined him.

"I'm not sure," Beth confessed.

"Do you want me to go after her?"

"No," Beth said, but she appreciated his compassion. "I think it'd be best if we gave her a few minutes alone. I'll talk to her later."

"What happened?" her son asked again.

"She's…in a lot of pain just now," Beth said absently, torn about what she should do.

"From the divorce?"

"Yes."

"Poor kid," Paul murmured, shaking his head.

Seeing Nikki's doubts made Beth all the more grateful that Paul had been spared discovering the truth about his father. At least he'd never know how Jim had betrayed them.

Nine

Mary Jane: So what did you think of Canada?
Beth: It was fabulous.
Mary Jane: Are you saying Washington State and British Columbia are heaven?
Beth: Not quite, but you can see it from here.

"Come on," Paul urged in a bored voice when Nikki lingered on the path leading down to the sunken garden. The four had caught the Port Angeles ferry at an impossibly early hour that morning for a one-day trek to Victoria, British Columbia. They were now in Butchart Gardens, just outside the city. This was Nikki's first trip to another country and she'd expected it to be more… foreign. But Canada wasn't all that different from the United States. If she hadn't gone through customs and had her papers checked, she would've figured she was still in the U.S.

Victoria was pretty, though, and there were dozens of things to see and do once they stepped off the ferry. Her dad thought it was important that they visit the provincial museum, so they'd gone there this morning, as part of a tour. The last thing Nikki had wanted to do was wander around a bunch of displays. Even if that statue of Native Americans in a canoe behind a curtain of water was way cool. The replica of an old ship wasn't bad, either. It creaked and everything when you walked on the deck. But she'd had enough history lessons for one day.

The only place she'd really, really wanted to go wasn't a tour or anything. She'd fallen in love with the Empress Hotel the moment she saw it from the ferry dock. The large Victorian-style brick hotel with its ivy covered exterior was quite possibly the most romantic building she'd ever seen. All she'd wanted to do was walk through it and buy a few postcards to show her friends.

Beth had been intrigued by it, too, so they'd had breakfast there. While they ate they'd discussed their agenda for the day and ended up on the all-day bus tour, which included the museum and a trip to Butchart Gardens. The beauty of the gardens had taken her by surprise.

"I want to talk to you," Paul said, his voice insisting that she hurry.

Nikki glanced over her shoulder and noticed that her father and Beth had lagged behind, talking.

"About what?" she asked.

"Your dad and my mom," he informed her as if it should've been obvious.

She tossed him a look that let him know she was beginning to find the whole thing downright tedious. It had become quite evident that their parents didn't need anyone's help to fall in love. The only problem seemed to be that neither one knew what to do about it. To be honest, Nikki felt a bit disappointed that her dad hadn't needed any coaching from her and Paul. She'd been ready and willing to tutor him if he asked—and even if he didn't. Thus far, he seemed to be doing fine without her assistance.

Nikki had never seen her dad like this, not in all the time he'd been divorced. Sure, he'd dated during the three years since her mother had left. Usually these were arrangements made by well-meaning friends. None had ever amounted to anything.

Beth was different.

Except for the past few weeks, she couldn't remember when she'd heard her father laugh. His eyes sparkled and he seemed to have a lot more energy. He was certainly eager to do more things than he'd been in ages.

It was what she wanted, what she'd hoped for, but at the same time Nikki wished *she'd* been the one to bring the life back into his eyes.

"Your mom and my dad," Nikki said with a deep heartfelt sigh, "don't need any help from the two of us."

Paul glared at her. "What's with you?"

Nikki shrugged, unwilling to admit how she felt, especially when she didn't *like* these feelings. She couldn't tell Paul she was jealous of his mother! Until recently she'd done everything for her dad—she'd cooked his dinner, reminded him of appointments, stuff like that. But he hadn't been happy, not the way he was now. But then, Nikki hadn't been happy, either....

"I like your mom," she said, and meant it. If her dad was

going to get involved with a woman other than her mother, then she… Nikki paused in midthought.

That was it. That was what bothered her most. She wanted her mother and father to get back together so they could be a family again. It wasn't going to happen, she realized with a sick sad feeling.

She sometimes dreamed about her mom and dad in happier times. Her favorite dream was having her mother come home from the hospital with a baby sister. But it would never happen, not with her mother already married to this weirdo she'd met on the Internet.

"Your dad's great," Paul said.

"You're just saying that because he let you drive."

Paul didn't agree or disagree. "I like him."

Her dad was a good guy and her mother was an idiot. Nikki guessed she fell somewhere in between. She just wasn't sure where.

"What do you think's going to happen with them?" Paul asked. They continued walking along the pathway, urged forward by the crowd. Nikki paused on the stairway leading out of the sunken garden and looked back. She was surprised to see Beth and her dad sitting on a bench, deep in conversation. They seemed oblivious to anyone else.

"Happen?" Nikki asked.

"Between them."

"How would I know?" She didn't own a crystal ball.

"Last weekend they were kissing, and then all week your dad went into the library after dinner. By himself."

"He had work to do," she said, defending her father. But she'd noticed it, too, and wondered. It was clear he'd been avoiding Beth. Then again, Beth hadn't exactly seemed eager for his company, either. But between the times her dad was in the library avoiding Beth, and the times Beth was running around avoiding him, they'd look at each other in a way that told her how they felt.

Those feelings scared Beth; Nikki could sense it. Three or four nights that week she'd disappeared after dinner. Nikki knew she'd taken long walks along the beach. She'd joined Beth a couple of times, and Paul had, too. It was like Beth and her dad had argued, but she knew that wasn't true. At mealtimes she'd seen the looks they exchanged. They couldn't keep their eyes off each other. Then as soon as dinner was over, they couldn't get away fast enough.

"It seems to me," Paul intoned seriously, "that our parents are falling in love and—"

"I already told you that," Nikki said scornfully.

Paul held up one hand. "Would you let me finish? The problem is, they don't know what to do next. *That's* what they need help with."

"No kidding, Professor. What do you suggest?"

"I…haven't got that figured out. I was hoping you had some ideas."

Nikki shook her head, glancing down at their parents. They sat side by side on the park bench without touching, intent on their conversation. So intent they were unaware that Paul and Nikki were no longer with them.

"Hey!" Paul suddenly laughed.

"What's so funny?" Nikki asked.

"If they don't hurry," he said, running up the stairs, "they're going to miss the bus."

Nikki glanced at her watch and noted the time, surprised herself. Laughing, she raced up the steps behind Paul. It would be a hoot if his mom and her dad got left behind.

It was midnight before they got home. As it was, they were fortunate to catch the last ferry to Spruce Island. By the time they arrived at the house, both Nikki and Paul were asleep in the back seat of the car.

Their day had been full from beginning to end. This venture into Canada had been one of the plans Beth had originally made with Mary Jane. She hated to be this close to British Columbia and not see Victoria. The city had proved to be just as charming as all the books and brochures had claimed. More so, she believed, because she'd seen it with John.

They'd spent the entire week avoiding each other. But once they were together, they couldn't seem to stop talking. It was as though they'd been friends for years. He told her about his work and she listened, intrigued. They discussed the kids; he said he was thrilled with the change he'd seen in his daughter's attitude. Beth felt the same way. She'd grown very fond of Nikki, and the girl was beginning to trust her. John had talked more about his ex-wife, too, and how he'd come to a new willingness to forgive her and let her go. He said Beth needed to do the same thing. Not all their conversation was so serious, though; they'd also laughed a lot.

At Rainshadow Lodge, John parked in the carriage house. They sat in the dark a moment, neither of them eager to leave the warm security of the car.

"I had a wonderful time," Beth whispered, wanting him to know she would treasure this day. There would be touching memories and some comic ones—including the mad dash she and John had made to catch the bus, and the sound of their children laughing when they climbed on board at the last possible moment.

"I had a good time, too," John whispered.

"I suppose we'd better get inside," she said, ready to open the car door. But she hesitated.

"How about a walk along the beach?" John said, rushing the words. "That is, if you aren't too tired."

"Sure." Beth wondered if he could guess how glad she was that he'd asked. "Give me five minutes, and I'll meet you on the front porch."

"Five minutes," he echoed.

Actually by the time they woke the kids, steered them upstairs and unloaded the car, it was closer to ten. When she met John, he was carrying a wine bottle and two goblets. "Are you sure you're not too tired?" he asked again.

"I'm too keyed up to sleep."

"Me, too." He led the way down to the waterfront. They heard the murmur of waves caressing the sand, and smelled the ocean's fresh briny scent. The moon showed a narrow foam trail that stretched along the beach where the tide had withdrawn.

They sat against the log they'd discovered the night of the fire. The night he'd kissed her for the first time.

"The wine was an inspired idea," she said as she watched him pour them each a glass.

"What shall we toast?" he asked when he'd finished.

Nothing came readily to mind. "To broken legs?" she suggested.

John chuckled. "And good friends."

"Good friends," she said, and they touched the rims of their glasses.

Beth sipped the wine, a mellow Chianti, with real appreciation. She'd always enjoyed wine and often recommended a bottle with the meals she catered. She told her clients that wine enhanced a meal and added a touch of elegance to a dinner menu.

After talking nonstop for most of the day, neither she nor John seemed inclined to speak just then. That was fine with her. She didn't object when he placed his free arm around her shoulder. Nor did he complain when she rested her head against his.

The moment was peaceful, serene.

"Thank you," John whispered. "For today, for everything, for more than I can mention."

"Thank you, too." She tilted her head upward, anticipating his kiss, and wasn't disappointed. His mouth settled on hers as if he'd been thinking of nothing but tasting her lips.

The hunger of his kisses stole her breath. Each kiss was longer and more intense than the previous one. Soon Beth forgot about her wine, about everything but this man who'd helped her confront the pain of Jim's betrayal. This man who'd helped her remember she was a woman with a woman's heart.

She broke off the kiss and braced her forehead against his chest, drawing deep breaths into her lungs while she struggled to regain her equilibrium. She wanted to blame the wine. But it wasn't a few sips of Chianti that had her head and heart spinning, and she knew it.

"We only have a week left," he whispered.

Beth didn't need that reminder; she was already well aware how little time remained.

"It went so fast," she whispered.

"Too fast." John's hands were in her hair, holding her against him.

Silence followed. She thought about the future and how difficult it would be to continue their relationship after this month. He would return to California and she'd go back to St. Louis, and for a time they'd remain in close contact. Phone calls, letters, weekend visits. Each would try... They'd try, but it would be impossible to recapture what they'd found here on this island paradise. Their private paradise. Back in the real world everything would be different. More complicated. There would be compromises and disappointments. Besides all that, she wasn't ready for a relationship. She needed to find her bearings first, reorient her life.

John tensed at the same moment she did, and she realized they'd allowed their friendship to develop too fast. Like teenagers at summer camp, they'd enjoyed a vacation romance, but they'd part and that would be the end of it.

"When are you scheduled to fly back to St. Louis?" he asked casually.

"Sunday afternoon."

"Nikki and I are catching a flight to LAX at six."

"Ours is at four."

"You might as well drive in with us."

"That'll work out great," she said, and leaned against the log, staring into the dark night. The only sound was that of the ebbing waves.

"I guess we'd better call it a night," John suggested as he got to his feet. He offered her his hand and she let him pull her upright.

"Thanks for a wonderful day."

It astonished her that they could be lost in a kiss one moment and act like polite strangers the next. But that was what he wanted, what she wanted, too. Wasn't it? A stolen kiss now and again, but nothing else and certainly nothing more.

Ten

Mary Jane: You know the problem with being in the middle of the road, don't you?
Beth: I have a feeling you're going to tell me.
Mary Jane: You get hit by cars traveling in both directions. I think it's time you and I had a little heart-to-heart.
Beth: Not yet, but soon. Not just yet.

A soft knock sounded on the closed library door. Emotionally and mentally drained, John glanced up from his desk and pinched the bridge of his nose. The day had been exhausting, full of the unexpected—including a job offer from a Seattle-based computer company. So many decisions... "Who is it?" he asked in a tired voice.

It could only be Beth or Paul. Nikki would have considered it her right to simply barge in.

"Paul."

John got up and opened the library door. It was early, still light out, and he had a stack of printouts to read this evening if he was going to hand in his report by the end of the week.

"Do you have a couple of minutes?" Paul asked with the politeness John had come to expect from him.

"Of course," he said, and motioned him into the room.

Paul chose to sit in one of the two upholstered wing chairs positioned next to the massive fireplace. John claimed its twin and patiently waited for the boy to say what was on his mind.

He liked Paul, and had given him four or five driving lessons now. He found Beth's son to be intelligent, quick-witted and respectful. All three attributes would serve him well in the future.

"It's about my mom," Paul said, staring intently at John. "I'd like to know your intentions."

"My…intentions?" John repeated, taken aback by the directness of the boy's question.

"Nikki and I've been watching the two of you—"

"Did my daughter put you up to this?" John wasn't sure what to think. "There's been nothing to watch," he added abruptly.

"We saw you kiss," Paul said in a tone that suggested a shotgun wedding might be in order.

"That's… It didn't mean… You saw?" The words tumbled out of his mouth, his thoughts confused. It'd been a long time since anyone had flustered him as much as this kid.

"Nikki and I think you're in love."

"Love?" John wiped a hand over his face, wishing he knew the best way to handle this and avoid any hurt feelings. "Paul, with all due respect, this matter is between your mother and me. Not you, me, Nikki and your mother."

"Do you love her?"

John opened his mouth to automatically deny it, then stopped himself in time. He thought about the word "love," and realized he hadn't made it part of his vocabulary since the divorce. But he had to acknowledge that he was attracted to Beth. He couldn't be with her and not experience a deep yearning to hold her and kiss her. Yet, strong as that attraction was, his feelings transcended the physical.

In fact, his feelings for Beth had changed just about everything in his life.

These past three weeks had shown a dramatic improvement in his relationship with Nikki, and that was due to Beth's influence on his daughter—her influence on him, too. He'd come to understand certain aspects of his failed marriage, as well as his own shortcomings in handling the situation between Nikki and Lorraine. He credited Beth with that revelation, along with the rest. Credited her with awakening his heart and reminding him that life had a good side, too. A side he'd too often ignored.

"I care for your mother," John admitted, "but as I said earlier, this isn't your business. What's between your mother and me is between your mother and me." Now, that was profound!

Paul seemed to accept that. "I realize it isn't my place to be asking you these kinds of questions," he said, "and I apologize for stepping over the bounds, but we don't have a lot of time."

As it was, they were scheduled to vacate the house in a few days. "I need to be sure you won't hurt her—not after my dad."

"Paul." John felt the boy's pain at the loss of his father and longed to reassure him. He leaned forward and held his gaze. "Your father died in an unfortunate accident. No man can guarantee how long he'll live. I can't tell you when I'll die. Loving someone is risky—"

"I'm not talking about my dad dying," Paul blurted. He clenched his fists and his eyes were wet with tears. "He was cheating on my mom, cheating on me. It'd devastate her if she knew."

It felt as if all the oxygen had been sucked from the room. Paul knew about his father's affair!

"Don't ever tell her," the boy warned, his soft brown eyes near panic. "It'd destroy her."

Mother was protecting son and son was protecting mother.

"Are you sure she doesn't already know?" John asked gently.

"Positive. Why would my dad do something like that?" Paul cried, and his voice cracked. "She loved my father."

"I know she did."

Paul nodded. "She needs someone to be there for her. So far, that's been me. Well, friends, too, like Mary Jane. But mostly me." He gave a quick shrug. "I'm going to get my driver's license next year," he added with the assurance of a young man who'd mastered the skill of parallel parking. "In a few years I'll graduate from high school."

"And be off to college," John said, yearning to comfort Paul and not knowing how to do it without embarrassing him. The boy struggled with his composure, and John realized Paul Graham was mature beyond his years.

Paul nodded. "I don't want to think of Mom living alone."

"In other words, you'd like her to remarry."

"I would," he said in all seriousness. "Someone I like and respect. Someone I trust, who'll make her happy, and who'll never cheat on her the way my father did." He hesitated, gazing confidently at John. "Someone like you, Mr. Livingstone."

Someone like you. To think one of the greatest compliments of his life would come from a teenage boy.

"She needs you," Paul continued, "and if you don't mind my saying so, you and Nikki need us, too."

John couldn't argue with the truth.

"Now, what's it to be?" Paul asked.

Following the evening meal, Beth puttered around the kitchen, putting away leftovers. She was going to miss this kitchen, with its spaciousness and state-of-the-art conveniences. But it was far more than the kitchen she'd be thinking about in the months to come. This summer would stay in her memory. Rainshadow Lodge, the beach, exploring the island. Their day-long expeditions. And, most of all, John Livingstone. He and his rebellious daughter had touched her heart.

"Hi!" Nikki sauntered into the room as though she hadn't a care in the world. She pulled out a stool at the island and plopped herself down.

"Hello, there," Beth said, looking for space in the refrigerator for the bowl of leftover green salad.

"Have you seen Paul lately?" Nikki asked.

"No, I can't say I have." Her voice echoed from inside the massive refrigerator as she rearranged the middle shelf.

"He's talking with my dad."

"Oh." It seemed odd that Nikki would ask her a question when she already knew the answer.

"Don't you want to know what they're talking about?"

"Do I?" The twelve-year-old seemed to have all the answers.

"I think you should," Nikki said.

Beth glanced over her shoulder and saw that the girl was slouched forward on the stool, both elbows on the countertop.

"Paul's asking my dad if he is interested in marrying you."

"What?" The salad tumbled out of her hands and crashed to the floor. The ceramic bowl shattered, and lettuce, tomatoes and other fresh vegetables colorfully decorated the tiles.

"Paul's asking my dad if—"

"I heard you the first time," Beth said as she reached for a broom. This was a joke. It had to be, and she'd fallen for it hook, line and sinker. "You're kidding, right?" she asked, sweeping the broken bowl and salad vegetables into the dustpan and dumping it all in the garbage.

"No, I'm serious."

"Nikki, this is crazy." Beth's face went pink with embarrassment.

"What would you say if my dad does decide to propose?"

"He won't! Nikki, why in the world is Paul doing anything so crazy?"

"It isn't only Paul. I'm involved in this, too. We both are. You didn't leave us any choice. We had to do *something*. It's fairly obvious you two were desperately in need of help."

Beth pressed the heel of her hand against her forehead as she tried to assimilate what was happening. "Help?" she repeated. "What do you mean, help?"

"You were both going to walk away as if this summer meant nothing. Paul and I couldn't let that happen."

Beth sank onto the bench in the breakfast nook, not sure her legs would support her.

"Paul and I talked everything over, and we realized we had to act quickly." Nikki took a banana from the fruit bowl and peeled it. "You love my dad, don't you?" she asked nonchalantly.

"I…"

"You don't need to answer that if it embarrasses you," Nikki said, smiling benevolently. "Besides, I already know you do."

Beth would've liked to say something witty, but she couldn't get her tongue to work. Not that she even *had* a comeback, smart or otherwise.

"I realized not long ago how much I wanted my mom and dad to get back together, but it's not going to happen and I have to accept that. Which means Dad will eventually remarry…and I think you'd make a wonderful stepmom."

Beth smiled weakly at the compliment.

"Besides, you're still young enough to have babies, if you wanted. You do, don't you?" she asked, and stuffed half the banana in her mouth.

"Where are Paul and your father?" Beth demanded. She

had to put an end to this before it got any more out of hand. She could only imagine what John must be thinking.

"I'd baby-sit," Nikki said, her mouth full of banana.

"Baby-sit?"

"My little brother or sister, but I'd rather you had a girl. I've wanted a baby sister forever."

Babies. This had gone on long enough. "Nikki, I'm honored that you'd want me as a stepmother, but—"

The kitchen door opened. John and her son stepped inside.

Paul gave Nikki a thumbs-up and she returned the gesture.

"Paul, I want to talk to you this instant," Beth insisted, then added. "Alone."

"Sure, Mom, but first—"

"But first," John interrupted, "I need a few minutes of your time."

"Mine?" Beth asked, flattening her palm against her chest. He nodded, then added. "Alone."

Eleven

Mary Jane: So you're going to marry John Livingstone, after all.
Beth: I didn't say that.
Mary Jane: No. Paul did, and he should know.

"John," Beth said after Paul and Nikki had left the kitchen. She pressed her hands to her cheeks, mortified to the very marrow of her bones. "I can't tell you how sorry I am."

"I'm not."

She couldn't believe what she was hearing. "You can't possibly mean…" Rather than put words in his mouth, she clamped hers closed and decided to let him talk.

"I take it Nikki's been discussing the idea of you and me getting married?"

She nodded. "She volunteered to baby-sit."

"Baby-sit?"

"Later." She motioned for him to go on. "You'd better tell me what Paul had to say."

"Simply that I need you in my life."

She wasn't sure how to comment or if she should.

"I don't know if Paul's given much thought to a career, but I think the boy would make a fine lawyer. His argument was very persuasive."

"You aren't actually considering… I mean…"

"That's up to you," John said.

"Me?"

"He's right. I do need you, Beth."

"But…" Her vocabulary seemed to be reduced to words of one syllable.

"Yes?" he urged when she didn't immediately continue.

"Marriage?"

"Well, that might be putting the cart before the horse."

She felt a flood of relief, replaced almost immediately by a surge of disappointment. "I… Naturally it's too soon. I mean, it's only been three weeks, and—"

"Could you love me, Beth?" he asked. His eyes were tender and vulnerable, almost as if he feared her response and at the same time hungered to know the truth.

Her reply was immediate. "Yes," she whispered. She was halfway there and struggling to keep from falling head over heels for him as it was. "Could you…love *me?*" she asked.

His smile told her everything she needed to know.

John held out his arms and she walked into his embrace. He hadn't so much as kissed her when there was a knock at the kitchen door.

"Can we come in yet?" Nikki shouted from the other side.

"Can they?" John asked. He'd slid his arms around her waist and smiled down at her.

"What did I just agree to?" Beth asked.

"To love me and my daughter."

"No problem." She smiled up at him, knowing her feelings shone from her eyes.

"To share my life."

"Marriage?" she asked again.

"In time, but I think it'd be better if we took a few months to really get to know each other first."

"I agree." They were older, more mature, and with maturity came a certain wisdom. Neither of them needed to rush into a second marriage, not with the numerous complications they already faced.

"Dad?" Nikki shouted. "At least tell us what's happening. We have a right to know."

"Hold on," John called back.

"Nikki mentioned another child," Beth said, her eyes avoiding his. John had no way of knowing how much she'd yearned for a second child. Jim hadn't been keen on the idea and found one excuse after another to put her off.

"Are you interested in having more children?" he asked, his face intent.

She nodded eagerly.

John's returning grin was bright enough to rival the sun. "Me, too."

"Where would we live?"

"I have a job offer in Seattle," he said to her astonishment. "Should be firmed up this week."

That was a possibility she hadn't even considered. Living in Seattle…

"Mom." Paul's impatient voice sounded from the other side of the door.

"All in good time," she promised him, "all in good time."

"Do you think I should accept it?" John asked.

"Well, moving to L.A. would be one option. Mary Jane and her family live there," she said, thinking out loud. They'd been friends almost their entire lives, and being closer to her definitely appealed to Beth. But starting over with John on fresh ground held an even stronger appeal. "I like the idea of moving to Seattle."

"Paul said—"

"Dad," Nikki complained loudly. "Just how long is this going to take? You love Beth and you know it."

John leaned his forehead against Beth's. "Why do I have the feeling those two are doing their best to keep us physically frustrated?"

Beth threw her arms around his neck. "Kiss me first. Just once."

He complied, slanting his mouth over hers in a kiss that was slow and thorough. When he lifted his head, Beth moaned in protest. She never wanted it to end. Then he was kissing her again with a need that had grown even more intense.

"They're kissing," Nikki shouted, and hurled open the kitchen door. "You've obviously agreed to something!" she declared, arms akimbo.

"We've agreed not to let kids meddle in our lives," John told them. He and Beth stood side by side, arms wrapped around each other's waists.

Beth caught a wink between John and her son.

"When's the wedding?" Nikki asked.

John and Beth looked at each other. "We don't know yet," Beth answered.

"When will you?" Nikki wasn't giving up easily.

Again John and Beth exchanged looks. "Soon," John promised.

"Soon for the wedding? Or soon you'll know?"

"I think we could easily have *two* attorneys in the family," Beth whispered.

John grinned and dropped a quick kiss on her lips. "Yes, to both," he assured his daughter.

Nikki and Paul shouted with joy and exchanged a high five.

"I told you all they needed was someone to point them in the right direction," Nikki reminded him, as though the whole thing had been her idea.

Beth felt a smile touch the corners of her mouth. "I suggest we save the debates for later. As it is, there's plenty to decide and even more to discuss."

"Why don't we all sit down and talk this out?" John suggested.

"That's what you said the day we arrived," Nikki remembered. She slid into the booth and patted the empty seat beside her for her dad.

Saturday night Beth found her son sitting on the beach long after midnight. "I wondered where you'd gone," she said, lowering herself onto the sand next to him.

"I was just thinking."

It was their last night at Rainshadow Lodge, and everything was packed for the trip out in the morning. Their last two days in the state had been spent exploring downtown Seattle. They'd ridden the monorail, gone up to the observation deck of the Space Needle, even toured underground Seattle. By all rights, Paul should be exhausted.

"Mom," Paul said, his voice little more than a whisper, "were you and Dad happy?"

She didn't know what had prompted that question. "I thought we were," she whispered back.

His chest heaved with a sigh as he turned to study her face in the moonlight. He frowned, and Beth raised her hand to cup his jaw, staring at him, noting his hurt and anger.

"How long have you known?" she asked, trying to keep her voice even.

He hesitated. "I…saw Dad with her about a month before the accident."

Beth swallowed tightly and closed her eyes against the unexpected flash of pain. "I…wanted to protect you."

"I didn't want you to know. I was afraid…"

"Of what?" she prodded, seeing her son struggle with the words.

"I don't understand why he did it," Paul blurted. "She wasn't even pretty."

"Paul…Paul." She wrapped her arms around him and hugged him tight, understanding that, in betraying her, Jim had also betrayed his son's trust and allegiance.

"Sometimes I think I hate him."

"Your father had his faults," she told him, and kissed the top of his head. "I can't—won't—defend his affair, but I can tell you this with complete and utter confidence. He loved you, Paul. You made him so very proud."

She felt the emotional conflict within her son and thought for a moment that he might break down and cry. He stiffened with the pain, then regained his composure and nodded. "I loved him, too."

"So did I," Beth whispered, and hugged her son close to her heart.

"Are you ready?" Mary Jane asked, opening the door to the master bedroom. Beth and Paul had moved into the Seattle house just that week.

Beth cast one last glance at her reflection in the full-length mirror and nodded. She doubted any bride had ever been more ready for her husband than she was for John. So much had changed in the past few months. Her house had been sold. His, too. A new job for him and one for her, with the same hotel chain that had hired her in St. Louis. A new start for them both. And a new start for Paul and Nikki, who'd helped bring all of this about.

"I've never known anyone to put together a wedding as fast as the two of you," Mary Jane said as she handed Beth the bridal bouquet.

"It was either marry the man or hand over my life savings to the telephone company. Besides, we're in love and we didn't want to spend the Christmas holidays apart."

Someone knocked gently on the door, and Nikki entered the bedroom. "He's a nervous wreck."

"Your dad?"

"No, Paul. He's never been a best man before. I've never been a maid of honor, but I don't feel like I'm going to throw up. Are we ready to leave for the church or not?"

"Ready," Mary Jane answered, and dabbed at her eyes.

"Mary Jane," Nikki chastised.

"Don't mind me," Beth's friend sobbed. "I always cry at weddings."

Dave met the small troupe at the bottom of the stairs. "Your chariot awaits you," he said, and made a courtly gesture toward the front door. A stretch limo was parked outside.

"By the way," he asked as Beth swept past him. "Where's the honeymoon taking place?"

She didn't get a chance to respond. Nikki answered for her. "Rainshadow Lodge, of course. Where else?"

* * * * *

ISLAND TIME

Susan Wiggs

Dear Reader,

Before I became a writer, I was a teacher, so I never really lost my childlike anticipation of that magical time of year known as "summer." For this reason, I wanted to bring that special feeling into the story *Island Time*. I'm also delighted to have the opportunity to be published with two of my favorite authors and dearest friends, Debbie Macomber and Jill Barnett.

Spending the summer at one particular place, year after year, conjures up a heady sense of romance and nostalgia for me. Even a pair as mismatched as Mitch and Rosie can't resist the spell cast by the idyllic Rainshadow Lodge, because summer is as much a state of mind as a time of the year. Like the sunshine and new growth, it's a season of possibility and promise—the perfect time to fall in love.

Wishing you many happy summers,

Susan Wiggs
Box 4469
Rolling Bay, WA 98061

To my grandmother, Marie Banfield,
who celebrates her birthday every summer.
I love you, Gram.

Thanks to Dianne Moggy of MIRA Books,
for her vision,
to Martha Keenan of MIRA Books,
for her re-vision
and to Joyce, Barb, Betty and Christina
for always reading and believing.

One

There was nothing Mitchell Baynes Rutherford III hated more than missed appointments. As he watched the ferry from Anacortes discharge the last of its cargo, he gritted his teeth and started to pace. A low-slung Corvette zoomed off, followed by a Winnebago the size of a Third World country. A station wagon crammed with squabbling kids and harried parents, followed by a convertible filled with college students. And then…nothing.

Not the person Mitch had been waiting for in the blistering August sun for the past hour. The so-called expert he had hired was nowhere to be found.

He stopped pacing, reached into the breast pocket of his suit coat and grabbed his cell phone. Flipping it open, he speed-dialed his office in Seattle, wondering if the unreliable island signal would work this time.

"Rutherford Enterprises," said a familiar voice.

"Miss Lovejoy, this Dr. Galvez person didn't show."

"I'm fine, Mr. Rutherford, and how are you today?" his secretary said pointedly.

He scowled, watching as a derelict Volkswagen bug, its exhaust pipe coughing up toxic smoke, limped off the ferry, the last of the last. Salsa music blared from the open windows of the little tangerine-colored car. Mitch covered one ear with his hand so he could continue his conversation.

"Sorry to be short with you," he said, not sorry at all. "That marine biologist you sent didn't show."

"Oh, dear." Miss Lovejoy sounded distressed, but Mitch knew her well. She was examining her manicure and looking out the window at the Seattle skyline. In front of her she probably held a voodoo doll in his shape, stuck with pins because he'd canceled her annual August vacation due to the current project. "I wonder what could have happened," his secretary added innocently.

The Volkswagen lurched along the exit ramp, then sputtered and died just past the ticket kiosk maybe twenty feet in front of Mitch. The driver, in a floppy sun hat and rhinestone-studded shades, banged her fists on the steering wheel and let loose with an angry monologue in rapid-fire Spanish. A pair of skinny dogs, their eyes bulging, stuck their light-bulb-size heads out the window of the car and started yapping over the tinny shriek and dull thump of the music.

Mitch turned away, pressing his hand harder to his ear. "What's that, Miss Lovejoy? I didn't hear you. I might be losing the damned signal."

"I said, ferry service is so unreliable in the summer. My son-in-law had a twelve-hour wait in Victoria—" The signal crackled, then died.

"Miss Lovejoy?" Mitch shouted into the phone.

But she was gone. Swearing, Mitch killed the power and

flipped the phone shut. The woman with the Volkswagen had gotten out and lifted the rear hood, exposing a steaming and cantankerous engine. He took a perverse comfort in seeing someone whose troubles far surpassed his own. Sure, it was irritating that his newest hire had missed the ferry, but he should be getting used to it by now.

Island time, the syndrome was called. He hadn't taken the expression seriously the first couple of days, but the concept was beginning to make a sort of annoying sense. People in the San Juans lived by their own inner clocks, not following any standard set by—God forbid—the business world. Workers came and went as they pleased, leaving a job half-finished if they got a better offer—like digging razor clams off Point No Point or climbing the Cattle Point lighthouse tower to watch a pod of whales swim by.

The tourists seemed to find the lackadaisical pace charming, but Mitch had a job to do and a limited time in which to do it. He had rented Rainshadow Lodge for the month of August. That meant he had just four weeks to get going on his latest project—planning a new forty-slip marina at the waterfront of Spruce Island.

Already the local planning inspector had stood him up. The marine architect had faxed some preliminary papers— and then everything had simply ground to a halt. The island sat like an emerald in the crystalline waters of a highly sensitive marine ecosystem. Before any work could be done, the entire area had to be evaluated to make sure the project wouldn't affect the local wildlife.

Now, it seemed, the latest contractor had let him down, as well.

And the clock was ticking on a very expensive project.

Mitch was about to go back to his boat—a 45-foot Bayliner he'd chartered for the month—when he walked around the rear of the Volkswagen. Glancing at the stranded motorist, he did a double take.

She wore a short tight red dress that fit like a halter on top, tied behind her slim neck. The hemline fell short enough to be declared illegal in some places but not, luckily, in the anything-goes San Juans. High-heeled sandals enhanced the effect of long slender legs, their polished olive hue rich and gleaming in the sunlight. When she bent over to inspect the engine, the pose made his mouth go dry.

And he hadn't even seen her face yet.

Who cares what her face looks like? his inner adolescent asked.

Apparently a few other inner adolescents had kicked in, too, because a handful of ferry workers started walking toward the damsel in the red dress. Propelled by a caveman territorial instinct, Mitch strode forward, reaching her first.

"Need some help, miss?" he asked.

"I guess I do," she replied, one slim arm propping up the rear hood, red-painted fingernails drumming on the metal.

The yappers in the car trebled their barking frenzy as Mitch drew near.

"Freddy!" the woman said sharply. "Selena! Hush up! *Silencio!*"

Surprisingly the rodents complied, glaring at Mitch but no longer barking.

"So," she said, pushing up the brim of her hat to reveal

a face that more than did justice to the lush body. She took off her shades and folded them, tucking one earpiece down between the cleft of her breasts. With a frank sweep of her dark-eyed gaze, she studied him. She seemed faintly amused. Something in her expression made him wish his shirt wasn't quite so crisply tailored, his trousers not quite so perfectly creased, his shoes not quite so gleamingly polished.

"You know how to fix cars?" she asked.

"I don't know the first thing about fixing cars," he admitted. "We should push it out of the ferry lane, though."

She lowered the hood. "Good idea." With a flash of her extravagantly gorgeous legs, she got in the driver's side and, mercifully, flipped off the radio. "You push and I'll steer."

Great, thought Mitch, taking off his suit coat and slinging it over the passenger-side window. The rug rats immediately set to sniffing it. Mitch didn't let himself watch. If one of the Chihuahuas decided to mark its territory, he didn't want to be a witness.

"Head for the lot over by the waterfront," he said, gesturing.

She nodded, tossing the sun hat on the seat beside her. Mitch glanced over his shoulder at the ferry workers. *C'mon, guys,* he thought, but since he'd beaten them to the punch, they had clearly lost interest.

"Okay, I'm in neutral," she called out the window.

Nice accent, he thought. Barely noticeable, just in the *r*'s and a few elongated vowels. Setting his palms flat against the sun-heated back of the car, he pushed, feeling the resistance lessen as the small battered Volkswagen started to roll. A moment later she'd managed to maneuver it into a parking space at the waterfront lot.

"Stay, guys," she instructed the dogs, then got out and came around the back of the car, nodding at Mitch. "Thanks."

"No problem." He tried not to stare, but she was gorgeous. Full red lips, hair dark and silky, eyes even darker and the lashes silkier. A single teardrop of sweat trickled down between her breasts. A tiny gold cross on a dainty chain lay against her smooth skin. He nearly groaned aloud. "Um, is there someone you could call? Do you belong to an auto club?"

She laughed, a bright staccato sound. "This car's older than I am. I always figured if it broke down, I'd just walk away."

He couldn't tell if she was joking or not. "Well, is there someone you could call?"

"Yeah, I'd better. I'm late for an appointment." She turned and scanned the ferry landing just as the boat blasted its horn and pulled away from the dock. She bit her lower lip. Mitch's inner adolescent came to full alert. "Someone was supposed to meet me, but I don't see him."

He yanked his gaze from her berry-bright mouth and forced his brain to kick in. "Whoa. You can't be Dr. Galvez."

Her face lit with a grin as generous and bright as the summer sun. Mitch didn't know many women who smiled so quickly and openly.

She stuck out her hand. "Dr. Rosalinda Galvez. My friends call me Rosie. You must be Mr. Rutherford."

"Mitch," he said quickly, his mind trying to reorganize

all his expectations. The fax from Miss Lovejoy had said only that he was to meet "R. Galvez, Ph.D." who would arrive on the afternoon ferry from Anacortes. Based on that, his unimaginative mind had pictured a professorial type. Middle-aged. Male. Probably balding and maybe a little paunchy around the middle. Thick-lensed eyeglasses, because all that peering into microscopes had affected his eyesight.

"Mr. Rutherford," she said. "Mitch. Is something wrong?"

"Me," he blurted.

"What?"

He shook his head. "Never mind."

She reached into the car, randomly picking up one of the Chihuahuas and stroking it absently. The dog nuzzled against her midsection. "I'm not following you."

He tried his best not to be jealous of a rat. "You're not what I expected."

"Oh." She did that lip-biting thing again; it was making him nuts. Her knowing gaze took in his custom-made shirt, Armani slacks, tasseled Italian loafers. "*You* are."

He spread his arms, feeling the sweat run. "I dressed for a business meeting. Old habits die hard."

"So I guess I should get my things, right?" she asked, tilting her head to one side. "I mean, your assistant said we'd be going to Spruce Island by private boat."

"That's right." He pointed out the Bayliner. "It's in a slip down there. I'll go get a handcart."

"Great."

"You need a parking tag from the attendant," he suggested. "Long-term."

She flashed her amazing smile again. "I like the sound of that."

"It's only a month."

She rolled her eyes. "The way my life has been going, a month is forever."

"I guess that means you haven't changed your mind."

She laughed easily and put the dog back in the car. "No chance of that, Mr.—Mitch."

A few minutes later he was still trying to get his bearings. His marine biologist was Carmen Miranda. She drove a Volkswagen bug older than she was, complete with plastic Virgin on the dashboard and fuzzy dice hanging from the rearview mirror. She had Chihuahuas named after deceased Latino singers and a smile he could live on for weeks. He couldn't decide whether this was a stroke of good luck or a joke played by fate.

He watched her open the front trunk of the car, noting the lyrical movement of long sleek muscles as she moved, and decided he could put up with the Chihuahuas.

"Here's all my stuff," she said.

He brought the handcart near. A medium-size suitcase, a case of Gainsburger and a large box of technical-looking apparatus lay in the trunk. "You travel pretty light," he commented.

"I had another big suitcase," she said a little wistfully, "but…" She let her voice trail off.

"But what?"

"I left it with a woman at the ferry terminal in Anacortes."

Mitch frowned, tossing the dog food into the cart. "Why'd you do that?"

"She needs the stuff more than I do."

He blinked. Homeless people were so sadly common these days that they'd become invisible to most passersby. It was unusual to find someone who actually did something about it. "That was pretty nice of you," he said.

"I didn't do it to be nice. I did it because she needed some things." She banged the trunk shut. "Freddy, Selena, c'mon." They scooted out the driver's-side door. She retrieved her hat and a box of cassette tapes and CDs, then took out a small cooler of water. "For the dogs," she explained. Lastly she drew out a big, bulging file box.

"And that?" Mitch asked, taking it from her.

"All my personal papers." Her gaze skated away from him. "I, um, gave up my apartment."

"This job isn't permanent," he reminded her.

She winked. "Like I said before, a month is forever."

Mitch helped her roll up the car windows. "That everything?"

"I guess so," she said, dropping a set of keys into an oversize tote bag with a faded chemical-company logo on it.

"Aren't you going to lock the car?" he asked.

She shrugged. "Hey, if somebody can find something worth stealing in this heap, more power to him. The speakers have been blown for years."

What a strange woman, Mitch thought as he wheeled the handcart down to the boat. Possessions didn't seem to mean a thing to her.

He held open the gate leading to the boat slips. "Ladies first," he said.

She treated him to that dazzling smile he was already

half in love with and preceded him down the ramp, the dogs skittering and dancing with joy at her feet.

God, Mitch thought before he could stop himself, what did those legs look like from the Chihuahuas' perspective?

Two

Mitchell Rutherford was a knight in shining armor. He couldn't know it, but he'd saved her life.

Rosie didn't dare tell him, though. He had that look about him. That look that said he'd take off running the minute he realized she had no place to go, no money, no prospects, nothing beyond this one-month assignment for his firm.

Free-falling without a net was nothing new to Rosie Galvez. Having grown up in a family of eight, she'd long ago learned the power of blind faith in the basic decency of the universe. But this last disaster had left her shaken. This time she almost hadn't survived.

"Let me know when you're ready to cast off," she called to him, angling her head to see him up on the bridge. Beneath a green canvas bimini, with blue sky and wheeling gulls in the background, he looked like an ad for aftershave. "I'll take care of the lines."

"Thanks." The twin engines came to life with a low-throated growl of power.

She unwound the line from the cleats fore and aft,

tossing them aboard and then shoving the boat, bow out, away from the dock. She hoisted herself aboard, gritting her teeth as she turned her ankle. The heeled sandals had been a mistake. She hoped her sneakers weren't in the big suitcase she'd given the homeless woman.

Another stellar moment in her crazy life.

As she bent over the rail, bringing in the large blue fenders, a wolf whistle sounded from the dock. She glanced up, seeing a pair of yacht-club rejects watching her. "Business or pleasure?" one of them called, elbowing his friend. Idiots, she thought, tossing her head. She disliked the assumption that she and Mitch were some rich guy and his Latino bimbo.

Of course, as her brother Carlito would say, you can't dress like that and expect people to call you Professor Galvez.

The trouble was, she liked wearing high-heeled sandals. She liked driving a funky old car and listening to loud music and wearing her hair too long and her dresses too short. Basically, she liked who she was.

Except the part about being flat broke.

She glanced guiltily up at Mitch, who was concentrating on getting the boat out of the harbor. "Need any more help?" she called.

"I'm fine, thanks. We'll dock at Spruce Island in about forty minutes."

The dogs, ever adaptable, had made themselves at home in the salon of the boat, which was furnished with a small sofa and club chair. Rosie slipped off her sandals and climbed the ladder to the bridge. She stood beside Mitch and, buoyed by the warm summer breeze that blew across the water, her spirits began to rise.

"I've got some drinks in the cooler," he said. "Help yourself."

She selected plain bottled water. "Would you like something?"

"I'll take a beer." He put on his shades and moved out into the channel. A flotilla of sailboats passed to the north of them, graceful as birds with their sails all bent into the wind. The summer day had the clarity of a diamond. No sky was ever bluer than the sky over the San Juans in August.

"It's beautiful," she said, lifting her face to the moving sea air.

Mitch took a heading to the southwest. "I guess so."

He didn't sound as if he meant it. She was usually pretty good at reading people, so as she sipped her water, she tried her skills on Mitchell Baynes Rutherford III. Handsome, of course, but not high-maintenance handsome. He had a certain easy grace about him. She suspected, studying the pleasing breadth of his shoulders, that he'd been blessed by natural athletic fitness. No doubt he kept himself too busy making money to work out in a gym or go to one of those nauseating male salons that seemed so popular lately.

The money, the looks, the aura of success, would all make him wildly attractive to women, but Rosie knew without asking that there was no one special in his life.

"You're looking at me like I'm some sort of lab specimen," he said.

She laughed. "You caught me. I was just telling myself you probably don't have a wife or a girlfriend."

"How did you guess?"

"I'm an expert at empirical observations."

He took a swig of his beer. "Are you interested in the position?"

She refused to let her gaze waver. "Are you looking to fill it?"

"No."

"Then no."

He grinned. "Good. Glad we got that settled."

She grinned back. "Me, too."

It was better, she told herself, to get this sort of thing out in the open. They had a business arrangement, and it wouldn't do to have all this unspoken tense interest seething around them while they worked. Because the tension was there, she acknowledged. It had been since the moment she'd glanced up from her dead car and seen him coming across the parking lot, looking like an *Esquire-* magazine layout.

They would get along fine, she knew, as long as they both stayed in their boxes. He in his self-made millionaire world, and she in her academic-with-an-attitude world. She knew instinctively that he'd better not find out she was in dire straits. Mitch Rutherford was definitely the type you wanted to deal with from a position of strength, not weakness. The moment he found out how needy she was, how desperate, he'd run the other way.

The moment he found out how utterly lonely she was, he might break her heart.

And as poor as she was, she certainly couldn't afford *that*.

"So how'd you find out about the job?" he asked, idly watching a rust-colored Japanese tanker nose through the shipping lanes toward Seattle.

"The Internet. Your assistant posted a notice on the UW bulletin board. The assignment looked intriguing." A white lie. A routine environmental-impact study was a total bore, consisting of predictable lab work and too much meaningless paperwork. But to an untenured professor who'd just found a pink slip in her mailbox, the position held the allure of a gold doubloon on the bottom of the ocean.

And since the project involved staying a month at a place called Rainshadow Lodge, doing undemanding work in an idyllic island setting, Rosie knew she'd have the chance to regroup and chart a course for the future. She'd never been much of a planner, but losing the best job she'd ever had had been a blow that left her stunned. Maybe it was a sign from the universe, a sign that said it was time to start acting like a grown-up, time to get her life in order and figure out what to do with the rest of it.

Seated on the high bridge of the Bayliner and seeing the islands rise like emeralds out of the sea, she vowed to do such a fabulous job on the study that her new employer would beg her to take a permanent position with his company.

"So you're familiar with what's involved in this sort of study, right?" he asked, blithely ignorant of her plan.

She nodded, taking a packet of gum out of her handbag and offering him a piece. He declined. She folded the stick of Wrigley's four times and popped it in her mouth. "I did a lot of field studies in graduate school. It's fun, but I take it seriously. I specialized in marine ornithology."

"What's that?"

"Birds. Especially the rare ones—cranes and such." She

held out her right arm, turning it so that he could see the jagged bruise-colored scar along her inner elbow.

"Jesus," he said, "how'd that happen?"

"When I was a grad student at UC San Diego, I got into an argument with a shark over a piece of camera equipment."

He gave a low whistle. "So who won?"

She laughed, tossing her head back and letting the wind muss her hair. "I never let the shark win, Mitch. Never."

Three

Bringing the boat alongside the private dock at Rain-shadow Lodge, Mitch had to keep reminding himself that Rosie Galvez was an employee, and a temporary one at that. But everything about this well-endowed gum-cracking woman surprised him. Though so far, nothing had surprised him more than her reaction to the summer place.

She stood on the dock while the dogs raced ahead, looking up at the old Victorian mansion as if it gave her a glimpse of heaven. Her sandals dangled, apparently forgotten, from her fingers, and her pretty bare feet were flush to the sun-warmed wood of the deck. He waited, her suitcase in one hand, and watched her. Something happened to her lush extravagant beauty as she studied the place where she'd spend the next four weeks. A softness came over her, a vulnerability, and that vulnerability did strange and unwelcome things to Mitch.

He didn't want to see it. Didn't want to see the need and loneliness and stark unhappy emotions the sight of the house seemed to evoke in her. Didn't want to wonder where her need came from. And most of all, he didn't want to be the one to answer that need. It was stupid and just asking for trouble, to get emotionally involved with an employee.

"It's perfect," she declared, her gaze fastened hungrily to the painted gingerbread woodwork that trimmed the wraparound porch. "It's like a place that time forgot, don't you think?"

"I understand that was the case with the plumbing until recently," he said. "Come on. I'll show you your room."

She walked ahead of him up the long flight of open wooden steps that led from the dock to the front lawn. The flared hem of the red dress flipped enticingly in the breeze. He tried to be good, tried not to stare, but the inner adolescent, the one his mother had once said would be his downfall, made him look.

He was sweating by the time he got to the top of the steps. And he'd changed his mind about getting involved with an employee. Because, after all, she was perfect for him. She had signed a contract to work with him here for one month and not a day more.

So why the hell not? he asked himself. It would be just like a one-night stand, only this would be a one-month stand. As long as they both understood this from the start, their month at Rainshadow Lodge might prove to be damned enjoyable. As well as profitable.

The one drawback was that, if she was anything like a lot of women he'd known, she'd have trouble letting go at the end of the month. Mitch didn't consider himself worthy of being clung to, but women did, anyway. They clung. They hung on way longer than they should, and then he had to do something that hurt them just to get them to go away.

He hated hurting people. But he was willing to do it in order to keep his distance. With weary reluctance, he surrendered the brief fantasy of a wild affair with this woman. He had too much work to do.

"Here, I'll get the door." He set down the suitcase. The Chihuahuas kept skittering around the yard, marking territory. So much for croquet, Mitch thought with a rueful smile. He wasn't a croquet kind of guy, anyway.

He unlocked the door and held it open while Rosie walked inside. Her sandals hit the vestibule floor with a clunk. "It's great," she said, her voice almost reverent. "Oh, Mitch. How did you find this place?"

"Miss Lovejoy found it. She didn't tell you about it?"

"Only that lodgings and meals would be provided. I had no idea *this* was what she meant by lodgings."

"I'll show you your room," he said, interested by her reaction. When he had walked into the lodge, he hadn't experienced any particular emotion other than irritation when he realized there was only one phone jack in the whole house. He liked setting up his computer and fax machine and phone on separate lines, but the old-fashioned lodge wasn't set up for that.

They walked up the stairs. He'd made a fairly random selection of a room for her, choosing one on the third story because it had an adjoining bathroom with a big fancy Jacuzzi tub he couldn't imagine ever using. But when she turned to him and smiled, he was glad he'd picked this one.

"So I guess this means you like it."

"You could say that." She went to the window and brushed aside the curtains. The distant Cascades, snowcapped even in summer, rose like white teeth across the Sound. "A beautiful view and all this luxury. Mitch, I couldn't ask for more."

He had to train himself to quit staring at her, but it was hard when she stood there with the sunlight streaming over her, a dazzling smile on her face and a look in her eyes that went straight to his heart.

"I'll let you get settled in," he said uncomfortably. "Just holler if you need anything."

"I might holler, anyway," she said, then laughed that easy uncomplicated laugh.

And it seemed to Mitch, as he turned away to hide a physical reaction that could drive nails, that fate was laughing at *him*.

Four

Mitch woke up to the racket of salsa music and Jacuzzi jets churning at full speed. Staring at the ceiling, he pictured that long luxuriant form in the oversize tub, and his body reacted with pitiless immediacy. Wondering what further trials the day might bring, he hurried through his shower and dressed quickly, determined to get downstairs before Rosie.

He wanted to be the one in charge here. It was only right, since he was the employer.

The house had been remodeled with a gourmet kitchen, which some of the summer residents no doubt valued, but to which Mitch was indifferent. He was indifferent, too, to the imported brass-and-chrome espresso machine. Some people enjoyed fussing for five minutes over a thimbleful of thick bitter coffee, but Mitch settled for instant.

He wondered what she ate for breakfast. He had all the bachelor staples—Pop-Tarts, bananas, a gallon of milk. If she wanted more than that, she was on her own.

Mitch thought that sounded good. Where Rosie Galvez was concerned, he had to be ruthless. Had to keep his distance. Had to keep telling himself she had a job to do, a month to do it in, and then they'd never see each other again.

Of course, there was no law to this effect, but it was the way Mitch wanted it. It was the way he wanted his life. It was the only way he knew how to be.

The Chihuahuas came skittering down the stairs, lifting their paws delicately and shrinking back when Mitch looked at them. "Weenies," he muttered under his breath. He picked up the sack of dog food Rosie had brought and poured some into a cereal bowl. The dogs crept forward, sniffed at it suspiciously and sat back on their haunches. "Suit yourself," Mitch said, turning away to fix his coffee and staring out the window over the sink. He'd heard there were killer whales in the area. "So where are you guys on the food chain, huh?"

"I heard that." Rosie appeared just as he was stirring the granules of instant coffee into a cup of hot water. Freshly bathed, her damp hair curling around her smiling face, she looked like something he used to dream about—back when he remembered how to dream.

"Good morning," she said. "The dogs are bilingual, so watch what you say about them. Don't you like dogs?"

Mitch lifted an eyebrow. "Is that what they are? I was thinking maybe fish bait or shaved hamsters."

"Very funny. I'll bet you don't even have a dog."

"I have a ceramic Dalmatian. It's an umbrella stand a business acquaintance gave me."

"It figures." She bent and cuddled the yappers against her briefly, then stood. "You're up early."

"It's a workday. Coffee?" He held out the mug to her.

She glanced at the jar of instant on the counter, then took

the mug and dumped it into the sink. "Please. I have my standards."

"Instant is fast," he said, annoyed.

She gestured at the espresso machine. "Do you mind if I make a latte?"

"Go right ahead. But hurry."

"You can't hurry a latte."

"Fine, then take your time," he forced himself to say.

She grinned at his impatient foot. He hadn't noticed he'd been tapping it. "I intend to."

"We should get started before it gets too late."

She found milk and a sack of Starbucks in the refrigerator. "After my coffee, I'm all yours."

He wished she hadn't put it that way. He found everything about her suggestive, although today she'd dressed in denim shorts, a tank top and frayed sneakers. Yet oddly, he found the outfit every bit as provocative as the red sundress.

"I'll show you the site—"

"Proposed site," she corrected him.

"Whatever. I'll show it to you, and then you can tell me what the procedure is." Mitch hoped she would catch his drift. If she was like other inspectors and officials involved in the building trades, she'd accept a generous check for her troubles and sign off on all the paperwork, declaring the project acceptable. Of course, she didn't look much like the other inspectors Mitch had worked with, but he had faith in the power of his checkbook.

Working deftly, she prepared two perfect lattes. Mitch sipped his, then looked up to see her watching him.

"Well?" she asked.

"Well what?"

"Admit it's better than instant."

"It's better than instant." He glanced at his watch. "But now we're running late."

"Do we have an appointment?" she asked, licking a line of foamed milk from her upper lip.

"No, but we have a schedule to keep. Are you familiar with schedules, Rosie?"

She laughed. "What if I said no?"

"I'd believe you. But I want to make it clear that this isn't a vacation. It's work."

Her smile faded a shade and Mitch felt unpleasantly guilty. "What I mean," he said, "is that my investors have certain expectations for this project. The economy of this island is in trouble, and the marina could save it. I can't afford to get behind."

"I understand." She had a seat at the table. It was in a hexagonal alcove with a window that bowed out over a view of the water. "But one cup of coffee isn't going to make or break your project." She took a deep breath. "The key is to make sure your marina isn't going to ruin what makes this island special in the first place."

Reluctantly he took a seat. Since he couldn't beat her, he might as well join her.

She smiled over the rim of her mug. He was amazed at the effect of that smile. It made something loosen and uncoil inside him, made him want to sit and stare at her while the clock ticked. "Can I get you anything else?" he asked.

"No, thanks. I usually skip breakfast. I'll bet you usually eat it standing up. Or on the run."

"You guessed it."

"So you must live alone, right?"

"Yeah. I have a place in the city."

"Let me guess again. A high-rise over Elliot Bay."

Mitch shook his head in mock dismay. "I'm so predictable."

She laughed. "Maybe I'm just smart."

"That's why Miss Lovejoy hired you."

She set her mug in the sink and went upstairs, returning a few minutes later with a lab kit and clipboard. "I'm ready."

They stepped out onto the porch together. Rosie took a deep breath and felt the sea air tingling in her chest. "It's wonderful here. It's so wonderful I can't stand it."

Mitch turned to her, frowning. "What's wonderful?"

"This. Everything!" With a sweeping gesture of her arm, she encompassed the water, glittering like diamonds in the morning sun, the backdrop of snowy peaks in the far distance, the rise of green islands out of the placid Sound. "How long have you been here?"

"Two days."

"Two days, and you don't think it's wonderful?"

"I'm here to do a job, Rosie."

They walked down a gravel path toward the water, then took a branch to the north and followed the shoreline. Driftwood logs the size of telephone poles littered the beach. Below the logs was a line of storm-smoothed stones that rattled as they walked over them. Cormorants swooped along the cliffs rising above the shoreline. Rosie felt herself getting closer and closer to the essence of the island. Yet it was a mystical essence, made even more enigmatic by the very remoteness of this place. Though people had inhabited Spruce Island since time out of mind, no one had conquered it. Instead, this island conquered *you*. That was its appeal, and its mystery.

And its complete and endless enchantment.

As they continued along the beach, she made an informal tally of the ecosystem, noting evidence of clams, crabs and a stunning variety of seabirds and raptors. Yet her gaze kept wandering to Mitch. There was something remote and unknowable about him, as well. A distance. She wondered if she only imagined a certain quiet melancholy that pervaded his life, or if that was simply her overactive imagination trying to rationalize her attraction to him.

And Lord, yes, she was attracted. He had dressed down for work today—khaki shorts, a Hilfiger golf shirt and Top-Siders. Yet even so, there was something innately formal about him. Even with her vivid imagination, she couldn't picture him less than perfectly groomed. Every sandy blond hair was in place, his shave was perfect and his fingernails were neatly trimmed.

"So what do you do for fun around here?" she asked.

"Fun?"

"Yes. As in, having a good time. Doing something for the purpose of enjoyment. Clam digging? Fishing?"

"Never done it."

"Scuba diving? Bicycling? Picnicking?"

He stuck his hands in his pockets. "I didn't come here for fun, Rosie."

"But if you happened to have fun while you were here, would it be the end of the world?"

"Of course not. I'm not a Nazi."

"But you know what they say about all work and no play."

"Maybe I like being a dull boy."

She couldn't help but laugh, looking at his broad shoulders and Tom Cruise features. "Nobody ever said you were dull, *jefe.*"

They walked along in a silence that was surprisingly companionable. Rosie wanted to fill herself with the matchless beauty of the place, the way the crystalline water lapped the beach, the towering cedars and Douglas firs that isolated them from the rest of the world, giving her the feeling they were the only man and woman alive.

They rounded a deep curve in the shoreline, leaving the driftwood logs behind. The stones thinned to sugar-fine sand the color of ground almonds. The cove formed by a jagged rise of rocks was a place of enchantment, with a spring trickling down the stone face and creating a shifting stream across the sand, down to the water.

"A salmon stream," she said, quickly noting it on the topographical map attached to her clipboard. "God, it's fabulous here." Unable to resist, she slipped off her canvas sneakers and sank her feet into the warm sand, savoring the almost orgasmic feel of it.

He sent her an odd look. "Just a little farther to the site."

"I'm in no hurry," she said.

He grinned. "It didn't take you long to adjust to island time."

"What's island time?"

"A misnomer. There *is* no sense of time on the island. No one's ever in a hurry around here."

"Except you," she said, unable to keep a faint note of accusation from her voice.

"Yes, well, someone has to get things done."

Five

Mitch told himself he shouldn't have been surprised by Rosie's reaction to the proposed marina site. Everything about Rosie surprised him, and this was no different. Instead of getting right down to work as he'd expected her to, she spent the day in some sort of weird Zen-like trance, exploring the area around the site to get a "feel" for the place.

This was something he'd never done, never seen the point of doing. To him, places didn't have any sort of feel. They just were. And most places, this island included, could stand some improvement.

The next morning, admitting that her way was a lot tastier than his, he waited for her to come down and make lattes. Bending over the table with the sunlight streaming in, they looked over maps and elevations and her pages of scribbled notes.

"When did you do all this?" Mitch flipped through the pages covered with her scrawling handwriting in peacock blue fountain-pen ink.

"I guess I did it on island time," she said, a teasing note in her voice.

He had to smile. So she was a hard worker, after all. He pushed a triplicate form toward her. "That's the first document the planning commission needs from us. It's a bunch of questions. I've filled in where I can, but it gets technical about habitat and populations and so forth. I figure that's your department."

She studied the paper for a moment, taking a thoughtful sip of her latte. "I'll have to take a lot more readings before I can complete that."

"Can't you just give your best guess on some of this stuff? I mean, do we really need to document the distance to the nearest foot? Or record bird-population density?"

She set down her mug and faced him squarely. "You hired me to do a job, Mitch. I intend to do it right. I won't gloss over this study. I'll do it correctly down to the last detail." She hesitated, biting her lip in that unconsciously sexy way of hers. "And, Mitch, I think you should know, I'll withhold my approval if it appears your marina will have a negative impact on the area."

He gritted his teeth. Over the entire course of his career, he had never let a client down, never abandoned a project. He prided himself on building, creating jobs, shaping communities and doing a damned good job of it. He could do the same thing here, and he wasn't about to let some self-righteous scientist stand in his way.

"This area is dying, Rosie. People are leaving the island in droves because they can't make a living here. The marina will add a dozen jobs, and indirectly, dozens more."

Scowling, he got up from the table. "I didn't ask for this project. The island residents came to me."

"I understand that. I don't want to stand in the way of progress, Mitch. But the islanders are the stewards of this place. I know for a fact they wouldn't want to introduce something detrimental to the environment just to drum up a few jobs. They could put a copper smelter here and employ a thousand people, but would it be the best thing for the island?"

"This isn't quite the same as a copper smelter," he said peevishly.

"Okay, I'm sorry. But I just want you to know I really intend to look at this."

"Fine." But he wondered if he meant it.

He watched her from afar that day. He worked in the front room with its bay window, glancing up too frequently from his computer screen. She walked with a strong purposeful stride, but she also had a way of slowing down that fascinated him. She'd be striding briskly along the waterfront; then she'd nearly stop as she inspected something or other.

And when she sat at the water's edge at sunset, with the fine evening mist coming down over her, he noticed a curious stillness about her. She was, at her center, as tranquil as the quiet tide pools they'd found on their explorations. Just being near her had a calming effect. He discovered he was in no hurry to be somewhere, that his normally impatient nature somehow found the patience to stand back and let her do her work in her own way.

You're good for me, Rosie.

The thought drifted through his mind, as enticing as her

laughter while she clapped her hands to summon the Chihuahuas. Rodentlike, they streaked down the yard toward her, and she gathered them up in her arms. For the briefest of moments Mitch entertained a fantasy—that he and Rosie were together like this, really together. Not just working on a project but spending time getting to know each other, talking and laughing, totally at ease.

He chased the fantasy away, slapping at it as if it were a mosquito about to bite him. He and Rosie Galvez were too different. She wasn't his type, much as he wanted her to be. In fact, he didn't have a "type" at all. Miss Lovejoy had been pointing that out for years as if it was some flaw in Mitch. He was too exacting, she'd say. His standards were unrealistically high.

Forcing his gaze back to the computer screen, he tried to put the thought out of his mind, but it nagged at him, this sense that he was incomplete and would always be that way because he made sure the perfect woman for him didn't exist.

His idea of the perfect woman was Barbie with a brain, but not a mind of her own. Yet now—his gaze wandered again—he kept looking out the window, seeing a tranquil dark-eyed woman and wondering, what if…

"I want to go out in the kayak," Rosie announced late the next morning.

"We both have work to do," Mitch said automatically.

"Yes. In the kayak."

Feeling his eyebrows descend in a scowl, he looked up from the letter he was composing to a financial group. "Going kayaking is work?"

"That's what I said, *jefe.*"

"Quit calling me that. It's insulting."

"Whatever you say, boss."

"So explain to me about this kayak business."

"We need to go out and explore the shores and reefs. The sea kayak's the best way to do it, because we'll be low to the water, and we'll be so quiet we won't disturb any of the wildlife."

He studied her for a long time. He, who had been ruled all his life by discipline, suddenly didn't want to have anything to do with discipline. He wanted to go kayaking with a beautiful woman. And because he wanted to go so badly, he said, "No."

"What do you mean, no?"

"I've got work to do, Rosie. Whatever needs to be done in the kayak, you'll have to do by yourself."

She crossed her arms beneath her breasts, drawing his attention there against his will. "It's a two-man kayak."

"I said I was busy."

A dangerous anger flickered in her eyes. He had the swift impression that her sweet nature could quickly detonate into a fiery temper.

But the expected outburst expressed itself as a brilliant smile. "Fine, then. I'll wait until you're finished working."

"That's not what…"

She was gone before he finished his protest. Muttering under his breath, he went back to what he was doing. A few minutes later he saw something—a glint of movement—from the corner of his eye. Knowing it was Rosie, he ignored the movement. For as long as he could.

Which amounted to about ten seconds. He looked up from his computer and saw her walking across the yard, heading down toward the beach.

His eyes nearly popped out of his head. She wore an iridescent bikini that pretty much ensured he wouldn't get another lick of work done. She sat in a chaise longue, took out a bottle of sunscreen and applied the gleaming polish to her long limbs, shoulders and stomach. Watching the languid stroke of her hands over her sun-warmed skin, Mitch groaned aloud. By the time she finished, he was pretty sure he was half-insane.

She stood and went to the end of the dock, the dogs capering at her feet. When she dove off the end, they started yapping furiously. She broke the surface, her inky hair slicked back from her face, and began paddling lazily through the water. And as he watched, he acknowledged that he wouldn't even look at his computer as long as Rosie was wearing a bikini and cavorting in the water.

He snapped his laptop shut and went down to the dock, pausing at the chaise to pick up a thick green beach towel. "You win," he called. "We're going kayaking."

She laughed, the bright sound dancing across the water to his ears. "Thank God. I'm starting to freeze in here." She swam to the wooden dock ladder and climbed out.

Mitch stared, even though he knew it was rude. "I guess that water *is* pretty cold," he remarked, holding out her towel.

"Pervert." She stepped into it, and just for a moment his arms came around her in an embrace, circling her from behind, wrapping her lush but shivering form in thick terry cloth. She smelled of seawater and sunscreen, and when she turned her head to look back at him, he nearly forgot to step away.

"This moment," he confessed, "is about one heartbeat shy of awkward, wouldn't you say?"

She shrugged, hugging the towel around her. "I'll be down at the boathouse in about fifteen minutes." As she started up toward the house, she turned to him. "Hey, Mitch, the answer to your question is no."

"No what?"

"No, it wasn't awkward. I thought you'd want to know that."

He couldn't stop a grin. He didn't even try.

Six

As Rosie dipped her paddle into the placid crystalline water, a glorious feeling of well-being washed over her. Sure, she was broke, jobless and homeless, but not at the moment. At the moment she was paddling through paradise with a gorgeous man behind her and a pair of bald eagles soaring overhead.

"God, I love this," she said, dazzled by the natural aquarium. "I haven't been spending enough time in the field." There. She'd found it. The silver lining. She knew she'd find it if she looked hard enough. "I'll have a lot more time for that now."

"How do you mean?" Mitch asked from behind her.

She gave a guilty shrug. "Being up here," she hedged. "For the past couple of years I've been in the classroom. It's nice to be out in the field once again." She trailed a hand in the water as they passed over a rocky undersea wall. Anemones in rainbow colors waved lazily in the watery sunlight. "I spent a summer up here as an undergraduate, studying the reproduction habits of tube worms."

He laughed. "You're kidding, right?"

"No, not at all. It was a great summer. My first away from my family."

"So where's your family?"

She was pleased to hear a personal question from him. He usually seemed so remote. She'd been shameless in trying to get his attention, but shamelessness often worked. "Wenatchee, just over the Cascades. My parents work in the apple industry."

"Everyone in Wenatchee does."

"Just about. Including my five brothers and sisters. I turned out to be the black sheep of the family, being fascinated by marine life, of all things. My folks kept thinking I'd grow out of it, but instead, I decided to make it my career. It was a little scary going off on my own."

"I can't imagine you being scared of anything, Rosie."

"Thank you. Being brave is something I work on. What about your family?"

"You've got me beat in the family department. Haven't seen my dad since I was nine years old. A few years after that, my mother remarried. She lives in La Jolla with a securities analyst. Between the three of them, they managed to keep me in therapy until I got tired of 'processing my emotions' for someone who charges 375 an hour."

He spoke jokingly, but Rosie stopped paddling and twisted around to look at him. Her gaze probed his lean face and chilly blue eyes, trying to see the abandoned boy he'd been, the boy with too much money and too little love. "I'm sorry, Mitch."

"Don't be. It's ancient history. And after all that psychoanalysis, the answer turned out to be pretty simple."

"Really? Then I wish you'd tell me what it is."

"This job," he said simply. "Building things. It's amazing how your own problems shrink when you don't have time to think about them. I never was that comfortable being the whining overprivileged kid, anyway," he added with a self-deprecating grin.

"You're serious, aren't you?" Rosie asked, incredulous. "You really think staying busy is the answer."

"Sitting around wringing my hands and processing my emotions sure as hell wasn't."

"But what happens when the work's over, Mitch? What happens then?"

"I don't have to worry about that. I've got enough irons in the fire to keep me hopping until I keel over."

"Don't you ever worry about that? About keeling over?"

"No."

She turned back, puzzled and vaguely saddened by him. "Let's head for the President Channel," she said. "A marina would increase the boating traffic there, so we should check it out."

They paddled in a comfortable rhythm. Summertime meant smooth clear water and sunlight strong enough to penetrate to three fathoms. Rosie felt the wind ripple through her hair, and she put her head back, trying to take everything in. It was glorious, all of it, the marshes and meadows running down to the water's edge, the slow-moving boat traffic passing idly by, the flocks of auklets and cormorants nesting in the hillsides, the dark flashes of fish schools below the kayak.

She refused to let herself be depressed by what Mitch

had told her. That he owed his mental health to unceasing hard work.

If that was the case, she was doomed.

The thought of returning to Seattle and starting the demoralizing process of job hunting depressed her even more. She enjoyed teaching. She was good at it. But the past couple of years the classroom walls had pressed in on her. Now, rafting along a glittering channel of Puget Sound, she knew what had been missing. The fieldwork. Being at sea, not in a lecture hall; studying habitats, not lab samples.

Landing a position in the field was even harder than a tenured teaching position. Sure, she could find something at a commercial aquarium, but the contained controlled environment had always made her feel claustrophobic. She might find seasonal work giving tours for tips at the Mermaid Whale Watching Expeditions. She'd heard the tips were good, particularly for guides in bikinis.

The very thought made her shudder, so she tossed it off and refused to let it spoil the day. They glided on, their silence companionable in the way it had been from the start. She wondered why that was, why she felt so relaxed and comfortable around this man who was so different from her, who held all but the very surface of himself away from the rest of the world.

In the distance, near the shore of Waldron Island, shadows flickered just beneath the surface of the water.

"Is that what I think it is?" Mitch said quietly.

She nodded, her chest filling up with the thrill of discovery. "Three family groups have been identified in this area. This is a pod of about twenty individuals." A trio of dorsal fins broke the surface, and her breath caught.

"Will we scare them?" Mitch asked.

"Not if we're slow and easy."

"Will they eat us?"

"Not unless we're easier to catch than a salmon."

The kayak glided nearer, and they saw more whales, mostly females and calves at varying stages of maturity. "Wow," he said. "Look at them all. They're colored like golf shoes."

"You would say that." Rosie would never tire of the beauty of the orcas. She loved their coloring, their family groups and the way their mouths lifted in a perpetual smile. She loved the way they hunted, swiftly and purposefully.

"Hey," Mitch said. "Look at that— Whoa!"

A large female shot out of the water, breaching only a few yards from the kayak. A tidal wave of water sprayed up, drenching them.

"My God," Mitch exclaimed. "Did you see that? It was the size of a bus!"

Rosie watched the trail of bubbles in the whale's wake and suddenly she felt overwhelmed. She couldn't help it, couldn't stop herself, and even though her back was turned from Mitch, she knew she couldn't hide her darkening mood. She laid her paddle across her lap skirt and lowered her head, wishing the month could go on forever, wishing she didn't have to go back to her real life.

"Hey, what's wrong?" Mitch sounded vaguely suspicious and fearful.

"It's…just…s-so beautiful," she said, feeling foolish and trying to keep control.

"The whale, you mean?"

"Just…everything."

"I agree with you, Rosie. But hey, get a grip. It makes me nervous as hell when people get emotional."

She heard him rifling around beneath his lap skirt; then he handed her a navy blue bandanna. "Here, Rosie. Please don't cry."

His gesture only made things worse. He muttered impatiently under his breath, and then the kayak began to glide swiftly to the nearest shore. Moments later he'd beached it and climbed out, undoing Rosie's lap covering and taking her by the shoulders, helping her to stand.

"Better?" he asked, taking the bandanna from her and awkwardly wiping her cheeks.

She swallowed, but the lump in her throat was still there. "Oh, Mitch," she said, leaning against him, feeling his arms go around her. "You probably won't believe this, but this is the best day I've had in a very long time. And it's all because of you."

"Hey," he said hastily, "you were the one who forced me to go kayaking."

"But you're the reason I'm here in the first place." She bit her lip to keep from confessing everything to him, about losing her job after working so hard, but it all seemed so overwhelming. She didn't know what had brought on the tears. It was the contrast, she supposed, between the glistening perfection of the day and the shabby mess her life had become.

Poor Mitch. She wanted to explain, but she couldn't really explain it to herself. She wasn't even certain she wanted to. So she simply settled against the remarkably comforting wall of his chest and let go.

Seven

The clink of glass and the liquid gurgle in the throat of a wine bottle were the only sounds in the dining room of Rainshadow Lodge that night. For the past three nights the local gourmet shop had provided the evening meal, a gangly teenager in an old station wagon delivering the meal neatly arranged in paper cartons. As he had the previous two nights, Mitch laid everything out on the charmingly mismatched antique dinnerware. Then he poured the wine, a vintage Burgundy he'd brought along from his private cellar in Seattle.

And then he waited. And waited.

His stomach growled. And his mind wandered. He couldn't stop thinking about Rosie. God, had he ever given in to his emotions so completely? If he had, he didn't remember. She'd simply collapsed against him as if the weight of the world pressed on her shoulders.

And finally, when she'd been able to get a grip, she'd confessed that the day with him had been the best she'd had in a long time.

It made him nervous as hell. Mitch had never been
anyone's best day before.

He wasn't comfortable with big sweeping displays of
emotion. After Rosie's declaration, he'd held her awkwardly for a while, then set her away from him. "I'm glad
you like your work," he'd said, wincing even now at how
lame that had sounded. "Look, it's been a long day. Why
don't we go back?"

She'd nodded and moved away from him. "All right. I'm
sorry. I didn't mean to lose it on you. I've been under a bit
of strain lately."

She'd been quiet on the way back, and he'd sensed that
same stillness in her, that absorption, as if she were no
mere observer of the world around her but right in the
middle of it. He'd wondered if she knew there was something special about that. Probably not. If it came easy, it
didn't seem special.

A quiet tread on the stairs alerted him. He set down the
wine bottle and watched her come into the dining room.
Freshly bathed, her hair in damp strands down her back,
she exuded a soft femininity that made him ache. Barefoot,
she wore the red dress and a tentative smile.

"Hi there," he said, holding out her chair. "You hungry?"

"Starved." As he scooted in her chair for her, he had
a swift powerful urge to move his hands to her shoulders, to skim them over her golden brown skin and feel
its warmth.

But he didn't. It had been powerful enough holding
her today, confusing enough. He was better off keeping
his distance.

He took a seat across from her and passed her the pasta salad. "Thanks," she said, sampling it. "This is really good."

"We're lucky to have a decent deli on the island. Here, try the rosemary chicken."

She took a bite, smiled appreciatively and said, "I take it you don't like to cook."

"I've been known to grill the occasional steak, but that's pretty much it. The local seafood restaurant is supposed to be good. We'll have to try it sometime."

"I'm a great cook," she said. "I'll fix dinner for you one night."

"Deal," he said, lifting his wineglass and tilting it toward her.

Just when he was starting to feel comfortable around her once again, she set down her fork, leaned across the table and said, "Mitch, about this afternoon—"

"Don't worry about it," he cut in.

The little gold cross spun on its chain as she leaned earnestly toward him. "I wasn't worried. I just wanted you to know that even though I get passionate about my job, I'm very professional. You have my word on that."

"Your professionalism has never been in question," he said, and that was true. She had startled him, yes. She wasn't what he'd expected. But all the work she'd done so far reassured him that she was a pro. He grinned. "Your passion is just sort of a bonus."

She leaned back and let out a sigh, as if she'd been holding her breath. The cross settled in the shadow of her cleavage. It was driving him crazy.

"I'm glad you feel that way. I was afraid you'd think I was being overly dramatic."

"I can handle drama," he lied.

"Good. When you come from a family the size of mine, you learn how to grab center stage pretty quickly. Otherwise you're in danger of disappearing."

He looked across the table at her, taking in her voluptuous figure, vivid coloring and gorgeous smile. "I doubt you'll ever go unnoticed, Rosie."

They ate in companionable silence for a while. Then, over sips of wine, they discussed the agenda for the following day. "I think we should go snorkeling," Rosie said.

"What will we be looking for?"

"We'll know when we find it."

Mitch hadn't been snorkeling since he was a kid and his folks had packed him off to summer camp in Kauai. The water was cold up here, but then he remembered watching her swim today. "Okay," he said. "How about dinner out tomorrow night?"

Her trademark smile flashed, then disappeared like heat lightning. "Um, maybe not. I didn't bring much with me. I don't think I have anything to wear."

"That dress is fine."

"A man would say so. But it's not a going-out-to-dinner dress."

"You can get something in town. There's a couple of shops and boutiques."

For most women he knew, the idea of shopping perked them right up. Rosie kept her gaze fixed down on her plate. "I'm not really into shopping." She pushed her wine-glass away.

Mitch had a bad feeling about the moment. Damn it. This was why he didn't complicate his life with relationships. It was like walking on thin ice. You never knew when you were going to fall in a hole.

"Rosie, what is it? Really."

She drummed her fingers on the table. Still, she evaded his eyes. "I'm having a bit of a cash-flow problem."

Ah. At last something Mitch could comprehend. He had never experienced it firsthand, but when it came to dealing with money, he was in his element. "How much of a problem?" he asked.

"The advance on my contract went to paying off my credit cards. The bank hasn't called yet to say I'm overdrawn, but I think I'm getting close."

"Can't you tell based on your last statement?"

She burst out laughing. "That's a good one."

"Did I say something funny?"

Relaxing back against her chair, she sipped her wine. "I know you're not going to like this, but I don't balance my checkbook."

She said it in a rush and then held up her napkin like a shield. At first Mitch thought she was kidding, but she wasn't, not in the least.

"You don't balance your checkbook."

"Nope. Sorry."

"Don't apologize to me. It's your life. But damn, Rosie. Don't you feel a little irresponsible?"

"Sometimes I do. But I always make excuses when the

time comes to deal with finances. I keep telling myself one day I'll get on track, but I never do."

"I can help," he heard himself say. He wanted to kick himself the moment the words were out, but the look on her face made the pledge worthwhile.

"Really, Mitch? I mean, it's asking a lot…"

"Don't worry. After dinner, you go get your checkbook and whatever statements you have. We'll drink some port and get it all sorted out."

"You might need something stronger when you see the state of my banking."

He laughed. "How bad can it be?"

"You have nine cents in this account," Mitch said an hour later.

Rosie folded her hands carefully on the top of the table. He shouldn't look sexy to her just now, but perversely he did. With his hair mussed from running his hand through it, horn-rimmed glasses perched just so and his sleeves rolled back to the elbows, he looked so sinfully attractive that she almost forgave him for figuring out she was only worth nine cents.

"You're sure of that," she said tentatively.

"I double- and triple-checked. Based on the statements you managed to find, and assuming you recorded all your transactions, I think it's a pretty reliable figure."

"Nine cents." She took a gulp of her port. After the wine was done, they'd switched to an interesting bottle of Whidbey Island Port. She wasn't sure she liked it yet, but it made the nine cents go down a little easier. "I suppose, based on my record keeping, that's about all I deserve," she said with a self-deprecating smile. She had endured hard times in the past many times, but she'd always landed on her feet. Why did this time scare her? Was it because, pushing thirty, she really was a grown-up now? Was it because she had depended too much on luck in the past and now it seemed to be running out?

He rifled through the stack of old mail she'd brought down with the bank statements. She'd shoved it all in a box when she'd moved. "So what about your other bank accounts? Are they in this shape, too?"

Rosie couldn't help herself. She laughed again. "Are you ready for a shock?"

He took off his glasses and pinched the bridge of his nose. "Shoot."

"I don't have any other bank accounts. That's it."

He idly tapped the buttons of his calculator. "Very funny, Professor."

"I'm not kidding, Mitch."

Very slowly he put the glasses back on. A single curl of hair hung down over the middle of his brow, making her think of the Beach Boys songs the Anglos used to listen to on their car radios when she was small.

"Are you saying this is the only money you have in the world?" He started toying with a pencil, rolling it between his palms.

"Practically. I have a pension fund started with UW, but since I only taught there two years, it doesn't amount to much. And I can't touch it until I'm retired. Or if I do, I have to pay it all back if I ever try to get a teaching job again— Oh." She clapped her hand over her mouth.

Too late. The pencil in Mitch's hands snapped in two. "Wait a minute. Back up here. I thought you were a professor at UW."

"I was. That was no lie, Mitch."

"But you're not anymore?"

She wanted to look away from him, from those blue Anglo eyes, from that controlled cleanly chiseled face. But she made herself confront his question. She'd never enjoyed lying and was terrible at it. "I was downsized. I think that's what they called it. My department just didn't get the funding to keep untenured staff." She forced a smile. "So you see, spotting Miss Lovejoy's ad was a godsend. I had to give up my apartment, anyway."

He set down the broken pieces of the pencil. "I don't get it. You're saying you have nine cents in the bank, no job and no home."

"You've summed it up pretty well," she said, wondering if he was being knowingly cruel about this. "And don't forget the car."

"Oh, that's right. You've got a car that won't run." She thought she detected sarcasm embedded in his disbelief. Then he startled her by adding, "In spite of all that, you're just about the happiest most well-adjusted person I've ever met."

"Except for the financial part."

"Yeah, except that. I don't get it, Rosie. Why aren't you in panic mode?"

She propped her elbows on the table and cradled her chin thoughtfully. "Would panicking change my situation any?"

"No, but—"

"Then why should I panic?"

He stared at her for a long moment. She felt like an exotic animal in a zoo, something he'd never seen before. He didn't quite know what to make of her.

"I just think panic would be in order in your situation. Or at least a certain level of stress."

"Something will work out for me, you'll see."

"How can you be so relaxed about all this?" He swept the papers and checkbook register into a pile.

"Mitch, look. I grew up the daughter of apple farmers. I have five brothers and sisters. You think I didn't go through lean years when I was growing up? Blight, fungus, fire—they all happened. Some years were *too* good, and we produced so many apples their market value sank. So I guess I learned right from the cradle that it does no good to panic about money. I'm thankful for my health, my education, my family, my dogs." She sent an affectionate smile at the two Chihuahuas curled on the afghan she'd spread on the parlor couch.

"But suppose the day comes when you can't afford dog food?" he demanded. "I know they don't eat much, but they have to eat something."

"What do you suggest I do?" she shot back. "Ask you for a raise?"

"You might start by deciding to care a little bit about money."

"Oh, right. So I can be as happy and well-adjusted as you, Mitch Rutherford?"

"What the hell's that supposed to mean?"

Agitated, she got up from the table and paced, arms folded beneath her breasts. "You have all the money in the world," she said. "If you keep going at this rate, you'll have all the money in the next world, as well. You can buy anything you want. Go anywhere, do anything. And what do you do? You work. And when you're through doing that, you work some more. It's all you do, Mitch. Is that any way to live your life?"

His face darkened a shade, but he didn't move. "I'm building things. Employing people. I wouldn't exactly say I'm wasting my life."

"Not in that way, no," she admitted. She knew she should stop, but it was too late. Her mouth had gone on way ahead of her common sense. "But there's something else people need, Mitch. An *inner* life." She stopped pacing and stood in front of him, studying him. Something about him broke her heart. He was as mesmerizing as the sun. As strong as a tree. Yet there, in the very center of him, she sensed something tender and vulnerable. Something she wanted to cherish.

Not him, reason told her. Don't fall for him. He's all wrong.

"I look at you, Mitch," she said, "and I see someone who's empty. Missing something, I guess."

"Then your eyesight isn't so good, because I'm doing just fine."

"Are you? I don't mean to insult you, but to tell you that you shouldn't keep everything all on the surface."

"And how do you know I do that?"

"I just…know. I see how smart you are about money and business. How organized, how efficient. But when you look back on the day you had today, what was the most important moment?" She held up her hand to keep him from speaking. "Don't think about your answer. Just tell me what the most important moment was."

"Holding you in my arms," he blurted.

Eight

Mitch couldn't believe he'd just admitted it.

Neither, apparently, could Rosie. Her cheeks flamed in the prettiest blush he'd ever seen. "That wasn't the answer I expected."

He moved quickly to cover his gaffe. "You have to admit," he said with a laugh, "you're a lot less scary than a killer whale."

"That's a relief," she said. "It's something I worry about."

"Finally you admit to worrying."

She folded her hands, twisting her fingers together. "Mitch, I'm sorry about what I said earlier. I was way out of line. It's not my place to criticize the choices you've made. Bad habit of mine, and for all I know, I was totally wrong." She hesitated, took a seat again at the long split maple table. "So was I?"

"Were you what?"

"Wrong about you. For all I know, you have a house with a white picket fence and you're a deacon in church and do volunteer work every week."

"What if I said all that's true?"

She smiled wickedly. He was getting to enjoy her smile way too much. "Is it?"

"No."

"I didn't think so."

"And you think this is something I should want?"

"Maybe not specifically. But a person needs connections other than business connections, Mitch."

"What for?"

"Because without them, you're...no different from that laptop computer." She gestured at the slim Thinkpad on the table.

"My computer's very happy."

"Mitch..."

"Okay, I know what you mean. But I didn't hire you to psychoanalyze me. You're supposed to be doing environmental studies."

"Well, I came here to do that." She gestured at the stack of envelopes and papers. "Instead, I'm getting a financial makeover I didn't ask for."

"So that makes us even. We've both butted in where we don't belong." He took out a fresh pencil. "Do me a favor, Rosie. Let me show you some ways to keep track of your money. It's pretty simple, and you'll feel better about everything."

She eyed him skeptically. "Is that a guarantee, Mr. Rutherford?"

"It is, Dr. Galvez."

"Fine. On one condition."

He nodded, absurdly grateful that she'd let him duck away from his comment about holding her in his arms. "Name it."

"You have to let me teach you something *I'm* good at."

"Yeah? And what's that?"

"I'm not going to tell you. You'll just have to trust me." She tucked her knees under her and planted her elbows on the table, leaning toward him. "Now, Mr. Wizard, show me how I can get my finances in order."

For the next two hours, he went through her statements and registers line by line. He discovered that an entry-level college professor made amazingly little money, and if that money was mismanaged the slightest bit, it amounted to next to nothing. He also discovered that she was basically a happy person in spite of all this. That amazed him even more. If his finances looked like hers, he'd be slitting his wrists the long way.

"What's this notation here?" he asked, pointing the register toward her.

"Oh. That's a loan to my oldest nephew. The little squiggle in the margin means I forgave the loan."

"You have a lot of squiggles," he observed.

"I have a big family."

"But they're not all your responsibility."

She blew out her breath. "We take care of each other." Pointing at a line in the register, she said, "That was a loan to buy some landscaping equipment. Eddie started his own business last year. When I need help, he'll be there for me."

Mitch wondered what that was like, knowing there was a family out there to catch you when you fell. "Will he be around after this month is up?" he asked pointedly.

She pursed her lips. "If I need him to be. But I won't."

He waved the balance sheet in front of her. "Nine cents, Rosie."

"Nine cents, plus the exorbitant amount of my contract with you."

"Is it exorbitant? Miss Lovejoy never told me it was exorbitant."

She fished around in the box for a while, then pulled out the document. Mitch scanned the pages, recognizing Miss Lovejoy's fine hand—and her meddling nature—in the short contract. He wouldn't have called the settlement exorbitant, but now that he'd had a glimpse into Rosie's salary history, he could see how she might think so.

"Well?" she asked.

"It's fine. I told Miss Lovejoy to hire the best, no matter what the cost. I want this project to go right."

She sent him a melting look. "Oh, Mitch. Thank you."

As compliments went, he thought he was being pretty oblique, but she'd picked up on it.

He flipped through the revised checkbook register. A folded bit of paper drifted out, and he opened it. "You know," he said, filled with exasperation, "one of the first principles of personal finance is depositing paychecks in a timely manner."

She snatched it from him. "My June check! I was looking all over for that." Her face lit up. "I'm not so broke, after all."

He took out a fresh piece of paper. "So here's what you do." He spent the next hour outlining a plan for her. It wouldn't make her rich, but if she stuck to it, she'd get by.

She listened with the sincere absorption of a natural student, and her attention gratified him in a way that felt strange…but good.

"You're right," she said at last, looking at the financial plan on paper. "I didn't want you to be right, but you are." She shivered, though she was still smiling. "It's a little scary, knowing I'm going to have to be financially responsible and stay that way."

"I can think of worse dilemmas," Mitch said.

"Money won't make me happy," she said urgently, intensely. "I found that out a long time ago."

"Aha," he said. "So now the truth comes out. Let's see, you were traumatized at a young age by vast sums of cash. Did a rich person drop you on your head when you were a baby?"

"Very funny." Her dark eyes, with fire in their depths, failed to hide the hurt.

Contrite, Mitch covered her hand with his. It felt odd, all this touching, this human connection. "Sorry. All kidding aside, Rosie, you really have a problem with this. I wonder why. I want to know."

She stared down at their linked hands, studying them. "I fall in love too easily. And I fall too hard."

Skepticism must have flickered across his face, because she added quickly, "It's true. Three times in the last six years. Does that make me a slut?"

"Of course not. You said it was love. But I don't see how this ties in with your attitude toward finance."

"Each time I thought the guy was the man of my dreams. The prince on the white horse. The happily-ever-after."

Her words touched him in a soft place he didn't know was in him. At the same time he felt an insane stab of envy. He knew it was impossible, but *he* wanted to be her happily-ever-after.

"And I guess," he said, "each time it didn't work out."

"That's right." She took her hand away from his, rubbing her temples as if a headache had come on. "Each time, it was because money became more important than our relationship. With Rudy, it was a job promotion he couldn't pass up, and he dumped me because I wouldn't drop everything and move to Fargo with him. Rafael worked sixteen hours a day, sometimes more, and he refused to slow down even when I begged him. And Ron— God, I loved that man—"

"Just tell me how it ended." Mitch wasn't interested in details about these losers.

"Um, well, you remember that big bank withdrawal you spotted on the statement from last year?"

"The one that made the next eight checks bounce? Yeah."

"Ron's parting gift to me."

"He cleaned you out?"

"Uh-huh."

"He must've been a real prince."

"I'm beginning to think I'm a real chump." She started rifling through another box. "Anyway, the best times of my life always happen when I'm broke."

Like now? he wanted to ask. He really wanted to ask.

Instead, he said, "I think you're looking at it all wrong. You claim money can't buy you happiness. That should also mean money can't make you sad."

"It means I should steer clear of men who are caught up in finance." She took a CD out of the box. "Okay. My turn to return the favor."

"What favor?"

"Straightening out my finances." She walked over to the stereo, flipped on the power and fed in the disk.

"And what are you going to straighten out?" he asked, filled with suspicion.

"Your priorities." Rosie rolled up the area rug in the middle of the parlor. She turned to him with a huge smile and held out her hands to him.

He scowled. "Meaning?"

At that moment the CD kicked in. Salsa music wailed out.

"The Macarena!" Rosie yelled over the lead-heavy beat.

He made a sign against evil. A nervous laugh escaped him. "Oh, no, you don't. I don't dance. I never dance."

"Coward." Hips swaying to the relentless tempo, she moved slowly, deliberately, across the room toward him.

"It's easy," she said coaxingly. "Anyone can do it."

"Sorry, Professor." He acted nonchalant even though he was on fire inside. "Just not my cup of tequila." But he couldn't take his eyes off her. She was mesmerizing, a vision in scarlet, a flame from the heart of a fire—beautiful, hypnotic, shimmering. And, God, burning hot.

She moved in front of him, nearly touching him. Her warmth became his warmth. He could feel the rhythm; it seemed to emanate from her, not the speakers. Her hips rolled, her breasts shimmered, and her bare feet on the wood floor made him want to howl at the moon.

"Get up, Mitch," she said with laughter in her voice.

He wondered if the double entendre was intended or if his condition was that obvious.

She captured both his hands in hers. "Hey, Macarena," she sang with the music. Then she gave a tug. "Come on. I didn't want to work on my bank account, but I did it to humor you. And guess what? I actually learned something." She bent forward, her incredible bosom hovering just inches from his face. "So humor me. *You* just might learn something, too." She gave one more tug on his arms. Like a snake charmed out of a basket, he stood and moved forward, pulled along by her. And every moment, she was dancing, moving to the belly thud of the beat, shimmying to the sinuous blare of the brass.

She led him to the middle of the parlor floor. "Okay. Ready?" She seemed blithely unaware of her effect on him.

"Ready as I'll ever be," he said.

"Top of the beat. Just do exactly what I do." The rapid-fire vocals filled the house with Spanish. Half closing her eyes, Rosie put one hand, then the other, to her hips.

Mitch tried to mimic her.

"Good," she said, "but don't just stand there like an outrigger. Feel the beat." She reached over and turned up the bass. "Feel it?"

"I guess."

"Okay, new move." Her body swayed. She touched first one shoulder, then the other, hugging herself. The pose deepened her cleavage, and Mitch couldn't take his eyes off her as he fumbled through the move.

She showed him the next sequence, and he knew he was

in the presence of a master. When it came to the Macarena, this woman was without peer. A wet dream come true. And Mitch was as stiff and awkward as GI Joe.

"You're like Al Gore at a head-bangers' ball. Loosen up!" After she led him through footwork and hand movements he knew he'd never remember, she gave him a smile filled with tolerant sympathy. And good-natured condescension.

"So how does it feel, Mr. Wizard?" she asked.

Like I need a cold shower. "How does what feel?"

"Being pushed out of your comfort zone. Being pushed somewhere you don't want to go?"

"I'm just so bad at this," he said. "And I don't see the point."

"Aha. I rest my case." She gave him a smile filled with secret knowledge.

And then he got it. She'd felt exactly this way when he was teaching her about banking.

"You're just not feeling the beat," she said. Then inspiration gleamed in her eyes. "You're too disconnected, Mitch. Take off your shoes."

He knew it was useless to protest, so he slipped off the Gucci loafers and kicked them aside. The floor vibrated under his soles, moving up through him. He felt easier, looser. Maybe there was something to this. He tried the footwork again.

"You've got it!" Rosie exclaimed, her face shining with delight. "I knew you could do it."

No wonder you fall in love so easily, Rosie.

"All right, now the hands." She called out the movements and demonstrated. "Hips, hips, shoulder, shoulder…"

He blew it then, just couldn't get the hand movements to coordinate with the beat. "Rosie—"

"Don't give up!" she cried. "You've almost got it. Here." She moved in front of him, her back against his chest. The sensation of her next to him, the lavish perfume of her skin and the smoothness of her shoulders filled him, overpowered him. She took his hands. "Keep your feet moving. See? It's good. You're feeling it."

"I'm feeling something," he said through gritted teeth, but she didn't seem to hear.

"Ready," she said, gripping his hands. "We'll go through the sequence together. Hips, hips…"

It was so damned easy, with her placing his hands in all the right places. So easy that he put back his head and laughed. So easy that even when she took away her hands and moved away, he was still dancing.

Jesus. *Dancing.* Who could've known it would feel so damned good?

"Look at you," she crowed, dancing along with him. "You're wonderful! Hey, Macarena!"

"Hey, Macarena," he sang, slightly off-key but not caring a bit. Dancing in the middle of the room to the incessant salsa beat shouldn't give him such an absurd sense of accomplishment, but it did. Damn, it did.

"You're hot, *jefe,*" she said with a merry laugh, and spun around.

"I'm not sure I'm ready for the fancy moves." He caught her as she spun back to face him. His unexpected touch made her catch her breath, and he liked that. He, who preferred predictability in all things, liked catching her by surprise.

And God, he liked touching her. She was so damned soft and giving.

When the shoulders-and-hips sequence started up again, he turned the tables, putting the moves on her this time.

She watched him incredulously but went along with him, her lush body swaying even as she surrendered the lead to him.

Surrender. Damn, he wanted her to.

When he heard the song winding down to its finish, he kept hold of her, backing her up against a bookcase, his hands still obeying the fading lyrics—shoulders, shoulders, hips, hips...

And by the time the raucous dance ended and the next song had not yet begun, they were still touching, crushed together, breathing hard in the silent space between numbers. Mitch felt a trickle of sweat inch down his back, and he noticed her face was flushed and moist from exertion, her full lips so damned close he could almost taste the berry sweetness of them.

The next song on the album was a love ballad in Spanish. The yearning notes spun out and played along Mitch's nerves, tingling and taunting until he leaned closer to her ripe mouth and caught her scent of bubble bath and shampoo. He was close, almost there, almost tasting, and—

"Hey, Mitch," she said with a bright laugh. "I think you've finally figured it out."

Before he could stop her, she ducked under his arm and hurried over to the stereo, quickly turning it off.

He turned to her, frustrated by her quick nervous rebuff even as he understood why and knew it was the right thing to do.

He echoed a phrase from the song. "What does that mean?"

She backed up even farther. "I will worship your body in the fond light of dawn," she translated. "It's a big hit in Mexico."

His gaze roved over her, over that incredible body that had just been so close to his.

"I can see why."

"Yes. Well, thanks for helping out with my financial records, Mitch. It's getting late." She hurriedly popped out the CD and put all her stuff in the boxes.

He watched her go up the steps, unapologetic as his gaze clung to the hem of her short red dress where it brushed the backs of her thighs.

"Good night, Rosie," he said.

Nine

Rosie looked out the window the next morning and experienced a sinking sensation in the pit of her stomach. Rain. Long cold sheets of rain.

She'd been counting on getting away from the house today, far away. From Mitch Rutherford. After last night, she needed space, far from him. Time to think.

Not that it took a rocket scientist to figure out what was happening. She was falling for him. She, who had declared herself free of men, bachelorette number one, was doing it all over again. Falling for the wrong man.

She rifled through her small supply of clothes and found an appropriately frumpy set of sweats. Standard-issue gray, with the nauseating purple-and-gold UW husky logo. Perfect for the suddenly nasty weather. She brushed her hair into a ponytail, put on a pair of sneakers and went downstairs, determined to be strong when it came to Mitch Rutherford.

So what if he knew how to hold her when she cried? So what if he didn't mind if she laughed at him? So what if he was the most adorably klutzy man she'd ever danced with? So what if the mere thought of his mouth on hers made her IQ drop fifty points?

She was going to be his associate, not his girlfriend. His employee, not his lover. They both knew that was best.

In the library she discovered that he'd made two lattes and a fire in the huge central grate.

All the resolutions she'd made up in her room started to melt like hot fudge. "This is so cozy," she said, hoping her vaporizing resolution wasn't obvious. "Perfect for the weather today."

"That's what I thought. So much for snorkeling." He sat at the table, his horn-rimmed glasses on the bridge of his nose and the *Wall Street Journal* spread out in front of him. "Sleep well?" he asked as she slid into the chair across from him.

"Fine," she lied. Truthfully she'd lain awake for hours reliving the moment when the love song had started to play. "Hey, isn't today the day you were supposed to meet with the bulkhead contractor?"

"Yep."

"Well?"

Mitch glanced up. "Island time," he explained.

"He's not coming?"

"No. He called from Eastsound this morning and said the weather's too squally to risk coming over."

She sipped her latte. It was perfect—the foam consistent, the coffee warm and nutty. "I think you're getting used to this," she said.

"I can't beat them. I don't have much choice but to join them."

She was almost convinced until he picked up the newspaper and she saw three broken pencils on the table in front of him. "Oh, Mitch. I'm sorry. This must be such a headache for you."

"I'll live, Dr. Galvez."

She smiled and helped herself to a banana and yogurt for breakfast. Her misgivings about the marina nudged at her. "I suppose I could go over the surveys one more time."

"What else is there to do?" he asked.

She cradled her chin in her hand and looked at the book-lined walls of the massive library. The bay window with its leaded and beveled fancy panes framed a day that was growing gloomier by the moment. The dock wasn't even visible; the rain and the fog were that thick. The case clock struck nine, and the fire snapped in the grate.

"I know what I'd like to do."

"What's that?" he asked, toying with one of the broken pencil pieces.

"I'd like to explore this old house."

"What's that got to do with the project?"

"Not a thing, *jefe,*" she said, miffed. "Forget I mentioned it."

"Okay, okay, I'm sorry. Since the weather is going to keep us in today, you might as well take some time off. Spend it however you like."

"Thank you. I think I will," she said, walking toward the kitchen.

"So what are you going to explore? It's been a summer place for years. I doubt you'll find anything of value."

"That depends on how you define valuable." She took

her cup to the sink and threw away the banana peel. "Didn't I see a flashlight somewhere?"

"Under the sink," he said. "Take your pick."

She selected a large one. "So what are you going to do?"

He tapped the cover of his computer. "It's the information age. I can stay busy all day."

She sent him a wry smile. "Congratulations." Switching on the flashlight, she went down a narrow hallway and headed for the stairs. As she opened the door that led down to the dark pit of the basement, she let out a sigh of relief. Breakfast had gone well. Exceedingly well. They had both been perfectly cordial, emotionally neutral. Exactly as they should be.

Despite the recent renovations to the house, the owners had not gotten around to the basement yet. She trod carefully on the steps, wincing as they creaked and ducking her head well away from the cobwebs that draped the passageway. The dank smell of old concrete permeated the air. The basement consisted of four rooms divided by stout timbers. The first room was empty save for an abundance of spiders. Shuddering, she backed out and peeked into the next, finding a jumble of ancient yard furniture. The third room contained tools even older than the lawn chairs. The last room was empty. But just as she was backing out, the flashlight beam touched off a dull glitter low in the far corner.

Curious, she crept forward. She had no idea why she was being quiet, but it seemed the thing to do. She found an old wine rack, hung with cobwebs. A half-dozen bottles lay on their sides. Gingerly, with her thumb and forefinger, she pulled one out and held it to the flashlight beam. To her dismay, she saw that the liquid had separated into something that resembled water and sludge. All but one of the other bottles was in the same condition. She took the one that seemed promising upstairs with her.

Mitch sat frowning at the screen of his computer. He glanced up when she emerged. "Find anything interesting?" he asked.

"Maybe." She grabbed a paper towel and dusted off the old bottle. "What do you suppose this is?"

He got up and looked over her shoulder. "It's hand-labeled. Bootleg reserve from the twenties. I'll bet it was produced illegally during prohibition."

"I wonder if it's still good."

"We'll find out tonight."

"You mean you want to drink it?"

He shrugged. "Why not?"

"It's not ours."

"Finders keepers, isn't that what they say?"

"It's probably gone bad."

"If it's bad, we'll have a great big salad tonight."

She laughed. "Whatever you say." She flicked off the flashlight. "There was nothing else down there. Hardly anything. I thought I'd check the attic."

"Be my guest. I found a hurricane lantern. It gives off better light than the flashlight." He struck a match and lit it for her, creating a soft golden flame.

"Thanks, Mitch."

He sat back down at the table and she left the kitchen.

This was getting easier and easier, she realized. They'd both gone a little crazy last night, probably because she'd stupidly broken down and cried in his arms and then she'd been euphoric because he'd saved her from financial disaster. Today everything was evened out, flat as the foggy light outside the window.

She put a small stepladder under the opening in the third-story hall ceiling. She pulled the rope, and a ladder unfolded from the hatch covering in the ceiling. Climbing into the attic, she surveyed her surroundings. Each gable end of the roof had a fan-shaped window. Gray daylight slanted down over the cobwebby interior. In the center of the attic rose the chimney, made of fieldstone. Thanks to Mitch's fire, the chimney gave off a kindly warmth that mingled with the glow from the lamp and created a cozy atmosphere.

The contents of the attic were much more interesting than those in the basement. She felt as if she were in an antique shop or a jumble sale. Ancient furniture, wicker baskets, intriguing round paperboard boxes and old toys lay in heaps everywhere. In a stack of musty books from the twenties, she recognized only one title, *The Sheik*. She picked over the stuff, trying to imagine where it had come from, who had used it. What shy young couple had made the four-poster their marriage bed? Who had rocked her baby to sleep in the old chair? Who had pinned up the fading Notre Dame pennant? What child had spun the rusty metal top? Had some woman read *The Sheik* and fantasized about an exotic lover?

Hours passed as she happily explored, letting the old mementos sweep her away to another place and time. Her two favorite discoveries were an ancient steamer trunk with creaking hinges and a big Victrola phonograph with a stash of 78s in the storage compartment under it. She blew the dust off the disks, reading the song titles. "Stars in My Eyes." "Picture Me Now." "Harvest Moon Waltz." They all sounded funny and quaint to her. She picked out "Dancing in My Dreams" and cleaned it off on the knee of her sweatpants, then set it on the turntable. She cranked the side handle and put the needle down on the spinning disk. To her delight, the trumpet-shaped horn crackled, then let forth a corny but oddly charming song. "I see you dancing in my dreams…."

While it played, she pried open the steamer trunk and picked over the contents. A brittle fan with yellowed ivory ribs. A pair of lacy gloves. A slip or camisole. A hilarious-looking striped tank top and shorts that had probably been worn as a bathing suit. Hats, shoes—everything a lady from a bygone era might need for a summer at the seaside. When Rosie found the gold silk dress, she couldn't resist. She had to try it on.

Quickly stripping off her sweats, she donned the camisole first, feeling the warm whisper of old chambray against her skin. The sensation was sweetly sensual in a way she couldn't explain. Then, careful not to strain any of the seams, she put on the old silk dress. It fit well enough for her to feel it smooth against her sides. Rows of tiny amber beads ornamented the bodice. The drop waist gave the skirt a natural swing that pleased her.

Feeling like a little girl playing dress-up, Rosie quit pretending any sort of scholarly interest and dived in. She discarded the tie holding her ponytail and donned a fabulous hat with a spray of yellow feathers across the brow, the lace-up boots, the dainty gloves. Holding out a pockmarked shaving mirror, she inspected her image. She didn't look anything like herself, but resembled a girl from another time, bathed in yellow from the lamplight, clad in delicate moth-light silk and lace, a shimmer of beads to catch the light, the brim of her hat framing her face.

She gave the Victrola another turn and started the song again. Closing her eyes, she swayed to the music. Her imagination ran wild, and she thought of the way Mitch had danced with her last night, the way he'd almost kissed her. She imagined a time and place where she would have been free to let him, where she wouldn't have been afraid of the consequences. After a few minutes she just thought of Mitch and pretended he was her partner. She heard the sweetness of the song through the roughness the years had scratched into the record. She heard the rain drumming on the roof, heard the hiss of the wind under the eaves.

And then she heard Mitch Rutherford's voice. "Who are you dancing for, Rosie? You look like you're a million miles away."

"Oh!" Her eyes flew open and she froze. "Darn." Feeling her cheeks flame, she blushed to the roots of her hair. "I guess I must look pretty silly to you."

He crossed the room, stepping into the golden radiance of the hurricane lamp and looking amused and sympathetic all at once. "Maybe you just look pretty."

She blinked in surprise, then blushed even deeper at his compliment. "I thought all these things were so charming, I couldn't help trying—"

"Rosie." With incredible gentleness, his fingers came up and touched her lips, stunning her into silence. The song on the Victrola came to an end, and the needle bumped against the label. "You don't have to explain." Then his touch left her mouth and his hand traveled down her arm, tracing its inner length, fingers coming to rest at the pulse of her wrist. A pulse that had begun to race.

"I don't?" she whispered, nervously reaching back to lift the needle from the record.

"No." He chuckled, the sound silky in the new silence. "After the Macarena last night, nothing could seem silly to me."

"Oh." She gave a small nervous laugh. Yes, she was nervous, because as he stood there looking as relaxed and neatly groomed as a golf-resort poster, she wanted him with a fervor that bordered on madness. "I guess I'm the cause of that."

"Uh-huh." He took a step closer, and she could feel the brush of warmth from him, and the tips of her breasts began to tingle. She remembered that she wasn't wearing anything under the dress and camisole. "So what else did you find?" He picked up the stack of old 78s and flipped through them. "Let's try this one."

She swallowed. "Are you sure?"

"Sure of what?"

"Sure you want to take time out of your schedule to listen to old records?"

"Tsk, tsk, Rosie. You told me I was being a dull boy. I'm trying to loosen up."

As he turned and cranked the Victrola, she watched the

sinuous fluid motion of his arm and whispered, "It's working."

"What?"

"Um, nothing."

The music turned out to be a waltz. Mitch turned to her, holding out both hands. "Shall we?"

"I don't know how to waltz."

"Neither do I, so we're even."

She laughed, suddenly getting past the nervousness and starting to enjoy herself. "Since we're pretending, let's pretend we know this dance."

He took her by the hand, and his other arm slid around behind her. They lurched along clumsily for a few steps. "You forgot to feel the rhythm," Rosie pointed out. "We can learn this if you'll just feel the rhythm. *One,* two, three, *one,* two, three..."

And within a few moments, it began to work. Perhaps it wasn't a perfect waltz—they wouldn't win any prizes— but they moved together in time with the music, which, after all, was the whole point. Round and round the attic they went, with the rain drumming down and the trumpet of the Victrola spilling out a song no one had heard in decades. For Rosie it was magical, like something out of a dream or a fairy tale.

By the time the record ended, Mitch had danced her into the far corner of the attic where shadows hung and the ancient bedstead stood. She felt one of the posts of the bed pressing into her back and suddenly it wasn't so much fun anymore. It was like last night, when desire had started raging through her and she'd felt herself falling, tumbling headlong in love with Mitch Rutherford. She told herself to duck beneath his arms, to make some excuse, but instead, she just stood and felt his hands slide up her arms to cup her shoulders, then slide down slowly, evocatively, massaging the back of her neck and then her shoulder blades and then lower.

"Why, Professor," he said in a voice that was rough with teasing and desire, "I believe you're naked under this dress."

"I believe," she whispered, falling and falling and now not caring, "you're absolutely right."

After the initial exchange, he was quite deliberate and matter-of-fact in his seduction. With focused and unhurried movements, he pulled out the hat pin and let the broad-brimmed hat drift to the floor. Next he took first one hand and then the other, removing each glove with almost clinical precision. Finally he cradled her face with his fingertips, lifting it up so that she looked him in the eye.

"I want you," he said, his tone neutral but his gaze intent.

"I know. I want you, too."

"That's what I hoped." His mouth quirked in the briefest of smiles, and then, still so slowly she nearly screamed, he bent and kissed her.

It was everything she had imagined his kiss would be. No, it was more than that. Her appetite whetted by days of unrequited attraction, she was so ready for this kiss that she moaned into his mouth and pressed forward, feeling the hardness of his chest even as she savored the softness of his mouth. She skimmed her hands over his arms and shoulders, then down his back. The fabric of his shirt was warm and taut over his muscular frame.

He ended the kiss when she wanted it to go on forever. He lifted his mouth from hers, and she made a small sound of protest, but he only laughed, so softly. It was the sexiest sound she'd ever heard. Then he amazed her by going down on one knee in front of her. Perhaps what amazed her most was the slowness of his movements. He was controlled, yet at the same time sexy and compelling. He took one of her shoes, cradling the heel in his hand while he unlaced it, then slid it off, setting her bare foot on the plank floor. He did the same for the other foot, but instead of setting it down, he held it in the palm of his hand and bent his head, kissing the sensitive bare inner arch.

Rosie steadied herself by holding the bedpost. Mitch's hand slid up her leg, smoothing along, up under the hem of her dress, higher and higher, and then his lips followed, tongue flicking, touching her ankle and calf, the back of her knee, and then when he straightened up, she nearly implored him not to stop.

Shouldn't they talk about this? she wondered wildly. Shouldn't they debate? Plan? Come to a conscious decision like the adults they were?

It didn't help matters that his hand was buried under the gossamer hem of the dress. It didn't help that suddenly her legs felt as if they were made of butter. When she sank helplessly back onto the bed, she clutched at him so hard that they both wound up reclining, speechless with wanting.

And she knew then, as his hand slipped down her back undoing the buttons one by one, that they *had* considered this. They *had* made this decision. They had decided to be lovers yesterday, though neither had acknowledged it.

They'd landed their kayak at a remote cove and she'd wept in his arms.

Later that night they'd underscored the decision by sharing. She had given him her finances—a gesture of deep trust by any definition—and he, who never danced, had danced with her.

And at the moment, any conversation or debate would be superfluous, so she didn't even try. She wound her arms around his neck, studied the dreamy glow of diffuse lamplight on his face, looked deep into his eyes and said, "Now."

He had an endearingly awkward moment of befuddlement, as if he'd been braced for rejection, but the hesitation ended quickly and he stood, drawing her to her feet and removing the dustcover from the bed to reveal yellowed linens and embroidered pillows redolent of ancient lavender sachets. He parted the shivery-light fabric of the dress, watching as it slipped down and pooled around her bare feet. He tugged at the ribbon of the camisole, inching it down her body.

The look on his face—his controlled, disciplined, businessman's face—told her everything she needed to know. The small nonverbal sound that came from somewhere in the depths of his throat paid her a higher compliment than any pretty flattery she'd heard too often from gaping undergrads.

He shed his clothes and took her in his arms, and she burned up with awareness of him. He had a body that was naturally athletic. She'd never been an admirer of the pumped-up look; it only meant a man spent too long sculpting his own body. A shallow pursuit and one practiced by too many of her students.

Mitch was simply a creature smiled upon by fortune—good bones and good genes. The passion that had been building in her for so many days made him look like a god to her.

They fell back on the bed again, and the old perfume of antique fabric and dried flowers surrounded them. She found it heady and erotic—the brush of old bed linen against her bare skin, the slow drag of his fingers down the length of her, then up again, circling and brushing over her breasts, then reaching around to skim her back, starting at the nape of her neck. He put his mouth to her ear and whispered a suggestion that made her dizzy, and he kissed her neck where his hand had been and then traveled lower, his moth-wing kisses, his feathering touch chilling her with an eroticism that took her breath away.

He was as inventive with his foreplay as he was conventional in the rest of his life. She felt stunned, and maybe even a smidgen betrayed, because nothing about him had prepared her for this. How could she have known he would turn out to be the Sheik in bed? The Sheik in pinstripes. But he was, in the way he touched and stroked and coaxed her, and she was possessed by the urge to explore him, to know him. She caressed and kissed him everywhere, filling her senses with him and feeling so warm and connected and aroused that her senses whirled in wonder.

The endless minutes spun out into honeyed strands of desire, and when finally they joined, she felt the silky-moist fit of their bodies, and everything came bubbling up to the surface, rising, roaring, and she clutched his shoulders and cried out his name and felt her own spasms trigger his. There was a moment, a breath, a heartbeat of complete and utter mutual shock, and then he poured into her, holding and cherishing her and then kissing her long and languidly while their bodies kissed, too, sweetly, but with an edge of pleasure so sharp it bordered on pain.

Rosie couldn't move, and with Mitch lying atop her, even breathing was an effort. This was usually the awkward moment, the oh-God-what-have-I-done moment, but the regrets didn't come. Instead, she savored the heavy warmth of his body collapsed on hers.

After a time he cradled her in his arms. She studied the antique pillows, perfumed and tied with ribbon, one of them embroidered with the woman's words to her bridegroom: *For you, for always.* The beautifully embroidered pillow, redolent of ancient roses and filled with the promise of a magnificent love, brought tears, foolish tears, to her eyes.

She blinked them away quickly, and at the same time Mitch braced himself on his arms to kiss her, long and deeply. It was that particular kiss that undid her, because it was so heartfelt and so unexpected.

When he moved away she saw him discard the condom and she was confused. She hadn't even remembered him pausing to take precautions. But she was grateful he had; it was typical of him to be discreet. Considerate. And always prepared.

He slipped on his boxers and twill slacks, then, with a gentle smile playing about his lips, he sat on the side of the bed. "You look incredibly beautiful," he said softly.

Suddenly too conscious of her nakedness, she pulled an

old quilt over her. The delicate fabric released a wafting of cedar and lavender.

"So," he continued, stroking his finger down a lock of her hair, "is this the start of the painfully awkward stage?"

"That was way too wonderful for me to have regrets so soon."

"My thoughts exactly, Professor."

Ten

Late that afternoon the rain stopped, leaving a clear wash of light and fresh shining green everywhere. Rosie, who had been reading *The Sheik* by the fire, looked out the window and smiled. "Sun's out again."

Mitch took a blueprint pencil from behind his ear. "I forgot to call the deli for dinner."

She set aside her book and stretched luxuriously. He couldn't take his eyes off her. All day she'd had a tousle-haired, full-lipped, well-loved air about her. She made it hard to concentrate, but somehow, he got a lot of work done. Amazing.

"We'll make dinner," she said. "Remember, we've got a great bottle of wine to drink with it."

"We don't even have anything to cook."

"So we'll go to town and get something."

"It's a long walk."

"No need to walk." She took his hand and led him to the old carriage house that served as a garage. "I found this while I was poking around."

It was a tandem bicycle, slightly rusted around the rims but otherwise in working condition. "I haven't ridden a bike in twenty years," Mitch confessed.

"I'm so surprised," she said wryly, wheeling the tandem out onto the gravel drive. "Get on. They say you never forget how."

She took the front position. "Ready?" she said over her shoulder.

"I suppose."

They took off, wobbling at first but then finding their rhythm and gliding out onto the smooth asphalt road. The deep old-growth forest gleamed with moisture, filling the air with the fecund aroma of evergreen. Sunlight, filtering down through the massive Sitka spruce and cedars, took on a misty greenish glow.

"It's beautiful," Rosie called over her shoulder. "Isn't it beautiful?"

He looked up from his contemplation of her derriere and studied the forest. She made him see the wild splendor as if for the first time. The glitter of raindrops on lush ferns. The rich red of madrona blossoms. The rise of a pheasant from a grassy field, and patches of sky through the forest canopy. She made him think about it. Cherish it.

"Yeah," he said at last, watching the way the wind lifted her hair. "Yeah, it is."

The sleepy island village consisted of a chandlery and delicatessen, a tourist shop and clothing boutique, and a small but well-supplied grocery and farmers' market. Rosie insisted on buying things he had never bought in his life— a bunch of cilantro, local prawns, a sack of masa harina, some homegrown tomatoes and onions, a lime, a pound of butter. She selected Rainier cherries for dessert and a stack of postcards to mail to her family.

An hour later she was in the kitchen, salsa music blaring, a bossy air surrounding her as she chopped and sautéed, making a huge mess and creating the most mouth-watering aromas. Mitch was relegated to chief gofer, setting the table and hanging around the stove. At eight o'clock she came into the dining room looking adorably disheveled and a little smug. "How about you open that wine, *jefe?*"

She laid the table with a stack of homemade tortillas, the grilled prawns and vegetables, and sour cream and salsa. Mitch opened the wine, a little concerned when the cork broke in two.

"The moment of truth," he said, pouring some into a glass. He took a sniff, then a sip. Surprised, he handed the glass to Rosie.

She tasted it, a ruby droplet adorning her lip. "It's delicious."

"That's what I thought." He filled his own glass and then his plate, his palate ecstatic over the spicy prawns and nutty-warm tortillas. "My teeth are singing."

"Oh, please. Now you're a poet."

"You're a woman of many talents, Dr. Galvez," he said, tilting his glass in her direction.

She laughed. "While everyone else was learning money management, I was learning to cook."

There was something simple and pleasant about sharing a meal they had shopped for and prepared together. They lingered at the table, savoring the food and the wine and each other's company. Even doing the dishes had a comfortable domestic feel to it, and when they were done, Rosie took the bowl of yellow blushing Rainiers from the refrigerator.

"Ready for dessert?" she asked.

She was doing it again, looking unbearably adorable.

"Yeah," he said. "I'm ready for something sweet."

"It's nice out tonight. We could have them on the front porch."

He took the bowl from her and pressed her up against the edge of the counter. "We could have them in bed," he said just before he kissed her.

"Your bed or mine?" she asked.

Rosie had never had such an interesting time with a bowl of cherries in her life.

Mitch conceded, in the days that followed, that Rosie had a lot to teach him. He'd never seen the point of lying in the grass and watching the clouds go by—until Rosie. He'd never flown a kite—until Rosie. He'd never watched a spider spin a web—until Rosie.

She showed him how to thaw out and enjoy the moment. She convinced him to walk barefoot on the beach, to listen to crickets at twilight, to take a nap in the hammock in the middle of the day. From Rosie he learned to roll a kayak and spot a school of fish, how to make tortillas and a chain of daisies.

Until Rosie, he hadn't known the meaning of free spirited.

She wasn't an employee, Mitch rationalized as he made love to her in the days that followed. He had always honored a personal policy of not getting involved with employees.

Rosie was someone with whom he'd contracted. For professional services.

He clung to that distinction because he wanted this affair with her, wanted it more than he could ever remember wanting anything.

After the day in the attic, an idyllic time began. They did their work, yes, but it was different. A magical glow seemed to gild each moment, and a sense of euphoria filled him when he was with Rosie.

He explained to her how he worked, and she showed him how to play. Seated at the scrubbed maple table, he helped her put her curriculum vitae on-line so she could start looking for another job. In turn, she took him swimming, fishing, cloud watching, beachcombing. They took long meandering cruises in the Bayliner and anchored in secluded coves where they could make love on the open deck.

He gave up trying to understand his need for her, his hunger. He'd always had a healthy libido, had always had an eye for a beautiful woman, but it was different with Rosie. She touched him on a level no one had ever reached before. She made him laugh. Made him angry sometimes. Filled him with passion—always. And he realized one day, when she came out of the bathhouse wearing a neon orange bikini and holding a box of snorkeling gear, that she was the first woman he'd ever met who had the power to break his heart.

* * *

The days all slid together into golden ribbons of sensual moments, aglow with the secret laughter only lovers share. The nights were woven of soft black velvet, when all the world seemed to sleep except two restless lovers, who stayed wakeful deep into the heart of the night.

They talked of everything: her unwieldy raucous family and the scarcity of sandhill cranes. His lonely childhood and her love of romance novels, his dislike of Barbra Streisand movies. Everything seemed important and relevant, everything from the proper amount of foam on a latte to the brand of the Chihuahuas' favorite dog biscuit.

In the middle of the third week on the island, as they sat together on the porch swing, the cellular phone rang. Mitch was startled by the sound; almost no one on the island returned calls. Leaving Rosie rocking dreamily on the swing, he answered the phone and was a little disconcerted when the caller asked to speak to Dr. Galvez.

Mitch brought the phone out to Rosie, then went inside to get some brandy for an after-dinner drink. As he heard the low murmur of her voice through the screen door, he frowned. He was starting to like this far too much— watching sunsets, sleeping late, hearing her voice as she sat on the front porch. The thought of Seattle—the bustling downtown that used to give him such a shot of energy— now seemed bleak and gray. He couldn't believe he'd spent so many years in a high-rise. If someone were to hold a gun to his head, he could not have said what color the walls of his condo were painted.

Strange. He could recite from memory the color of every room in this house, and he'd been here less than a month.

He poured the brandy and brought it out in two snifters. Rosie still sat on the porch swing, talking on the phone. She wore her red dress, and had one foot tucked up underneath her, the other trailing over the planks of the porch floor, causing the swing to rock.

"Thank you, Dr. Olsen," she was saying, a slightly thunderstruck expression on her face. "I'll have my decision for you by the end of the month." She listened a moment longer, then said goodbye and turned off the phone.

Mitch handed her the brandy. "News?"

She took a gulp, then another. "That was a job offer."

Something sank inside him. He had an instant flash of disappointment—she'd just received a dream job offer in the Florida Keys or off the Great Barrier Reef. He took a gulp of his own brandy.

"And?" he prompted.

She smiled broadly. "And you're a genius, Mr. Rutherford. Dr. Olsen saw my credentials on the Internet. He wants me to work for the Puget Sound Underwater Biosphere. Huge corporate funding. I'm dazzled."

He went down on one knee in front of the swing. "That's in Seattle, right?"

"Yes. Near Pier Seventy-one."

He set down his brandy glass and picked up her bare foot in both hands. Bending, he kissed her smooth tanned knee.

"So are you going to take it?" He pushed up the hem of her dress and nipped at her inner thigh.

She gasped. "It sounds like…a great position."

"Mmm." He pushed the hem higher. Since they'd become lovers, she'd developed the delightful habit of not wearing any underwear, and tonight was no exception. He teased and then tasted her, coaxing an involuntary cry from her, and he realized that he loved her like this, helpless and open to him while at the same time completely in command of him. The swing made for an unorthodox but fascinating position, one he found wildly exciting. When he could no longer wait, he reversed their positions, sitting on the swing and lifting her up to straddle him. He entered her recklessly, swiftly. She put back her head and he kissed her throat and the valley between her breasts, and the surge of movement created by the swing brought him to a swift searing climax.

She touched her damp forehead to his and then kissed him. She tasted of brandy and the faint salt of sweat, and he wanted to hold her like this forever, wanted to forget that their time here was coming to an end, that she had to find a job and he had to move on to other projects.

"So," she said with a shaky laugh, "do you want to hear more about this job offer or not?"

He stood, reaching around behind her to unzip her dress. "Later, okay?"

She sighed. Helpless. Spellbindingly sexy. "Later."

Mitch had never considered sleeping with someone a treat before. But with Rosie, it was a sweetness beyond description. He didn't even mind the Chihuahuas, who showed him scant respect, though they slept curled in balls at the foot of the bed. Rosie was the essence of comfort, soft and warm and sleep-tousled, sighing lightly as she fitted herself against him with a natural ease. When he held her in his arms, breathed in the scent of her and felt the cool whisper of the bedsheets swirl around him, his spirit seemed to uncoil, to relax. He'd never experienced that before—that utter calmness, that perfect contentment to be in the middle of the moment.

He kept telling himself not to get used to this, not to expect this, not to want this to last forever, but his soul wouldn't listen.

Neither mentioned the fact that it was their last week at the summer place, but the reality bronzed every moment with the gleam of desperation. They made love more frequently than ever, sometimes not even getting through breakfast without tackling each other on the window seat or on the old-fashioned fainting couch in the parlor.

A hot afternoon might be interrupted with a languorous session in broad daylight when the warmth of the sun and the isolation of the place made them aroused and pleasantly drowsy afterward.

By the time their last day of fieldwork arrived, Mitch had come to a decision. He had only known Rosie Galvez for a month, but he knew her better than anyone else on the planet. And he knew he needed her in his life.

Since the phone call from the biosphere facility, she'd gotten two other interesting offers—one in Alaska and one in San Diego. Since Mitch got a sick feeling inside each time he imagined life without Rosie, he planned to ask her to accept the Seattle offer.

It was the only way he could stand to think of the future.

* * *

Rosie had long since stopped trying not to fall in love with Mitch. As she loaded the kayak with gear for the final study of the area, she hummed a tune and let herself savor the heady joy of losing her heart.

Yes, he was a no-nonsense businessman like the other men who'd disappointed her.

Yes, it would probably end once they returned to the real world. She'd fallen in love with the Mitch of Rainshadow Lodge, the Mitch who danced to old Victrola records and made love to her on the porch swing and let her dogs sleep on the bed with them.

The Seattle Mitch was bound to be a different creature altogether. He ran a multimillion-dollar enterprise and worked eighteen-hour days. His secretary kept up with his mother's birthday.

She resigned herself to letting this Mitch go, because being with him in Seattle would never work out. The San Diego job offer was too good to pass up, anyway.

But when Mitch came out of the house, tanned and smiling and ready to launch the kayak, she decided the news could wait. He looked different these past couple of weeks. He'd taken to wearing shorts, instead of creased slacks; T-shirts, instead of golf polos. He looked relaxed, happy.

The summer place had worked real magic on him.

"Where to, skipper?" he asked good-humoredly as they paddled out into the main channel.

"One last tour. Maybe the far side of the cove. Remember, it's the one we missed the day it rained."

He glanced over his shoulder, flashing her a grin that made her want to beach the kayak and attack him immediately.

"I remember that day," he said.

And as they paddled into the cove, she started thinking more about Seattle. Maybe, just maybe—

"Hey, Rosie. What do you think that is?"

Mitch pointed his paddle toward an outcropping of rock where the water was shallow, the tide pools crammed with starfish, mussels and urchins. A group of untidy nests made of plant fibers hid in the marsh reeds at the shore.

"Madre de Dios," she said under her breath. "I can't believe you found this."

"Found what? What'd I find?"

"It's the breeding place of the sandhill crane," she said. "Most biologists go their whole lives without seeing them in the wild."

"Cool. Are you going to take some pictures?"

She already had her camera out. "The world population of this animal is only 27,000," she said, fascinated. "This is their nesting ground."

"Damn, Rosie. Are we good or what?"

When they made love that night, Rosie was as ripe and eager as ever, yet she talked less.

"Are you thinking about tomorrow?" he asked, kissing her temple as she snuggled up against his shoulder.

"Yes."

"We knew the month had to end."

"Uh-huh."

"Rosie, I've been thinking…"

"Yes?"

"I want to ask you something."

She stiffened, stopped breathing. He couldn't see her face and suddenly wished he could. God, did she think he was about to propose marriage?

"It's about your job offers."

"What about them?"

"Have you decided yet?"

"I'm not sure."

And for some reason Mitch stopped there. He didn't want to push, to probe, to force something to happen that wasn't ready to happen. It just wasn't his way. And apparently it wasn't Rosie's way, either, for she sighed sweetly and drifted off to sleep without saying another word.

"We'd better hurry if we want to make the five-twenty-five ferry," Mitch said, loading the last of their bags onto the boat.

"I'm ready," Rosie said. She looked lovely and slightly nervous as she patted her thigh, motioning for the dogs to follow her down the dock.

"I hope I won't have any trouble hiring a mechanic to fix my car," she said.

"It's fixed. I had it done right after you got here."

She smiled, though melancholy tinged her smile. Once the dogs were aboard, she helped him cast off. Slowly the boat pulled away from the dock.

Rosie stood in the cockpit, facing back toward the house. Mitch put the engine on idle and went to her, arms circling her from behind, burying his face in her hair.

"Look at the house," she said. "Like something out of a storybook."

She was right; the old Victorian summer place gleamed on the green knoll, the white scrollwork porch railings brilliant in the afternoon sun.

"Rosie," he said, turning her in his arms, "something special happened there for us. Something I don't want to end."

"Mitch—"

"Wait, let me finish. I've been thinking about this a lot. I don't want to stop seeing you."

The edges of her smile trembled. "Do you know how badly I've been wanting to hear that?"

"Do you know how scared I've been to say it?"

She smiled and touched his cheek, then dropped her hand. "I have to finish that paperwork."

"I thought all the paperwork was done and we're clear to start the marina."

"Um…I have more work to do." She ducked her head quickly.

Mitch felt an odd twinge of foreboding. She was acting strange. As if she was hiding something. "Rosie?"

"We'd better get going." Her smile looked edgy. "You have to get to the ferry in time."

"Yeah. Ferries are the only thing that are on time around here." He grinned, mounting the ladder to the bridge. "I guess I don't mind so much. I could get used to island time."

She ducked into the salon without answering and picked up the thick file containing the study. Only after he pulled out into the channel did Mitch realize she hadn't given him an answer.

* * *

The ferry landing at Eastsound was a shock to the system. After a month in the heart of nowhere, Rosie was unprepared for the blare of horns and boom boxes, the reek of exhaust and baking pavement, the smells of fast food that greeted her as she parked the Volkswagen in the ferry line. She wished she could simply roll up the windows and disappear, but it wasn't possible. Mitch was waiting.

While she'd gone to get her car and park in line, he had gone over her final assessment. By now, he'd know the truth.

"Don't be a coward, Rosalinda," she said to herself, rolling down the car windows so the dogs wouldn't be too hot. "Go and face the music."

Mitch stood at the dock where his yellow-and-white seaplane was docked. The pilot waited in the cockpit, sipping a Mountain Dew and fiddling with his radio. When Mitch heard her coming, he looked up, and she could tell by the expression on his face that he'd finished reading the assessment.

"Nice of you to clue me in, Rosie," he said, his voice harsh with fury.

"Mitch—"

"I don't suppose you could have let me know sooner that you were going to recommend against building the marina."

"I didn't make up my mind for sure until yesterday."

"Oh, that's right. You work on island time. You do things when you feel like it."

She felt her cheeks redden. He had every right to be mad, but he was pushing her. "Mitch, in all honesty, I thought—right up until yesterday—that your plans to build probably wouldn't have a significant impact on the wildlife. But then, when we found the nesting grounds yesterday, I knew I couldn't risk it."

"Jesus, Rosie! If you ruin this project, you're gambling away the survival of the islanders. Jobs, tourist dollars—"

"If you destroy the wilderness, no one will want to go to the island, anyway."

"I don't want to destroy anything, damn it. I want to *build* something. You saw the plans. You know I'll be careful. We'll make every effort to minimize the impact on the environment. We'll make it work."

She forced herself to look at him, the man who owned her heart and her hopes, and felt both of them shatter. Determined not to cry, she swallowed hard and said, "Some things are just incompatible, Mitch. No matter how hard you try to make it work."

Then she turned and walked away, not looking back even though it took every ounce of strength she possessed.

Eleven

"It's not the end of the world, you know," Miss Lovejoy said, handing Mitch a stack of mail.

He looked up from his desk, blinking at the slanting light of the October sun. Sunshine was rare in October, but Indian summer had decided to visit Seattle. He had an urge to loosen his tie, unbutton the collar of his shirt, abandon work for the rest of the day.

"What's not the end of the world?" he asked distractedly, annoyed by his own thoughts. He wasn't the same person he'd been before going to Rainshadow Lodge. Instead of being focused on business, he experienced strange urges—like the desire to do something frivolous, to go out to lunch and never come back. Or visit the salmon ladder at the waterfront aquarium. Or go parasailing over Elliot Bay. Or get a Chihuahua puppy.

"This registered letter. I had to sign for it. It's postmarked Spruce Island."

He tried to pretend he was cool and calm as he picked it up. The return address indicated that the mail was from the group of investors who'd contracted for the marina. "Great," Mitch muttered. "They're probably suing me for failing to get clearance for the marina." He felt no particular alarm at the prospect. Lately, matters of business just didn't have the importance they used to. Rosie had stolen that from him—along with his heart.

He scanned the letter and his eyes widened. "I'll be damned."

"What? Good news?"

"They've dedicated their efforts to another project that's going to net them a lot more jobs than the marina."

"Really? What's that?"

"They're starting up kayak tours for whale watching, something they won't need a marina for." He turned over the glossy tri-fold brochure that accompanied the letter. The brochure featured gorgeous views of the island, including a shot of Rainshadow Lodge. Curiously, there was a small animal in the photo; it suspiciously resembled a Chihuahua. "That's funny," he said.

"What?"

"One of the photos just looked familiar for a minute." His gaze dropped to the credit line at the bottom of the brochure. *This project is funded in part by the Underwater Biosphere Foundation.*

"Are you feeling all right, Mr. Rutherford?" his secretary asked.

"Just a weird coincidence. The new enterprise is coming about thanks to an organization that offered to hire Dr. Galvez."

"That's no coincidence. She works for them." Miss Lovejoy sent him an innocent look. "Didn't you know?"

His throat went dry; he hurried to the watercooler to get a cup of water. "No. I didn't know. I thought she took the job in San Diego."

"You might want to thank her in person. If she hadn't proposed the whale-watching venture, they probably would have sued the pants off you." Miss Lovejoy checked her watch. "If you hurry, you can catch her on the four-forty ferry. She lives in a bungalow on Bainbridge Island now."

"How the hell do you know all this?"

"If I have to explain everything, you'll miss that ferry."

He was already halfway out the door. In the reception area, he paused to steal the fresh flower arrangement from Miss Lovejoy's desk and dashed out of the office. In the elevator he took off his tie and suit coat, knowing it would be a fast hike to the ferry. The commuter ferry across the sound from Seattle docked several blocks from his office. He ran the whole way, knowing for the first time in weeks that he was doing something right.

After being so wrong about Rosie.

Shoving his fare at the ticket clerk, he scanned the flow of passengers moving along the walkway toward the massive triple-decker boat. He pushed through the press of commuters—women in Birkenstocks and no makeup, bringing their home-schooled kids back from a field trip in the city. Attorneys from law firms along the waterfront. Studio artists lugging art supplies. People who liked living in the heart of nowhere.

Miss Lovejoy had been wrong, he decided, standing on

the bridge while the cars flowed onto the lower deck of the ferry. Rosie wasn't on the boat.

Then he heard it.

Faintly at first, but growing sharper as it got closer. Salsa music.

He looked down at the cars driving on and saw the tangerine Volkswagen lurching aboard, disappearing into the belly of the boat. His heart thudded louder than the aggressive beat of the music as he watched her park near the front of the ferry. He couldn't feel the steel stairs beneath his feet as he went down to find her.

He approached the car, and Freddy and Selena started yapping madly. He went to the driver's-side window, and Rosie looked up at him.

She had just blown a bubble with her gum, and it rested weightlessly on her lips as she stared in shock. The dogs fell quiet, perhaps remembering him as the tolerant guy who let them sleep on the bed.

Very gently, his heart rising, he took the bubble gum between his thumb and forefinger and tossed it overboard. "I was wondering," he said, bending low, "if we could find something else for you to do with your mouth."

Before she could reply, he bent and kissed her, feeling her lips harden in protest, then soften in surrender as he pressed closer. When he drew away, her eyes stayed shut and she had a rapturous expression on her face.

But when she opened them, suspicion clouded her gaze. "What's this about, Mitch?"

He handed her the flowers. "These are for you."

"Thank you." She took the flowers. "So I guess you learned about the kayaking venture."

He grinned. "Yeah, just now. It was brilliant."

"So you're here because I got you out of trouble with the marina deal."

"Yes—hell, no, Rosie."

"Then why did you wait until today?"

"Why didn't you tell me you'd stayed in Seattle?"

"Why didn't you tell me it mattered to you?"

Frustrated, he opened the door, pulling her out of the car and pressing her against it, not caring who was watching. "Everything about you matters to me, Rosie. I've missed you."

"You have?"

"Yes. And I'm sorry for going off like that when you rejected the project."

"You are?"

"Yes. And I love you."

"You do?"

"Yes." He was amazed at how easy it was to say it, how true and how right it felt. "I never thought I'd feel this way about anyone, but you changed my life, Rosie. I guess that's why I ran you off. It was different, and it scared the hell out of me."

"It did?"

"Yes. But I discovered something even scarier."

"What's that?"

"Being without you. I need you, Rosie."

Tears welled in her eyes. "Really?"

"Really."

"Oh boy." The tears spilled over, making silvery tracks down her cheeks.

"Ah, Rosie. Please don't cry."

"I told myself you were wrong for me. You're exactly the kind of guy who keeps breaking my heart."

"Not this time. This time I'm exactly the right kind of guy. I've changed, Rosie. I don't live for work anymore. Ask anyone. I went bowling Thursday night."

She smiled as the tears continued to flow. "Ask me what my checkbook balance is. Just ask me."

"Okay, what's your checkbook balance?"

"It's 1,869.54. Not counting the book of ferry tickets I just bought."

He kissed her again, long and crushingly, and she swayed against him. It felt right, perfect, just like coming home. And then he did something he'd never in his life imagined doing. Keeping hold of her hand, he sank down on one knee. Some part of him realized that a small crowd had gathered on the passenger bridge high above them, but he didn't care. It was time to take this step, and if the whole world saw him do it, all the better.

"Marry me, Rosie," he said. "Please marry me."

"I want to." She tugged at his hand so he was standing again, looking down at her and knowing he'd never ever get tired of holding her in his arms. "I love you."

"Then say yes. We don't have to live in the condo. I'll get a place on the island, anywhere you want—"

"Yes."

Her emphatic reply brought a strange thickness to his

throat. This was it, then. The big plunge. He was so ready for it he nearly burst.

"On one condition," she said.

"Damn, Rosie, you name it." He meant it. The moon, the stars, the world on a silver platter. He would lie down and die for her if that's what she wanted. "Anything."

"I want us to go away every August. Every August for the rest of our lives, I want to go with you to that summer place."

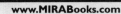

A new Shenandoah Album novel
by *USA TODAY* bestselling author

EMILIE RICHARDS

Gayle Fortman has built a good life for herself and her three sons in the Shenandoah Valley of Virginia. Divorced from charismatic broadcast journalist Eric Fortman, Gayle has made a success of *Daughter of the Stars*, a popular bed-and-breakfast. And Travis Allen, her closest neighbor, has been a loving surrogate father to the boys and her own best friend.

Then one day, Eric returns. After nearly losing his life in Afghanistan, he needs a place to recover. Gayle and Eric are all too aware that the love and attraction they once shared are still there. But can the pieces of their broken lives be mended, or are they better laid to rest?

Touching Stars

MIRA®

MER2561

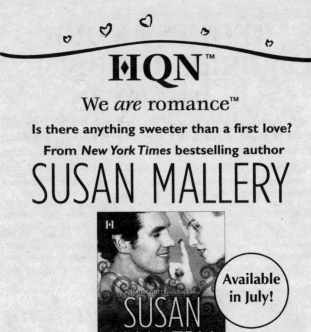

REQUEST YOUR
FREE BOOKS!

2 FREE NOVELS
FROM THE ROMANCE/SUSPENSE
COLLECTION PLUS 2 FREE GIFTS!

YES! Please send me 2 FREE novels from the Romance/Suspense Collection and my 2 FREE gifts (gifts are worth about $10). After receiving them, if I don't wish to receive any more books, I can return the shipping statement marked "cancel." If I don't cancel, I will receive 4 brand-new novels every month and be billed just $5.49 per book in the U.S. or $5.99 per book in Canada, plus 25¢ shipping and handling per book plus applicable taxes, if any*. That's a savings of at least 20% off the cover price! I understand that accepting the 2 free books and gifts places me under no obligation to buy anything. I can always return a shipment and cancel at any time. Even if I never buy another book from the Reader Service, the two free books and gifts are mine to keep forever.

185 MDN EF5Y   385 MDN EF6C

Name _____ (PLEASE PRINT)

Address _____ Apt. #

City _____ State/Prov. _____ Zip/Postal Code

Signature (if under 18, a parent or guardian must sign)

Mail to **The Reader Service:**
IN U.S.A.: P.O. Box 1867, Buffalo, NY 14240-1867
IN CANADA: P.O. Box 609, Fort Erie, Ontario L2A 5X3

Not valid to current subscribers to the Romance Collection,
the Suspense Collection or the Romance/Suspense Collection.

Want to try two free books from another line?
Call 1-800-873-8635 or visit www.morefreebooks.com.

* Terms and prices subject to change without notice. N.Y. residents add applicable sales tax. Canadian residents will be charged applicable provincial taxes and GST. Offer not valid in Quebec. This offer is limited to one order per household. All orders subject to approval. Credit or debit balances in a customer's account(s) may be offset by any other outstanding balance owed by or to the customer. Please allow 4 to 6 weeks for delivery. Offer available while quantities last.

Your Privacy: Harlequin is committed to protecting your privacy. Our Privacy Policy is available online at www.eHarlequin.com or upon request from the Reader Service. From time to time we make our lists of customers available to reputable third parties who may have a product or service of interest to you. If you would prefer we not share your name and address, please check here. ☐

BOB08R